THE COMMON LAW
#6 in the Peter Sharp Legal Mystery Series

By Gene Grossman

From Magic Lamp Press
Venice, California

Magic Lamp
Press ™

If you purchased this book without a cover, you should be aware that this book is stolen property. It was reported 'unsold and destroyed' to the publisher and neither the author nor the publisher has received any payment for this "stripped book."

This is a work of fiction. Names, characters, places, and incidents are the entirely products of the author's imagination and used fictitiously or with permission.
Any resemblance to actual persons, living or dead, is entirely coincidental – or possibly intentional.

THE COMMON LAW
Peter Sharp Legal Mystery #6

All rights reserved
Copyright © MMVIII Gene Grossman

This book, or parts thereof, may not be reproduced in any form, stored in a retrieval system, or transmitted by any means, electronic, mechanical, photocopying, recording, or otherwise, without written permission from the author. For written permission, contact: Gene Grossman c/o Magic Lamp Press, P.O. Box 9547, Marina del Rey, CA 90295.

http://www.legalmystery.com

ISBN: 1-882629-39-6

The Complete Peter Sharp Legal Mystery Series

Single Jeopardy

…By Reason of Sanity

A Class Action

Conspiracy of Innocence

…Until Proven Innocent

The Common Law

The Reluctant Jurist

The Magician's Legacy

The Final Case

An Element of Peril

A Good Alibi

Legally Dead

Available at bookstores, and Amazon
Now also available as eBooks

http://www.legalmystery.com

1

Marriage can be a great institution, but I don't do well in institutionalized situations, so mine didn't work out – and that's too bad, because my ex-wife Myra was elected as our county's District Attorney and I missed out on those fancy black tie events offering free food and an open bar.

We got along just fine during the first couple of years we were married, but then she decided to start law school. Why not? I guess she figured that if I could do it, anyone could. It was all down hill from there. I think that some females are born with a prosecution chromo-some so that no one around them can ever get away with anything. Most women utilize that trait as mothers; others become teaching nuns or deputy district attorneys. Myra was fortunate in having been able to achieve her maximum genetic potential... she's the chief prosecutor of Los Angeles County. My law practice requires that I do some criminal defense work, so she now gets some opportunities to do to me what I used to enjoy doing to her.

At first there was a feeling in the legal community that because the D.A. is my ex-wife I'd be getting some preferential treatment from her office. Unfortunately though, all the feelings have been proved wrong. Aside from my being wrongfully arrested a few times in the last year or so, I'd say that I've been getting treated fairly by her gang, but anyone who spends time in the downtown Criminal Courts building knows that there's no love lost between us. As a result of my helping her to get elected she gave me her private telephone number so I now have instant access to her, but that's all the thanks I ever received. So much for gratitude.

My good friend Stuart Schwarzman is the complete opposite. He hasn't got a prosecutorial bone in his body, is easygoing, and always concerned about the rights of every person. He isn't married at the present time, or at least I don't think he is, so when he calls to ask my advice about a domestic situation he claims to be involved in I remind him of my general rule to not do 'phone law' and invite him to stop by my boat later this afternoon so that we can talk about his alleged issue face-to-face.

With the help of a certain computer freak who rarely talks to me, my law practice has been doing quite well, and I was able to afford a partnership share in this 50-foot Grand Banks trawler-yacht here in Marina del Rey, California, which is where I live and run my practice. We're out on the western edge of Los Angeles, so the constant ocean breeze protects us from most of the city's smog.

I normally wouldn't have a mini-family living with me on the boat, but in Mel's last Will and testament he requested that I be appointed Suzi's legal guardian. She's an adorable little 12-year old Chinese girl with exceptional logic and computer skills. I never thought that the court would approve me, and I still suspect that Myra must have had something to do with the judge's decision. Like everyone else, both Myra and the judge fell in love with Suzi at first sight and couldn't resist her plea to be allowed to continue her lifestyle of living on a boat in the marina, like she did with her stepfather on his houseboat. A portion of the multimillion-dollar settlement I was able to get her from Melvin's death made her my partner in this boat, and allowed us both to move up: her from Mel's small old houseboat, and me from a client's old wooden cabin cruiser I was staying on. Our Grand Banks is a beautiful boat, but pales in comparison to the 138' mega-yacht everyone says is owned by George Clooney that ties up out on the end tie of our dock. One of these days I hope to bump into him, but so far all of my efforts at meeting him have failed.

After Melvin was gone I discovered that Suzi is a home-schooled genius and was always the brains behind her stepfather's small law firm and her huge beast is a great watchdog. He knows who the 'friendlies' are and Stuart is one of them, so there's no growling whenever he comes to visit the boat.

The other friendlies who can come aboard at will are Stuart's employees Vinnie and Olive, my investigator Jack Bibberman, Suzi's adopted big sister, my ex Myra, all of our dock neighbors, and just about every cop on the west side of town who make frequent visits to the boat to avail themselves of Suzi's computer skills and access to secure criminal databases – with passwords she probably 'borrowed' from Myra's computer during one of her sleep-overs at what used to be our house in Brentwood Glen.

Suzi is always trying to create some scheme to get Myra and I back together again, but we're both onto her plan, so we just play along, so as not to upset her. Unfortunately, the good ship *reconciliation* has already sailed, and I'm afraid I've missed the boat.

The loud knocking on our hull is probably Stuart. The way this 40-ton boat is starting to rock means that he's coming up the boarding ladder, and we're glad it's a strong one, because he'll never see 250 again... if he can even see the scale at all, while he's standing on it.

"What's up Stu? I haven't heard from you in a while. By the way, did that deal you were working on to sell your house last year ever come through?"

"It's funny you should ask, because that's the problem. I'm facing a big capital gains liability."

"That's what happens to successful people Stu. They buy low, sell high and pay taxes on their profits. But that's not exactly a domestic situation... it's a tax problem. "

"I think I've figured out a way around that. My accountant says that as a single guy I'm allowed to avoid paying taxes on the first quarter million of profit. But if I'm married and filing jointly with my wife, the exemption is doubled to a half mil... and I'll be going for the much bigger exemption."

"Yeah Stuart, I've heard about that law. I think you'd have had to be married and living there with your wife for two of the past five years in order for that exemption to kick in. Maybe you can find some girl to marry and backdate the marriage certificate. Don't look at me like that! I'm just kidding." It's hard to feel sorry for Stuart and his tax liability. He's got several successful businesses going on and as a result of some cases I've settled for him in the past, he's also got a couple of million dollars stashed away somewhere. Another thing he's always successful at is never failing to surprise me.

"I was married. I mean I'm still married. I mean, I have a wife, and we file joint returns."

"Stu, are you telling me you're currently married? How come I've never met her?"

"You have met her Pete."

"What are you talking about? You've never introduced any woman to me as your wife. Are you secretly married to someone?"

"Well yeah, I guess you could say that."

"Is it someone I know? What's this lucky female's name?

"Her name's Priscilla and you've met her… at least you've seen her around my office."

I'm struck silent for a minute. Of all the times I've been to Stuart's office the only woman I've seen there is Olive, and she's engaged to Vinnie - Stuart's other employee.

My thoughts are temporarily interrupted by the sound of large paws approaching. It's the beast and its master. Usually she just opens the door to her private forward stateroom to listen in on the conversations I have, but this time it must have gotten too interesting, so they've decided to come out into the open and eavesdrop in person.

As I rack my brain trying to remember Stuart introducing me to any dame named Priscilla, Stuart saves me the trouble.

"Don't strain yourself Pete. Priscilla's not a woman. I mean, she's female, but not a woman."

"What do you mean it's not a woman? You mean you're married to some girl child named Priscilla?"

I'm dead serious, but this last question of mine forces a giggle out of the kid. It's the first time

I've ever seen her do that since a funny car commercial we saw last year.

"Calm down Pete. Priscilla is my cat. You've seen her at the office a million times. She sleeps on top of my warm computer monitor during the day."

"Come on Stuart. This is getting a little too weird for me. I never expected this kind of craziness, even from you."

"I know it sound nuts Peter, but I had to do it for tax purposes. By the way, all this stuff we talk about today is privileged, isn't it?"

I can't believe what I'm hearing, but I think I know where he's going with this. The kid obviously figured it out already because behind me I hear large paws leaving the room and then the foreward stateroom door being closed. "Yes Stuart, it's privileged."

"Pete, please listen. I'm not crazy or weird. A couple of years ago when I saw how the property values in my neighborhood were starting to go through the roof, I knew that my old house would be a valuable item. I bought it over twenty years ago for only thirty-five grand, and now others not even as nice as mine down the street started selling for over four hundred big ones. Over the years I put in a nice pool, air conditioning, a big family room addition and lots of other improvements to make it the nicest place on the block.

"Several local real estate agents told me that if property values in my neighborhood kept going up like they were, I might be able to get over six hundred G's for the place, so I made some tax-saving plans.

"The government doesn't come out to verify what a person's wife looks like, so I applied for and received a social security card for Priscilla and started filing joint returns with her as my wife. My tax guy isn't a close personal friend, so he never knew. I only contact him once or twice a year, and didn't retain him until about a year after my cat marriage, so he never questioned it.

"As husband and wife we took the full half-million-dollar capital gains income tax exemption instead of one half that size. And there was no misrepresentation either, because it was our main residence for at least two of the past five years. We were just following the law."

I put my hand up as a signal for him to stop talking. I need a brief period of silence to gather my thoughts. As I rub my forehead, I find that no words are coming to mind. This new stunt of his has left me completely speechless.

"Okay Stuart, here's the way I see it. You're not really married to that cat, and there are so many reasons why, that I don't even want to start to explain them all. Suffice it to say that if you want to play out this little charade for tax purposes, my advice is to not do it.

"With your marriage plan, the State of California's refusal to recognize common law marriage probably doesn't apply because you're not using it for purposes of inheritance, insurance, property rights or any other reason where the state's law comes into play. The I.R.S. doesn't care about most individual state laws with respect to domestic relations, so maybe you can get away with it. I don't know, but I advise against it anyway."

I don't know what else to say. He's really gone over the top this time, and I don't want to dignify this ridiculous situation by responding to it with any type of discussion about the law.

"Thanks for your input Pete, but I think that as long as I've reported all my income, the worst that could happen during an audit is that they'd disallow the extra exemption and I'd have to pay the tax. As long as you report your income, they don't get too mad at you. From what my tax guy tells me, you have to fail to report at least fifteen percent of your income before a criminal investigation kicks in, and I've reported every penny of mine. Everyone cheats a little on deductions. Nobody goes to jail for it and believe me - my tax guy is an expert on that subject."

The secret of Stuart's financial success has always been an uncanny ability to find some small way to change the odds just a little bit toward his favor. The way he once explained it to me was like a game of blackjack in Las Vegas. As far as games go, Stuart thinks that blackjack is the one with the best odds of a customer winning. Those odds are still with the 'house,' but at blackjack the player has some kind of chance if he doesn't do anything stupid. The question Stuart asked me was "what if you played blackjack in Las Vegas, but were legally allowed to see what card the dealer had face down on the table?" His logic becomes apparent. Even if you could see the dealer's 'hole' card, there's no guarantee that you'll win every hand, but just that little edge gives you a slight boost in the odds, because of your knowing when the dealer will have to either hit or stand pat.

This marriage scam of his is no different. Once again he wants to skew the odds. I can see there's no sense in continuing to argue with him because his mind is obviously made up, and that's that. But who am I to question him? He's avoided being arrested so far in his life, and he's wealthy, so maybe he's right and I'm wrong.

"By the way Pete, are you doing anything special next Thursday afternoon?"

For some strange reason I don't like the sound of his question. It's too innocent. "I don't know, Stu. What do you have in mind?"

"Well, I got this letter from the I.R.S. and it seems that they'd like me to stop by their office next Thursday to clear up some questions they have about my capital gains tax marriage exemption."

The other shoe just dropped. I had a feeling he might be leading up to something like this.

"Stuart, I might be wrong about this, but I think that's what they call an audit. I don't know too much about tax law, so you'd be much better served by having your C.P.A. go there with you... and bring your checkbook, because they might not look favorably at your wife not exactly being human."

"You mean I might get arrested?"

"I think that commitment to an asylum would be more likely. Talk it over with your C.P.A. He'll handle it for you. I also think that if a representative appears on your behalf, there's no need for you to be there. Come to think of it, that would be a good idea. If your representative doesn't know anything about Priscilla's lower classification in the food-chain, and you're not there, there's less of a possibility of that little detail leaking out."

"That's a slight problem Pete. My tax guy can't make it next Thursday."

"If he's a C.P.A., there's probably someone else in his office that can handle the appearance for you. He is a C.P.A., isn't he?"

"Not exactly."

"That's okay. Even if he's not a C.P.A., as your accountant, he can still make the appearance on your behalf." He is a real accountant, isn't he?" I can tell by the hesitation what Stuart's answer probably is to my question. I just hope he hasn't been having his taxes done in some storefront fortune-teller's place.

"C'mon Stuart. If he's not a C.P.A. and he's not even an accountant, what the hell is he, your gardener?"

"No, no, it's nothing like that. He really knows his tax law, it's just that he's unavailable next Thursday."

"That's no problem. I'm sure you can get a continuance of your appointment until your guy is available."

This causes more hesitation on Stuart's part. It looks like he's racking his brain for another excuse he can make for his accountant.

"They might not want to continue the appointment until he's available... I mean, it might be a while.

"You mean he's that busy?"

"No. He's out of town."

"Exactly where out of town? Timbuktu?"

"3901 Klein Boulevard. That's in Lompoc, California."

For some strange reason that address sounds familiar. Whoa, it just hit me. Some time ago I had to go up to Lompoc to visit a former client, and if my memory serves me correctly, that's the location of a correctional facility. "Stuart is your accountant currently a guest of the federal government?"

Stuart looks down towards the floor. Why am I not surprised?

"Stuart, I suppose you know that address is a federal penitentiary. Is your tax accountant a convicted felon doing hard time?"

Stuart's silence says enough.

"How did you happen to find this criminal? His ad in the yellow pages?"

"No. We met in a tax chat room on the Internet. He sounded really knowledgeable, so we made a deal for him to do my income taxes, and at first I didn't know he was in prison. I knew he wasn't local because all my written correspondence to him was sent to a P.O. Box in Buelton, California. I now know that's a town near Lompoc, where some of the prisoners are allowed to receive mail.

"He did my taxes for the first two years and I was really satisfied with his work. It wasn't until I wanted to meet with him in person to discuss my capital gains problem that he confessed to me he was serving time. He let me know that he would understand if I decided to pull my business and find another accountant… one on the outside.

"I appreciated his honesty with me, went up there to visit with him a couple of times and realized that I'd have to find someone on the outside to help me with the audit.

"And that's where it stands now. I know that you're not a tax lawyer Peter, so there're no hard feelings in your not wanting to go with me next week. I'll find someone else. There're a lot of accountants in the San Fernando Valley."

I'm glad he understands my reluctance to get involved in his beastial tax matter.

Ever since Stuart started classes at some fly-by-night correspondence law school his main purpose in visiting our boat is to meet with Suzi, who is tutoring him in his studies and helping him brief some cases.

Realizing that his discussion with me has now come to a dead end, Stuart goes to the foreward stateroom, knocks and enters. As he closes the door behind him I hear the kid's voice. "Hello Stuart. How's the wife?"

2

Sometimes when things get dull around here after dark I've been known to take a leisurely stroll over to the Marina del Rey Liquor Store to pick up a six-pack and some wine. I use them to calm my nerves and improve my social life. If my timing is right, by the time I get back to the dock my neighbor Laverne will be in the window of her houseboat waving two wine glasses at me. She can smell her favorite box of wine a half mile away.

Notwithstanding the fact that she's not exactly a '10,' I'm glad she rents on of the small houseboats on our dock. I would guess that we're about the same age, but because she's a slender 40-

something, she still looks pretty decent. On a good evening I'd give her a 6+.

We have a routine. She puts my beer in the fridge, opens the wine, and starts us off with a toast, as we ceremoniously click our elegant plastic wineglasses together.

After the first box of wine is finished we usually agree that I've had too much to drink to safely get home, notwithstanding the fact that I live only five boats down the dock. To remedy that situation, we decide to spend the night in her stateroom, watching one of those dreadful television reality shows she loves. To make me happy, she turns the sound off and tapes the crappy show for her sophisticated video library, while we listen to some soft country music that all sounds the same to me: it's always about a guy who has lost his pick-up truck, dog and wife.

Whenever the kid notices that I'm not back on the boat by bedtime she's knows that I'm either in jail on another charge trumped up by my ex-wife, or down the dock on Laverne's houseboat. If she doesn't get a call from Myra telling her to come and bail me out, it means I'm spending the evening with Laverne. There's no way anyone can bother her while the dog is around, and if she needs me, she knows where I am

Knowing how close the kid is to Myra and how much she wants to see the two of us get back together again, she's not too happy that I'm cavorting with Laverne. I'm sure she knows for sure that there's no possibility of my falling for this dame, so there's no threat to her master reconciliation plan.

Notwithstanding the fact that Laverne's houseboat decoration motif is what could be classified as 'early whorehouse,' it's really not that bad. There's about as much room in here as a small one-bedroom apartment, and with the red-flocked wallpaper, the place can actually be quite cozy once the artificial fireplace is switched on. And thanks to the TV and country music, we don't feel any need to have a conversation.

In the late 1800's a French guy named Gustave Flaubert got so fed up with the dull conversation of his dinner companions that he compiled all of their hackneyed platitudes into what he called his 'dictionary of accepted ideas.'

I may not be a Flaubert, but I've come to the conclusion that there are three levels of conversation, and people locked into the bottom level are only capable of nouns. All they ever talk about is people, places or things. Their favorite entertainment is gossip, watching reality TV and reading tabloid magazines.

The second level of conversationists is comprised of people who not only talk about nouns, but can also mention events. This level is inhabited by sports fans, people who read the sound bites in Time Magazine, and are pretty good at regurgitating some opinion they've heard and adopted about something that was spouted off by Rush Limbaugh, Howard Stern, Don Imus, Bill O'Reilly, Al Franken or any of the other self-appointed pundits they idolize and believe are giving them a fair and balanced view of things.

On the other hand, all modesty aside, I like to think that I'm on level one, the rarified area where people who are actually capable of original thought reside. Level one people don't just talk 'at' each other with competing comments about nouns or events... they actually listen to what's being said and can respond with intelligence, whether they're in agreement or not with other parties to the conversation.

Unfortunately, Laverne is a level three person and like others in her strata, they haven't the slightest idea that higher levels exist. Like those guys with confederate flags on the back of their pick-up trucks, to them, anyone who appears to be a level one conversationalist is just some commie egg-head, to be despised and suspected.

Rather than spend an entire evening discussing the intense relationships between desperate losers in some survivor show, we just sit back, listen to some soft music and get embalmed. I'd prefer that the soft music not be country & western, but this isn't a perfect world, so I listen to those depressingly sad ballads about people who have lost everything but their ability to make records and appear on some award show at the Grand Ole Opry once or twice a year, to celebrate the millions they've made off of those people with pick-up trucks.

Thanks to the booze, by the time we hit the sack Laverne looks really nice - like the prettiest dame in the trailer park. Fortunately I'm still asleep when she gets picked up for work in the morning and as usual, there's a plate of greasy French toast waiting for me on her kitchen table.

This morning while I'm trying to digest a slice, a dog-mail gets delivered. Whenever Suzi wants to communicate with me she usually tucks a message under the dog's collar and sends him to wherever I am in the boat or on the dock. This morning he pushes Laverne's door open and is now sitting next to me, waiting for me to remove the message and give him his tip, which usually consists of a pat on the head and a scrap of whatever edible item is available. I don't know if this French toast meets the 'edible' requirement, but I might as well give it a shot. After removing the message from his collar I pet his huge head and toss a slice of my breakfast onto the floor.

He appreciates the pat on his head, but after a few sniffs of the breakfast tip, he looks up at me with one of those 'thanks anyway, but I think I'll give it a pass' looks, and exits the boat.

My message is an email from an old classmate of mine who conducts an annual review class for freshman law students preparing to sit for the California State Bar's First Year Law School Examination, or 'Baby Bar.' Passing this test is a requirement for all students of non-accredited law schools and it covers the three first-year subjects of Contracts, Torts and Criminal Law.

Peter:
　　I'll be conducting my semi-annual six-weekend Baby Bar Review Course soon and have added a few new sections that cover some of the finer points of writing an essay answer, the psychology of taking a State Bar exam, and how our present judicial system evolved from the Common Law of England.
　　If I remember correctly, you were pretty good in those areas, so I'd appreciate very much your

considering being a guest lecturer for two Saturday afternoons.

From what I hear of your recent successes, you're probably a high-priced lawyer now, but hope that you'll think about the satisfaction of helping out some desperate students who are now in the same position we used to be in.

Sincerely,

Bart Levin

This sounds interesting. I wonder what his real reason for contacting me is. As soon as I finish breakfast and do the dish, I'm going to call Bart and make arrangements to meet with him. Later this morning I'll be driving Suzi to the Board of Education's downtown offices so she can be given one of those periodic home-schooling tests. They usually accept results sent in by the home-school teacher, but Suzi's results are so much higher than any other student that they insist she come in to take the exams in person so they can see she's not cheating. Bart's office is also downtown, so after dropping off Suzi I can stop by and meet with him.

At first I thought the kid would resent being required to go downtown several times a year and not being trusted to take the tests on her own, but I was wrong. This way the need for her home teacher's certification isn't required. Come to think of it, I've never seen any home teacher. I'll bet the kid has the Board of Education believing that there actually is a home teacher, and is completely self-taught. I wouldn't put it past her.

Suzi often talks Myra into joining us on these test days, claiming she needs some moral support for the test. Myra and I both know that it's just another scam that the kid pulls to get us together for a part of the day. Unfortunately it won't work this time because Myra can't make it. I got a message from one of her assistants telling me that some idiot pedestrian caused a traffic accident in front of the Criminal Courts Building that involved a police squad car, so the Mayor asked Myra to supervise the taking of witness statements, to try and avoid another onslaught of non-meritorious lawsuits being filed against the city.

We usually draw quite a bit of attention during our infrequent car trips together. Aside from the fact that I drive a big yellow Hummer, it's probably more due to the huge dog riding with his head sticking up out of the open sunroof. And if that's not enough to get stares, he's been fitted with some fancy goggles made especially for dogs to wear while riding in cars. They're called 'Doggles,' and the kid ordered them to protect his eyes from specks of flying road debris. At first glance he looks a lot like some canine World War One air ace, with his goggles on and big ears flopping in the wind.

They won't allow the animal into the testing building, so I'm stuck dog-sitting him for the next hour or so while the kid's up there showing them how much smarter she is than they are. In the meantime, I've set up a meet with Bart Levin and it looks like he's recognized us, because like the other people milling around outside his office building, he's gawking at Baron Bernie, the air ace and me as we come to a landing. It becomes immediately obvious to him that there's no way the dog will be giving up his front seat co-pilot position, so Bart hops in the back seat and we continue our motor tour of the downtown Los Angeles business district, becoming a popular subject for every Asian camera-toting tourist we drive by.

After exchanging some small talk and catching up on our old classmates, I cut right to the chase.

"Bart, I think now's the time for you to tell me why you really want me to lecture at your review course. I was never a genius in those new sections you've added to your class, and you know it."

"Okay Pete, you caught me. The truth of the matter is that my decision was based solely on business reasons, and because of your ex-wife."

His answer catches me off-guard. I can't believe that Myra asked him to hire me. There must be another reason.

"Please Bart. We both know my ex-wife didn't call you. What's going on here? And if you don't tell me the truth, I'm going to order Baron Snoopy here to eat you."

"All right Pete. You've been in criminal courts lately. What do you see there? I'll tell you what I notice... the prosecutors and public defenders are mostly female. And that's not all. In the past ten years I've noticed a complete change of the gender composition ratio of my students. It used to be almost six-to-one male. Now it's fifty-fifty and it looks like the next year women will be in the majority for the first time. And what's more, they usually express an interest in going into government work... for the prosecutors or public defender's office."

"I don't understand Bart. What draws them to governmental service? The pay isn't that great."

"You're right. The pay isn't that good, but the experience is. In no time at all they can be handling preliminary hearings and misdemeanor trials. And take a look at the high profile criminal felony trials. Marcia Clark was on the O.J. case, Leslie Abramson tried the Melendez brothers, Kobe Bryant hired a lady lawyer, and all you see on the television law shows is females. It probably started with Ally McBeal, but there have been plenty others. Every one of them wants to become an Erin Brockovich or Gloria Allred."

"Well, I think we can both agree that there definitely is a need for more Gloria Allreds out there."

"I think another main reason is they feel that coming from unaccredited law schools they don't stand much of a chance of getting hired by some big law firm, and if they do get hired by one, it'll probably be because they look good in a sweater… and that won't lead to any trial experience. That's why many of them have requested you as a teacher."

"Why me?"

"Think about it Pete. Your ex-wife is now the District Attorney of Los Angeles County. If a female student gets friendly with you, there might be a possibility of your recommending her to Myra for a job there."

"C'mon Bart, you know it doesn't work like that. The position of Deputy D.A. is a civil service job. No matter what I might say to Myra, an applicant has to go through the regular hiring procedure."

"You and I know that Pete, but these are just desperate law students. They believe what they want to believe, so please think about it, because if you join our team your first lecture will be next Saturday morning."

"Bart, are you trying to tell me that if I teach at your seminar that there will be a large number of females trying to get friendly with me just because they think I can help them get a job? And, that they don't care one way or another about my brains, looks, legal talent, or teaching ability? That the only thing I'm good for is a job recommendation, and for that reason and that reason only, they'll be willing to cozy up to me? What kind of person do you think I am? You disappoint me Bart.

"By the way Peter, we don't have any rule against a teacher dating a willing student."

"Is it okay if I don't wear a tie?"

3

The telephone is ringing and my caller ID display shows Myra's private number. "Hello beautiful, what can I do for you today?"

"Cut the crap Petey, I just want to know how the little princess did on her tests."

I hate it when she calls me that, but at least she's calling. "You know how she did. She was the absolute smartest person in that whole administration building, and they should all know it by now. And believe it or not, she did it without you being there for moral support."

"Yeah, now she'll have to come up with some other scam to get us together again for lunch on the afternoon of her next test."

"You're the top prosecutor in the County. What do you think will happen when they find out she doesn't have a home teacher? Will you be coming out here to arrest her for fraud?"

"Of all the people in this world I'd like to arrest, she rates the lowest. I've seen the way she wraps people around her little finger with that cupie doll face, and there's no way I want to go up against her in a court of law. Where is she now? I'd like to say hello. I'm afraid I'm one of those people she's got all wrapped up… and I think you're one too."

"Sorry. It's the last Tuesday of the month, so she's holding court over at the Chinese restaurant around the corner, where the local cops are having another one of their interagency luncheons. Most of them are her computer clients now that she's figured out a way to hack into the secure criminal databases… thanks to you, Miss Frankenstein."

"Peter, do you think it's safe for her to drive that e-cart of hers around the marina to the bank, post office and that restaurant she probably owns a part of?"

"I think it's a lot safer than telling her not to, because then she'd probably figure out some way to commandeer my Hummer, and then she'd have to teach the dog how to drive because she can't see over the steering wheel or reach the pedals."

"Yeah, I guess you're right, but I'd still rather she didn't. Oh by the way, congratulations on your new professorship."

"How did you find about that? I just agreed to it the other day."

"One of the interns in my office is a law student and she's taking that phony-baloney review course."

"Hey, while we're at it, what happened with that accident in front of your office?"

"Watch the news tonight Peter."

This is no surprise. Myra never saw a camera she could resist, especially since becoming an elected official.

The kid won't be back from the restaurant for a little while. Her late mother used to work there and her uncle Charlie owned the place. Unfortunately, tragedy struck the family. Her mother died in an automobile accident shortly after marrying my ex-boss Melvin, to help improve her immigration status. Uncle Charlie was shot to death in the restaurant's parking lot during a dispute over parking spaces, and little Suzi, who was always sort of like the restaurant's mascot, spends quite a bit of time there getting petted on the head by all the customers. It gives her a chance to get away from me and be with a lot of nice people, so I really can't complain about her close association with the restaurant. There are four guys working there who have been nicknamed 'the Asian Boys' who not only wait tables and clean the place every night, but also do routine maintenance and varnishing on several of the boats on our dock, including ours. And whenever we have boat guests in the evening, Suzi arranges for the

Asian Boys to deliver a gourmet Chinese dinner, serve it, and clean up afterwards.

The only strict rule that I as guardian enforce is that she must be back at the boat before sunset, unless she calls in with a good excuse and lets me know exactly where she is. The few times that has happened, her and the dog were driven back to the boat by a squad car, while another cop drove her electric cart back here.

Most cops have their favorite spots for doughnuts, restrooms, coffee, lunch, and other needs. The Chinese restaurant is their most popular lunch place, and the parking lot usually has quite a few black-and-whites parked there from the California Highway Patrol, Culver City Police, L.A. County Sheriff and L.A.P.D. For the monthly interagency luncheons, uniforms from the nearby beach cities of Manhattan, Redondo and Hermosa also show up.

As a result of her crime-busting computer skills and popularity at the restaurant, I don't think it's possible for Suzi to ever get in trouble with the police. A retired cop who was once a client of ours gave her his badge when he retired and went cruising. Even though it's against the law, she wears it on a necklace when she goes to the restaurant, and not one cop has ever said a word to her about it.

Every couple of years I reread the most famous 'locked-room' mystery of them all, Jacques Futrelle's *The Problem of Cell 13*. It's the amazing story about a French Professor named Augustus S.F.X. Van Dusen, who was called 'the Thinking Machine,' who makes good on his promise to escape from a cell in the notoriously secure Chisholm

Prison, while under constant watch. I feel some kinship with the author – not because I'm a 'thinking machine,' but because like me, he's also had quite a bad experience on a boat. Mine was a horrific harbor cruise here in Marina del Rey but his was a little worse. He was a passenger on the Titanic.

Several hours mysteriously flew by while I've been reading and I feel the boat rocking slightly. This means that the kid and her 200-pound pet have returned from their appearance at the restaurant.

I climb down the ladder from our flybridge and avail myself of the signaling device to institute a dog-mail. It's a box of dog biscuits. All I have to do is shake the box a little and the Saint Bernard miraculously appears from out of nowhere. I tuck the note into his collar, hand him a biscuit, and off he goes to the forward stateroom that serves as the little princess' private domain. My message is a reminder that Myra will be on the news this evening.

Now that my chores are done, I might as well prepare some dinner for myself. I never have to worry about the kid because with all the food she brings back from the restaurant, she can probably survive for about six months without leaving the boat. And she's no fan of my cooking.

Tonight's delicacy will be the usual eight ounces of large elbow macaroni mixed with some butter, a dash of cream, and grated cheese that's a mixture of Parmesan and Romano. It's one of the simplest dishes I prepare, but I've enjoyed eating it ever since I was a kid, when my grandmother used to make it for me.

Unlike dear old grandma's instant heart-attack ingredients, the cream is imitation non-fat, non-cholesterol, as is the cottage cheese, butter and imitation grated cheese. When enough fake salt-free garlic salt is added for seasoning, it's almost edible.

With the pot of gruel now cooked a bit past *al dente*, I'm ready to sit down in front of the boob tube and watch my ex-wife on the early evening news.

As usual, the local broadcast starts out with the results of last night's high-speed car chase and we're treated to the image of some guy being handcuffed. In all the years of watching these stupid chases, I have yet to remember ever seeing a follow-up item that tells why the guy was trying to escape or what his ultimate sentence was.

Just once I'd like them to put one of those idiots on camera being asked 'why did you do that?' I think the public is entitled to see the stupidest members of our society. Publicly disgracing them on television would be tantamount to the historic use of 'stocks,' when criminals were shackled and put on display in the town square, with their head and hands stuck out of a wooden device like the kind they use on a team of oxen.

If the courts really want to get serious about putting the sociopath lunatic car-chase drivers away, they should consider imposing the maximum sentence of about six months for every stop sign and red light that the idiots go through without even slowing down. That would surely add up to a minimum of ten years for each chase. We usually learn that in addition to causing a dangerous chase, they're often driving while drunk.

I've heard of some jurisdictions where sentencing judges order people who get convicted of drunk driving display a mandatory rear bumper sticker indicating the driver has a DUI conviction on record. That would subject any car with a sticker like that to more attention at night, and hopefully deter future violations. There are now some websites where concerned parents can learn if a convicted sex offender is living in their neighborhood. Maybe they should expand those databases to include drunk drivers and guys who pick up street-walking prostitutes.

The blow-dried anchorperson is now reading some other details about things that aren't really news. They finally get to the only thing I want to watch.

"And now we have a report from downtown Los Angeles, where this afternoon our on-the-scene reporter interviewed District Attorney Myra Scot, who made a statement on the steps of the Criminal Courts Building."

There's Myra, looking as good as ever. She's probably going to talk about that accident in front of her office building.

"The Mayor has requested our office to make an investigation into the events that took place out here just a little while ago. Although all the facts aren't in yet, it appears that a pedestrian stepped back away from a parked vehicle and into oncoming traffic, where he was struck by a Los Angeles Police Department squad car.

"The squad car that hit the pedestrian contained two officers and when slamming on its brakes, caused the vehicle behind to crash into the squad car. Air bags were automatically deployed in both vehicles and four people were taken to the hospital for observation: the pedestrian, both police officers and the female driver of the vehicle that rear-ended the squad car. We aren't releasing any names yet, but our office will provide the press with a detailed statement once our investigation has been completed."

One of the reporters shouts out a series of questions to Myra.

"Miss District Attorney, is your office under the impression that a crime has been committed here? I mean, this seems like it would be more of a job for the City Attorney to handle, wouldn't it? How come they requested your office to look into it?"

Myra dodges that barrage completely by repeating her prior statement about a detailed statement that will be provided for the press.

That was simple. No crime appears to have been committed, so Myra won't have to waste any more time on this matter. I hear some large paws, so the kid must be making an entrance. I'm wrong. She's only going to the fridge to get some ice cream. For some strange reason she has long conversations with everyone but me. I might as well make some effort to communicate. "Suzi, did you get a chance to watch Myra on TV?" No response. I'll try again. "So, what do you think about that accident?"

As she enters her stateroom she decides to grace me with a few brief words. "The pedestrian was a thief."

How does she do that? How can she possibly know that the guy who got hit by the police car was a thief? It wouldn't do me any good to ask because I know there would be no answer forthcoming. She's already used up her quota of words to me for this week. As amazing as her statement was, I have a feeling that she'll wind up being proven right... she usually is.

It doesn't matter. I'm not involved with this non-case. I don't handle misdemeanor petty thieves and certainly am not interested in defending some lady who rear-ended a police car. Besides, I've got some preparation to do for my first lecture Saturday, and an appointment with my barber, Richard. Maybe I'll let him darken some of the gray this time. I don't want to disappoint my female audience or let them think some old fuddy-duddy is teaching them. I think I'll set some rules of engagement for myself with these students.

Let's see.... they have to be between twenty-five and forty-five. No, that won't work. I wouldn't know what to talk about to a twenty-five year old girl. Okay, any decent looking female student over thirty can have me. No, she should be over thirty-five. No, because that would mean she's probably married. This isn't going to work. I better not talk to anyone outside of class because I know that the D.A. has a spy in there, and I'd never survive what Myra and the kid would do to me if they found out that I fooled around with a student.

Stuart's employee Vinnie is calling. I hope he hasn't gotten arrested again. "Hello Vinnie, what can I do for you today?"

"Hi Mister Sharp. I have a little problem I'd like to talk to you about."

"I see by my caller ID display that you're calling from your apartment, so I'm going to take a wild guess and say that your problem has nothing to do with the police. Am I correct?"

"Oh yeah, Mister Sharp. I've got no problem with the police. It's worse than that. I've got a problem with Olive."

For quite some time now Vinnie has been working for Stuart at his Van Nuys warehouse office. When he started dating his now fiancée he talked Stuart into hiring her, so now Vinnie and Olive are engaged, working together and living together. That's a little too much togetherness for me to handle.

"You mean that same old argument you guys have been having about setting the date for your marriage?"

"I wish. This time she wants a divorce."

"Wait a minute Vinnie. How can she want a divorce? You two aren't even married... at least I don't think you are. Did you take her to Las Vegas for one of those quickie marriages recently?"

"No Mister Sharp, we didn't go anywhere. She claims that she's my wife because of some thing called a common-law marriage."

There must be something in the Van Nuys drinking water. First it's Stuart using a prisoner to do his taxes and marrying his cat. Now it's Olive, claiming she's in a common-law marriage with Vinnie.

"Listen Vinnie, I've got a lecture to prepare for but I think that the two of you should get out here. I can only spare about a half hour of my time, but I think it's important enough that we should straighten things out as soon as possible. I'll look forward to seeing you and Olive within the hour."

Vinnie thinks Olive is crazy, but he might be wrong. Up until a couple of hundred years ago people used to become married just by agreeing to do so. It was tough to find a preacher out in the prairies or boondocks, so people just married each other by acting as man and wife.

California doesn't recognize common law marriages, but about a dozen of the other states do, so if you get married that way somewhere else and then come to California, you're married here too. It's called the Full Faith and Credit rules whereby one State must honor certain things from other States. Judgments for debt and convictions are two prime examples, but there are others that also fit into the category. The same types of situations are now happening with gay marriages too, but that's not my problem today. Vinnie says that he and Olive didn't go to any other jurisdiction, so they're going to have to be satisfied strictly with California's laws.

The dog must sense that I've got some time to kill because he's now sitting here with his leash in his mouth. This is a new trick he's taught me and it works every time, so I hook the leash onto his collar and take him for a walk. He really doesn't need a leash because he's very well behaved and wouldn't think of running away or doing any harm to anyone. The leash is only a measure to make the people we encounter feel a little safer, because the dog is big enough to eat just about any normal person he sees. That feeling of safety works for everyone but me, because if he ever decides to take off after a cat while that leash is wrapped around by wrist, I'm in for the dragging of my life.

Our timing is perfect because just as we return to the boat, Olive and Vinnie are going up the boarding ladder.

Once on the boat they don't waste any time before starting to argue their respective cases. It seems to be standard procedure for people with opposing views to try and convince a neutral third person that one opinion is right and the other is wrong. They're really wasting their time, because outside of a courtroom it doesn't make any difference what anyone thinks about their arguments.

"Mister Sharp, would you please tell Olive that there is no such thing as a common-law marriage in California, and that it's against the law?"

"Oh no, Mister Sharp. Vinnie is totally wrong about that. Common-law marriage is perfectly legal in California and it's okay for people to live like that here."

They both stop trying to convince me for a second or two, waiting to see if I'm for or against either one of them. I take advantage of the brief silence to try and get a few words of my own in.

"You're both wrong."

This doesn't make them happy. They look at each other in disappointment, trying to figure out if they should put their differences aside and join forces against me for telling them what neither one of them wanted to hear.

"Why don't the two of you sit down for a minute or two and let me give you my idea of what the law of this state is with respect to common-law marriage. After you've heard what I have to say, maybe you'll be able to make your own decision as to your domestic status.

"People have been getting married for thousands of years... a long time before civil ceremonies and officials came into being. One by one, the various states started to set down written laws governing marriage. They also created procedures for people to use in civil or ceremonial marriages. And that was good, because a lot of rights depend on the status of marriage, with respect to inheritance and other issues.

"The problems started to arise when common-law marriages created before the new laws became enacted started to conflict with the new regulations. In 1877, Massachusetts and Michigan tried to invalidate all marriages that were in place prior to the passage of the new domestic relations laws.

"Fortunately, the United States Supreme Court disagreed with those two states and they struck down those statutes. But what was more important was a statement the Supreme Court made that still is in effect today. They said that marriage is a common right and the states can pass laws regulating how they will recognize marriages as being valid, but the states do not have the right or power to invalidate a common- law marriage."

Just as I feared, they both interpret what I say as supporting their own theory. Vinnie is first.

"Aha! You see, I was right! Common-law marriage isn't recognized in the State of California. We're not married, so you can't ask me for a divorce."

"Uh-uh Vinnie. What Mister Sharp said was that marriage is a common right that no state, not even California, can make invalid."

Another brief silence as they look to me for another opinion on their volley of opinions. This time they're also going to be surprised.

"Okay. You're both on the right track now. As a matter of fact, this time you're both right."

Now both of them are happy, but confused at the same time. I guess they could understand both of them being wrong, but both being right seems like a contradiction of logic. Olive is especially confused.

"Mister Sharp, how can we both be right? We're either married or we're not."

"That's right Olive, but that's not the question I was trying to answer. The both of you started out by making statements of what you believed the law to be. The first round of your statements were both wrong. In the second round, you were both right.

"Now as to whether or not you guys are legally married, let's go a little deeper into your own unique situation and not worry about the history of the law over the past couple of thousand years."

This seems to calm then down a bit. They now feel that we're finally going to get down to the nuts and bolts of their own relationship. That's what they really came here for, so they're sitting here paying attention. This is good practice for me because I've got some guinea pigs to try my lecturing skills out on. If I can make these two conflicted, uneducated, un-sophisticated people understand what I'm talking about, then I stand a pretty good chance of succeeding with the first year law students I'll be in front of this Saturday.

"For openers, you should be aware that of the fewer than about ten states that recognize common-law marriages, they all have a set of requirements before the marriage can exist. First, the relationship should be between two heterosexuals capable of being married and not encumbered with any previous existing marriage still in effect."

This makes Olive jump up with a thought. "Oh, then that must mean that Stuart isn't really married to Priscilla the cat." My, how observant she is.

"That's right Olive. Stuart isn't really married to the cat, notwithstanding his many tax contentions to the contrary, but if the I.R.S. thinks he is, that's okay with me. But getting back to the requirements, second is the issue of what's called 'holding out to others,' which means that the couple must lead the people they know to believe that they are married. Examples of this are the woman assuming the man's last name and the filing of joint tax returns. And no, that still doesn't mean Stuart is married to Priscilla.

"Third, they should cohabitate, or live together. This isn't a strong requirement, but it goes a long way toward the 'holding out' of the relationship as a marriage.

"And last but definitely not least is the most important requirement of all: they must both have the intent to be married. There is no way anywhere in this country that people can inadvertently fall into a common-law marriage, just because they live together.

"It looks like you two are only meeting one of the requirements... you're living together. There's no holding yourselves out as husband and wife, and from the way you're acting, I would say that there's definitely no mutual intent for you guys to be married to each other at this point in time. Yes, I know you're engaged to each other, but I would say that you both really know it won't be official until the preacher says so, and you open the wedding gifts from all of us.

"Now comes the important question. What does it matter whether you guys are into a common law marriage or not? To the best of my knowledge there's no issue of inheritance, taxation, litigation, child custody or support, or any of the other reasons that come into play in your domestic relationship."

This question brings out the real truth and Olive sheepishly admits it.

"Well if we're already married by that common law thing, it means that we don't have to go through with the ceremony and stuff. Every time we start to make plans, something usually goes wrong and we never get to be officially married."

At this point I see some tears in her eyes. Vinnie notices it too and finally realizes that she really wants to be married to him but is afraid of the formalities involved in getting there. He takes her in her arms and whispers something into her ear. They then both slowly leave the boat. On their way out, Vinnie gives me the 'thumbs up' sign.

Just as they're leaving, the phone rings. It's a friend of mine who clerks in the Superior Court's arraignment division. He asks me to come to the courtroom tomorrow around ten in the morning because the judge has something for me.

I'm sure the judge in that courtroom doesn't have a gift for me… it's probably some problem with a recent case in his court. Oh well, I'll find out soon enough.

There's a classic type of choreography that goes on in many courtrooms before the judge takes the bench. In this one, the first thing that happens is the clerk buzzing the judge's chambers to let him know that they're ready whenever he is. The judge puts out his cigarette, puts on his robe, checks himself out in the mirror and then buzzes the clerk's desk to let her know that he's going to come out.

Uniformed bailiffs run the courtrooms and each one has his or her own method of bringing out the judge. In this courtroom the bailiff walks in front to the center of the room and makes his announcement. "Remain seated and come to order. The Honorable Ronald B. Axelrod is now presiding." When he finishes his announcement, a side door of the courtroom opens and the judge dramatically enters, steps up to the bench and takes his seat.

I always suspected that judges periodically rehearse this entrance to get their timing right. Once on the bench the judge starts calling cases and one by one the criminal defendants and their lawyers enter their pleas on the record.

After about a half hour the judge takes a recess. As he leaves the bench he looks in my direction and with a nod, signals for me to join him in chambers. I comply.

"Good morning Mister Sharp. Thanks for coming in today. I've got a little matter here that I think you might find interesting. By checking with my brethren I've learned that you're not tied up with any other serious criminal matters now, so I'm confident you'll have the time to accept an appointment from me."

A court appointment is both an honor and a drag at the same time. Any lawyer should feel complimented that the court thinks enough of him to make the appointment, but at the same time, every lawyer prefers having the liberty of picking and choosing who he wants to represent... and when. A court appointment is a done deal and it looks like today is going to be one of them. There's no sense fighting it.

"Okay Your Honor, what's the guy's name and what's he charged with?"

"Well Mister Sharp, that's the problem. Nobody knows his name, and there aren't any charges filed yet."

"No problem Your Honor. I'll just sign one of these blank timesheets and leave it with you. Then, whenever you feel like it, you can award me whatever amount you think is fair, and we can go on to the next case."

"Relax counselor, it's not that easy. Your client will be the gentleman who was struck by the police car in front of the Criminal Courts building recently. I don't know his name because he's still drifting in and out of consciousness. As for the charges, we don't have any yet, but from the rumors I've been hearing, it'll probably be theft."

This is quite hard to believe. Neither the prosecution nor the court know at this time what charges will be filed against him. All they have is a rumor that there was some theft involved, and that's exactly what Suzi already told me.

"Yes, I believe that's what the charges will be."

"Amazing. Mister Sharp, please, how did you know that?"

"It's a long story Your Honor. Maybe some other time. My only question right now is, if there isn't a charge or a filing yet, how can you make an official court appointment? At this point, there isn't an active case number."

"Actually I can't. But I've been informed that the police want to question him, so I'm appointing you to be there when they do. This guy's in a daze. Hopefully he'll come out of it soon, and I don't want to see the prosecution take unfair advantage of a guy who has just regained his faculties. It's not uncommon for the court to appoint counsel to represent a testifying witness without a case being filed, so I think this will be okay."

"It looks like you've finally come around to the defense side of people's rights."

"Don't get me wrong Mister Sharp. If this guy is convicted of a crime in my court I want to make sure it'll stick and not get reversed by the boys upstairs. In the meantime, consider yourself on the clock. And I'd appreciate it if you would go over to the hospital and look in on him. You just might catch him in a lucid moment."

I hate hospitals. They're full of sick people. My guy is in a special psychiatric ward and there's a uniformed cop sitting outside his door. I've seen this cop around plenty of times, so he just waves me on into the room without asking to see my Bar card. The person on the bed is a white guy in his thirties with his broken leg in a full cast that's being held up off the bed by some type of sling contraption. His eyes are closed. I hate to bother him, but some communication should be in order here to justify at least an hour on my timesheet, so I quietly start to talk to him.

"Excuse me sir, I'm your lawyer. The court appointed me to help you. Can you hear me?"

His eyes open and he looks at me. He looks completely awake, which means that he's miraculously just been brought back to consciousness by the sound of my wonderful voice, or his entire coma routine was nothing but an act. When he starts to talk, I realize that my wonderful voice had nothing to do with it.

"What do you mean you're my lawyer? Do I need a lawyer?"

"Take it easy. No charges have been filed against you yet. My name is Peter Sharp and I'm here to advise you in the event that the authorities want to ask any questions, and to represent you if charges are brought. I'd like to start out with a few minor things. First of all, what's your name?" He looks at me with a blank stare.

"Please tell me your name. All they have on your chart and your wristband is a John Doe designation with a patient number. I have to have your name... at least for my timesheet. C'mon, give me a break. What's your name?"

The blank stare continues. His expression becomes pained. "That's the problem. I've been lying here in this bed for the past couple of days pretending to be in and out of a coma, because I'm afraid of something."

"Okay, don't worry. I'm sure everything will be okay. Just tell me your name, what happened the day of the accident and what you're afraid of, and I'll try to help you out."

"That's just it. I don't know my name. I can't remember anything."

4

This is nothing new. I've seen several cases where a defendant has tried to feign amnesia. The subject of amnesia has always been popular in the entertainment industry, with several television shows based on it, and movies like *Memento* and the one that was made of Robert Ludlum's *The Bourne Identity*, just to name two.

The only thing that a criminal defendant might hope to gain from faking a loss of memory is to possibly succeed in an attempt at some exotic defense. I think it's a valid argument that having no memory of the events upon which charges are based renders the defendant unable to adequately cooperate with the defense attorney. That is if the loss of memory is real, and not phony.

Before leaving the hospital I have a brief discussion with one of the guy's doctors, who tells me he has no idea when the patient's memory will return. It could be anywhere from hours to never.

I'm sure the prosecution will want to have their own shrinks examine this guy if and when charges are filed against him. Just to play safe, I advise him of his right to have counsel present if anyone other than the doctor tries to ask him questions. He has my cell phone number and will call if the need arises.

Back at boat I instruct our office to get a memo off to Judge Axelrod letting him know about my visit with Mister John Doe at the hospital, and then set aside some time to check out the Baby Bar exam procedure. I might as well have some idea of how the State Bar does things now because it's been more than twenty years since I went through that ordeal, and it would be nice to know what my students will be up against.

The internet is my favorite source of info, and when Googling the subject I note that there have been some small changes. When I took the Baby Bar it was two sessions, each containing four essay questions - and it was only given once a year.

Now they give the exam twice a year, which is a lot better, because if you fail it you don't have to wait an entire year before taking it again. Another change is that only the morning session is essay questions. The afternoon is for multiple-choice questions, which sounds like it might be easy, but actually can be a lot tougher.

The previous few years' passing rates average below thirty percent and show that this exam is no walk in the park. This means that more than seven out of every ten people taking it are not going to pass. Not very good odds. And not only will over seventy percent fail, but they'll pay quite a bit for the opportunity to get knocked down. The examination fees are in the neighborhood of four hundred dollars, with up to another hundred tacked on if you want to type the exam or use their software on your laptop.

With these statistics taken into consideration, it won't be surprising for me to be confronted by a large group of desperate law students who have been studying nights at unaccredited law schools, correspondence schools, out-of-state schools and some enrolled in study programs conducted in private law offices and judges' chambers. California is one of the most liberal states in the country when it comes to allowing people to qualify to sit for the Bar examination and become lawyers.

Bart asked me to come a little early so he can give me some pointers as to exactly what he wants me to cover with his attendees. I have to hand it to him for his business acumen and success in making arrangements to use several large classrooms in the Venice High School's adult education department. He breaks the classes up into four separate sections on Contracts, Torts, Criminal Law and Examination Writing. The course goes for six weekends and gives the students plenty of time to sit in on all the sections and then re-visit the ones they feel they're the weakest in.

I've been assigned to the legal writing section and have been asked to hammer home the common law bases of three subjects, along with proper approach to executing an answer that has some remote possibility of getting a passing grade.

When my group files into the room I'm pleasantly surprised to see that my fear has not come true. I'm not the oldest person in the room. I guesstimate that the average age is at least forty, with just a few under thirty and several up in the sixties. This first group is almost evenly split between males and females and many of them are already in different professions. The little cards that Bart has each one of them fill out doesn't ask for age, but it does ask the three things he's most interested in knowing about them: name, where they're studying law, and their current occupation. I now know that I am lecturing to three doctors, a chiropractor, two accountants, five secretaries, four receptionists, three cops, some clerks, paralegals, numerous other employed people, and some housewives.

I'm glad there are some doctors here today. Maybe I'll be able to get some info on amnesia from one of them. Now that they're all seated, I start my spiel.

"Good morning ladies and gentlemen. My name is Peter Sharp. I've been a practicing attorney for about twenty years and I went to an unaccredited night law school, so like the rest of you, I also took the Baby Bar.

"Checking out the State Bar's most recently published statistics, I see that recently, a total of four hundred and thirty-six people sat for the Baby Bar. Only ninety-two passed. That's a passing rate of less than twenty-two percent. If your exam has the same rate, then about eight out of every ten of you will not make it.

"My own personal opinion is that nobody passes."

This gets a round of confused gasps out of them.

"That's right, nobody passes. Almost eight out of ten fail. The graders don't know what to do with the rest of them, so they put them on the 'pass' pile of papers. The purpose of this lecture is to tell you how to try and avoid having your paper tossed onto the large 'fail' pile. In other words, it's not necessarily what you do that gets you through a Bar exam, it's what you don't do.

"For instance. Don't use the word "I." It's not proper legal writing form. You'd be much better off using "this writer" when expressing an opinion.

"Don't argue a case one way or the other unless the question's instructions ask you to do so. Present both sides and let the grader know that you recognize the different variables that the trier of fact can use to base its decision on."

The next couple of hours are spent going over some sample questions that Bart provided me with, and I point out things to avoid when composing answers to them. During one of the breaks a student expresses her difficulty in starting the introduction to each of her essay answers. When class re-convenes I answer her question for the entire class.

"I'll bet that most of you have difficulty in the opening for your essay answers. That's very common, and there's an easy way to avoid the problem. Forget about it." Another round of gasps.

"There's no law that says you have to write the opening paragraph first. Just leave some room on your paper for an opening paragraph and then get right into discussing the issues you think are important. After you've laid out all the things you feel the grader wants so see, go back to the beginning and drop in an opening paragraph that says something like 'to fully discuss the issues involved in this matter, we must cover the following.' Then take a look at what you wrote and insert those issues in the same order you discussed them. When the grader looks at your paper he'll think you've got a tremendous sense of organization. Not only did you tell him in advance what the most important issues were, you then proceeded to set them out in the exact same order you promised you would."

Success. They look at each other with smiles of understanding on their faces. Someone finally told them something useful that might help on the exam. Later that day Bart calls me over and congratulates me on doing a fine job. I guess he got some good feedback from the students. I still don't know if Myra's spy was in my class today. Looking through the cards they all filled out, it could have been any one of the females who put 'secretary' or 'clerk' down as an occupation. If either Myra or the kid lets me know what kind of a job I did today, then I'll know it was one of the secretaries or clerks.

Unfortunately, none of the females try to get friendly. There were only two or three that I would have looked forward to accepting advances from. They were at least in their late thirties or early forties and looked like they were high-maintenance ladies. Another problem is that I have no way of putting the cards together with the faces because there is no seating chart, name-tags or mentioning of names when they participate in the class discussions.

Bart Levin has a video camera set up in the back of the room and that means the entire session is being put onto tape. When I ask about it after class, he lets me know that he's considering using the videos from each classroom as a 'distance learning' device for people who can't attend the seminar in person. We'll have to work out a royalty deal first.

I also learn from Bart that this review course has more than eighty students involved, so my promise to the class that the ones who pass are invited to my boat for a victory party means that I shouldn't have more than fifteen or twenty guests. They all appreciate my invitation. It lets them know that I really care about their getting through okay, and word of the invitation seems to have quickly spread throughout the other classrooms as well.

When going through my emails back at the boat I see that there's one from Stuart. He's announcing a new business he started. It's called Auction Specialties. I've known Stuart for over twenty years now, and his entrepreneurial skills never cease to amaze me. In just the past year alone he bought an old Brinks armored truck and had it painted with the phrase "he's taking it with him." The truck is rented out to disgruntled heirs, who hire it to ride in the funeral procession immediately behind the hearse. Stuart hired Vinnie to do the driving, complete with armored-car guard uniform and holstered, but not loaded, weapon.

In no time at all business was so brisk that Stuart had to buy another armored truck for the fleet and hired Vinnie's girlfriend Olive to drive it. They had a slightly rough start after finding out that Olive forgot to tell them she never learned how to drive, but after a few minor accidents that little problem worked itself out.

Stuart also conducts his small claims suit business, going after people who send out unsolicited faxes and recovering hundreds for each one of them, in accordance with a federal law that was passed several years ago.

His most ambitious recent endeavors involve the purchase of recovered stolen vehicles and re-purchased factory lemons, having them trucked out here from the east coast and re-selling them at a nice profit. I don't know if he's still bringing girls in from Thailand and running his Siamese Introduction service, but it wouldn't surprise me if that was also still doing well, as well as his private investigation business.

His announcement about the auction business is centered around one single activity – selling things on eBay, the Internet's huge garage sale venue. From what he writes in his lengthy email, it all started out several months ago when he began buying government surplus, refurbished and lease-return laptop computers. When people found out that he was doing so well on eBay, they asked if he could help them sell their stuff online too.

Before long he had the beginnings of his new Auction Specialties business running. Stuart owns a warehouse out in Van Nuys, so he has plenty of room to do all the things that the average person doesn't want to get involved with. He offers a whole bunch of services that include storing the merchandise until it's sold, photographing it and building the eBay website, conducting the auction, collecting from the buyer and then packaging and shipping the item out. After the entire transaction is complete Stuart pays the seller of the merchandise, deducting a percentage fee for his services, which can be over twenty percent in come cases.

I think this is such a good idea, that I may use him myself. I've got quite a bit of junk in storage after my divorce and move to the boat. It's not doing me any good where it is, so why not auction it off? I've heard the old saying about one man's junk being another man's treasure, but thanks to Stuart and eBay, there's no need to take that adage on faith alone any more.

I checked out the items Stuart's service is now selling on eBay, and my old laptop will fit in there quite nicely. I call him to get started.

"Hello Peter, it's nice to hear from you. Did you get that announcement about my brand new auction service business?"

"Yes I did Stu, and I'd like to retain your services to sell my old laptop. Hey, while we're talking, how did your appointment go on Thursday? Did you get bruised up very much?"

"Not at all, thank you very much. In fact it went quite well. I don't owe a dime more than filed on my return."

"Hey, that's great! You must've picked a real hotshot to go with you. Who'd you get?"

"Sorry Pete, I'm sworn to secrecy on that one. My representative doesn't want it to be known how good the service is. We want to avoid being deluged by new business."

"Okay Stuart. I can tell by your answer that there's more to it than that, but considering the fact that your original return was done by a guy in the joint, I don't think I want to know any more about who represented you last week. I'll e-mail you the details on my laptop."

No sooner do I hang up than the phone rings again. It's Myra calling from her house.

"Hello beautiful. Yes, I'm available for a sleepover tonight, but you'll have to feed me first."

"In your dreams. I'm calling about your spaced-out client. We have a strange situation going on with that guy. First of all, we got all the tapes from about seven security cameras that cover the immediate outside area of the Criminal Courts building and it looks like Mister Doe pinched a laptop computer out of the back seat of a parked sedan.

"Unfortunately, after the accident, the owner of the sedan came out of the building, got in the car and drove away. It's taken us this long to get enhanced footage from one of the cameras to read his license plate and track him down."

"So what are you telling me? You'll be filing theft charges against my client?"

"Not exactly. The owner of the car denies owning a laptop and refuses to make a statement or press charges."

"Well in that case, I think it would be a good idea for you to get that uniformed cop away from his hospital door. It puts a terrible stigma on my client's status there."

"I don't think so. I smell something fishy here, and I'm going to try to keep him under observation at the hospital as long as I can. The purpose of this call is to see what your feelings are about his stay there. If you're not happy with it, I can always have him transferred to the hospital ward of County Jail."

"Naw, let's leave him in the private hospital for a while. Wait a minute... you said there was a laptop involved, right?"

"Yes, that's right."

"Did you have your computer people go through it to try and find out if there's anything on the hard drive that's worth either stealing or denying ownership of?"

"No, I can't do that yet. Without charges being filed the laptop isn't evidence, so I can't go into its files without a warrant. And at this point in time, I don't have enough for a warrant. We couldn't fingerprint him either. I'm afraid that because it's your client's personal property, we're going to have to release it.

"You're his attorney, so I guess it would be okay for you to receive it for him. And if you happen to know any small person who is really good with computers, maybe as his legal representative you can have it thoroughly examined... for his own good... to help him find out who he is."

I know that her threat to have him transferred to the jail ward was meaningless, because she really has nothing to hold him for. But, if making her think that I believe her threats makes her feel better, then so be it. We arrange to have the laptop messengered to the boat. I'm sure that Myra and Suzi have already discussed this matter at length and the kid is waiting to get her hands on it. My difficult task now is to make sure that the kid knows this is a delicate matter and that whatever she finds on the hard drive is privileged information and not to be put on a silver plate and delivered to the prosecutor's office. We'll share some info with Myra, but I don't want us to go so far as to give her the ammunition to build up a case against our client.

    I know that this is going to cost me. The way our agreement was structured, any fees I earn from court appointments are completely my own and our law firm doesn't share in them. In this case I'll have to make my fee a 'house account' to keep the confidentiality privilege intact. The kid seems to be a genius when it comes to taking portions of my fees. I wouldn't be surprised if she engineered this whole scenario.

    This might be a good time to swing by the hospital to see if Mister Doe has remembered anything new. While there, I might as well show him the computer… maybe it'll ring a bell with his memory. And speaking of ringing a bell, I now remember Myra mentioning that Mister Doe's fingerprints weren't taken. Could that have been a hint?

    While working another case recently I made the acquaintance of a unique gentlemen named Victor Gutierrez, who operates a business in the San Gabriel Valley. Victor has given his establishment the macabre name of 1(800)AUTOPSY, which is also its telephone number. Having worked for a large city coroner's office for some time, he decided to go out on his own. Many times the authorities refuse to perform an autopsy unless there is a crime involved or other question surrounding the cause of death. This is not good enough for many people, including companies guaranteeing life insurance policies and medical malpractice lawyers, so there is enough private demand for Victor's services.

In addition to independent autopsies, he and his staff all have extensive experience in criminal forensics, so I retain him occasionally to help me. This is one of those occasions. I instruct our office to have Victor meet me at John Doe's hospital room and to bring his fingerprint kit with him. As soon as the messenger delivers the laptop here I'll take it with me to the hospital.

After being waved in again by the uniformed police officer still stationed outside his room, I find Mister Doe awake, alert, and watching some mindless talk show on the television set perched on its raised platform across the room from his bed. Our conversation is brief. Aside from the leg still in a cast he's feeling fine and knows that Victor will be arriving soon to take his fingerprints.

I show him the computer that Myra sent over to me but it doesn't seem to spark any memory. Once the device is turned on, he puts it on his lap and I see his fingers flying over the keys so fast that his hands look almost like a blur. He has done some diagnostic tests on the computer and is now looking at me with a blank stare.

"That's pretty good John. I guess you know how to work a computer. At least your keyboard skills are topnotch."

"Yes Mister Sharp. I wish I could understand what I just did, because it's like my fingers were working on remote control. It wasn't until I looked down and realized what I was doing meant something that I somehow lost the ability to do any more. It was like Wylie Coyote in the Roadrunner cartoons. His legs would go really fast even after he ran off the side of a cliff. Then, while temporarily suspended in mid air, he'd look down and realize he didn't know what he was doing there off the edge of the cliff with his legs still moving fast. When he looks down, gravity takes over and he falls.

"I guess I was the coyote on this computer, until I went over the edge and looked down at the keyboard. Then gravity kicked in and reality took over again. I'm sorry, but I just don't remember anything about this computer, and I'm as stunned as you are that I was able to demonstrate such dexterity on it."

At this point there's a knock on the door and Victor enters. I make the introductions and Victor suggests I step outside to chat with the police guard while he does the fingerprinting. We both know that the hospital might not appreciate our fingerprinting one of their patients, so I stand guard out in the hall in case some nurse comes by and wants to go in. That would disrupt Victor's efforts and should be avoided, so in that event I'll have to stall a little to give him time to complete his efforts and pack up.

When the fingerprinting is finished Victor leaves and I stay to make some small talk for a little while and tell Mister Doe that I'll keep him posted if we come up with any information from the fingerprint research. He promises to keep me posted as to any luck with his memory.

I know that the kid is dying to get her little hands on this computer. She hated to see me take it away from the boat when the messenger got there. We've already agreed that John Doe's matter is a house account, so I feel I can depend on her to use discretion when talking to Myra.

By time I get back to the boat I see that the kid has unwrapped a package. I know this because there's a torn up carton from Comp USA in the garbage can. She must have had something delivered to the boat in preparation for her work on the mystery laptop. There's no need to knock on her door or send her a dog-mail. Before I can sit down to read the news-paper, the little princess and her beast are retrieving the laptop. She gives me one of those eye rolls letting me know that by taking it off the boat I've delayed her investigation. I type up a summary of my conversation with John Doe and email it to her.

The phone is ringing. It's Myra again.

"You must really miss me. This is the second time today."

"Well, did he remember anything about the computer?"

"So much for small talk. No, he didn't remember anything."

"Let me know the results of the fingerprint search."

"Did the kid tell you that? I'll wring her little neck. That was supposed to be privileged information. She had no business reporting to you."

"Oh Peter please stop being so paranoid. Suzi didn't tell me anything. I got a call from the guard at the hospital as soon as Victor showed his ID at the door. I didn't think you brought him along to do a post mortem on your client, so that leaves only one other possibility. Call me when you get the results, and you're welcome for the information during our earlier conversation about us not printing him."

I have to find a better exercise than jumping to conclusions. It's been the better part of an hour since Victor got back to his place. He has access to all the fingerprint databases, so I call him to find out if there was a match anywhere. He says that as far as the United States of America is concerned, my client doesn't exist. While Victor was in the hospital room he also examined Doe's clothing and couldn't find any leads there either.

The phone rings. It's Myra again.

"Myra, if you don't have a good excuse for this third call today, I'll just assume that you've still got a thing for me. C'mon now, admit it."

"You're right Petey sweetie, I do have a thing for you. It's an indictment of second degree felony murder against you client."

5

"You can't be serious Myra. How can he be charged with felony murder for the supposed theft of a laptop when nobody died and the alleged victim won't even admit the computer was his?"

"There was a death Peter. Remember the woman driving that Plymouth Acclaim? The one that rear-ended the squad car that hit your client? Well as you know, her airbag deployed, and after the accident she was taken to the hospital. My office got a call from the hospital. Unfortunately, she passed away this morning, and preliminary results indicate that death was caused by the accident aggravating an existing bad heart condition, so we're going in for a grand jury next week. I'll have no problem in getting an indictment on the evidence we've already got, even without any theft victim's testimony. We can bring in the security people who run the outside surveillance cameras and establish the theft by video evidence. I'm sorry, but whether we ever know his real identity or not, he's going down for this one.

"Forgive my error. I made this call as a courtesy – to give you a heads-up as to what's going on. I guess you just don't appreciate my courtesy anymore.

"Once the indictment is filed, the computer you've got becomes evidence. I'll be sending a messenger back to pick it back up from you."

"All right Myra, but as long as you're paying for the messenger, please have him bring over a copy of the theft video you plan on using. I'd like to show it to my client. Maybe being confronted by reality will jar his memory a little."

"Okay, I'll have one run off for you. Toodle-oo, Petey."

I don't know what's worse - the fact that she's indicting my client, or calling me 'Petey.'

I've never handled a felony-murder case, but was always under the impression that it only applied to deaths occurring during the commission of violent crimes like armed robbery, where a getaway driver would also be charged with the murder his partner committed inside the liquor store.

This case is one where a small computer was allegedly taken out of an unattended car. No people were threatened and no violence was involved. In addition to that, I have some question as to the defendant's ability to cooperate with his own defense. His complete lack of memory precludes him from telling me what the facts surrounding the alleged theft were. It may not have even been theft. What if he was trying to recover a computer that was previously stolen from him?

There's no sense in arguing this case on the telephone with Myra. I'll save my contentions for the judge. I instruct our office to start putting together some points and authorities for a motion to quash the indictment that I'll be making once the grand jury rubber-stamps Myra's presentation to them. And what the hell is she doing going to a grand jury anyway? That's supposed to be reserved for investigations meant to be kept secret or involving the misdeeds of public officials.

Her messenger will be here pretty soon to pick up the laptop. I guess I could fight giving it back now because as of this moment officially there are no charges against my client, but what the heck. There's no reason creating another battle that will eventually be lost once the indictment comes in.

Just to make sure there's no hanky-panky at the D.A.'s office, I scratch my initials into the bottom of the computer. I know that they'll be sending it out to their cybertechs, who will probably take it apart. I want to make sure that I can recognize it as the same one, when they present it in court.

I shake the dog biscuit box to summon the beast, attach a note to his collar and send him to the

61

forward stateroom. Suzi should know that the laptop will be picked up shortly, so if she's going to get any information out of its hard drive, it will have to be in the next twenty minutes.

I already told John Doe that something like this might happen, so there's no reason upsetting him now. I'll wait until the videotape and indictment come in and then meet with him and make plans to have him surrendered at the hospital ward of County Jail. In the meantime I've got a lot or research to do.

Myra's messenger takes the laptop and drops off the videotape. It contains footage from a surveillance camera that's mounted inside a fifth-floor window in the old Hall of Justice, directly across the street from the Criminal Courts building. The portion of this tape she sent me runs less than five minutes but covers the entire sequence of events quite nicely.

First we see the alleged victim's sedan luckily grabbing a parking space in front of the Criminal Courts building. The driver gets out of the car, locks it, and goes into the building. We then see John Doe cross the street and do the thing that I'm sure influenced Myra to press charges. He uses a 'slim-jim' to open the driver's-side rear door of the sedan.

I've seen that device used several times by AAA drivers who get called out to help people get into cars they've locked themselves out of. It's a thin strip of metal with hooks in its design. When used properly outside of a car, it can be slid down the between the window and the door and hook onto something that when lifted will unlock the vehicle's door. From the short period of time it took my client to get that rear car door open, I would say that he's had quite a bit of experience in using that nifty gadget.

Once the rear door is open, he reaches in, grabs the laptop, slams the door shut and then tries to pull the slim-jim up and out of the door. There's a problem, because it looks like the thing got stuck. He appears to be applying quite a bit of force trying to remove it. Suddenly it breaks free, and his efforts result in the slim-jim being pulled up and out of the door so quickly that it flies into the air causing John Doe to lose his balance and fall backward into the flow of traffic.

At that exact moment a black-and-white LAPD squad car is slowly driving past the building and strikes John Doe, causing a concussion, breaking his leg and knocking him to the ground. Strangely enough the computer is being held so firmly under his arm that it doesn't even hit the pavement. A split second after the squad car hits John Doe the lady in the Plymouth slams into the squad car's rear end and I see four airbags deploy. Two in each car.

The old adage about there never being a cop around when you need one just doesn't apply in front of the Criminal Courts Building during the daytime. In a matter of seconds there are at least a half dozen uniforms from different police agencies running out to assist the occupants of both cars and to comfort John Doe. Within another couple of minutes several red-and-white paramedic vehicles pull up and the emergency medical technicians take everyone involved away.

The next few minutes are just other police officers taking photos and marking off the accident scene and then the footage abruptly ends as the two trucks arrive.

Okay, I admit my guy broke into the sedan and removed the laptop, but it looked like such a professional job that the video asks more questions than it answers. Because it was taken from across the street, the tape I saw didn't have a very clear shot of my guy's face, but I'm sure that footage from other cameras combined with the squad car occupants and ambulance attendants' testimony will conclusively tie him into the events that took place. The evidence and testimony clearly show what happened. The only thing it doesn't tell is why.

I guess Myra couldn't get in front of a grand jury as soon as she wanted to because this week is almost up and I still haven't heard from her. John Doe is still in his hospital room, so I guess no indictment was returned. I'm sure Myra would at least give me the chance to surrender him. She's no softie, but I don't think she'd grab him out of a hospital bed without at least giving me a heads-up call.

I've been to the hospital several times and discussed his situation with him. I showed him the video and left it for him to review again at his leisure, which he has plenty of. Nothing seems to be working. He still doesn't remember a thing.

The weekend is almost upon us and I'm supposed to deliver another lecture this coming Saturday, so most of my time has been spent in preparation. I haven't received any proposal from Bart Levin about using the videotape of my lecture, but I'm sure we'll work something out. This week I'll be talking more about the common law and how it evolved into what we presently use.

I hear paws. It's another dog-mail. The maildog gets a pat on the head, so he's happy. I open up the envelope and see that it's a check from Stuart's auction service business. What a pleasant surprise. It's a check for three hundred forty five dollars, along with a statement showing that my old laptop was sold and the auction service's fee was deducted. This is nice. I paid about five hundred for it more than five years ago and didn't think it was worth more than a hundred dollars now. Stuart is really doing a nice job with this new business of his. I sit down for a minute to try and think of what other useless junk I can have him sell for me.

I look around and see that Suzi is in the galley getting some dog food for the beast. She calls him by some name that sounds Chinese, so I've given him the name of 'Bernie,' which is much easier for me to pronounce than his proper Asian name. I try to initiate a conversation with the kid, not expecting any great results.

"Suzi, that message you had Bernie deliver to me was a check from Stuart's new business. He sold my old laptop for three times what I thought it was worth. Do we have anything else on the boat that we can give him to sell? Something that's useless?"

Silence. I really didn't expect anything else. The dog is looking up at me and I'm looking down at him. She notices this exchange of glances and surprises me with a reply as she heads back to the foreward stateroom. "Don't even think about it."

The television camera is set up in the rear of the classroom again, so it looks like Bart is continuing with his distance learning plan. From the looks of how many seats are being filled up, I seem to have gained in popularity as a lecturer. I hope that some little bits of English history dropped into today's presentation don't put them to sleep.

I start to address the full house and notice that some lawyer-looking types are also in attendance today, sitting in the back row trying to look as inconspicuous as possible.

"Welcome to today's lecture, ladies, gentlemen and lawyers." This gets some smiles out of the crowd as some of them look to the back row, acknowledging the fact that I suspected the same thing they did.

"Today we'll be covering some aspects of the common law of England, and how it has crept into and influenced the laws we now work under, particularly here in California, where I suppose that most of you will be practicing.

"First of all, there's nothing common about the common law. I remember these trivial little details by recalling the name Hank William."

Some puzzled looks appear on their faces. They probably think I'm mentioning a country western singer and pronouncing his name wrong.

"The William I refer to is really William the Conqueror, who pulled off a little covert operation in 1066 called the Norman Conquest. One favorable result of his police action was to impose some stability on the law of England, which was previously governed by unwritten local customs that varied from community to community.

66

"Almost a hundred years later, the 'Hank' comes into play. That's really Henry the Second, who in 1154 became the first Plantagenet king... I'll tell you what that means in a little while. One of Henry's big achievements was to create a more unified system of law that was common to the whole country. Get it? It wasn't just *common* law, it was law *commonly* used throughout the Kingdom.

"The down side of Henry's work with the law was that he got into big trouble with a guy named Thomas Becket, who at that time was the Archbishop of Canterbury. It seems that Henry's common law system was competing with Tom Becket's church courts. I think that Henry might have originally been from New 'Joisy,' because after putting up with Becket as long as he could, he had some of his own crew whack poor Thomas. Problem solved.

"The result of this contract hit was that the common law started to get a lot more popular and was finally all put down in writing by Sir William Blackstone in 1765, when he published his *Commentaries on the Law of Eng*land. In today's terms, you might call it a blockbuster. It was four volumes that covered the rights of persons, the rights of things, private wrongs and public wrongs, which is much of what you're now studying in preparation for the Baby Bar. The huge work was so popular that it reportedly sold almost ten thousand copies in its first year of availability, thanks to Joe Gutenberg's new printing press, invented a couple of hundred years earlier.

"And like popular movies nowadays, a guy named Oliver Wendell Holmes Junior thought that a sequel was in order, so over a hundred years later in

1880, he published his work. It was much shorter and simply titled *The Common Law*. It also became a classic and still is to this day. If you're curious, you can order it from Amazon.com.

"What does all this have to do with what we're studying here in this review class? Well, depending on how you look at it, either nothing or everything, because modern statutes that reflect the English common law are usually interpreted in light of the common law tradition. And that can be helpful because so much of it was recorded for our research purposes.

"For instance, take the Second Amendment. That issue polarizes a lot of our citizens because there's a conflict over whether or not the framers intended permitting gun ownership just for organized militias, or whether the right also extended to private citizens. Well what if there had been guys like Blackstone and Holmes who covered that Amendment in their works, and it was definitely stated somewhere that the Amendment either was or wasn't meant to apply to private citizens who wanted to pack heat? That would've solved a lot of problems.

"Fortunately, we've got a lot to look back on for discussion of the laws you're now studying, because as Alfred Newton said, 'if I can see farther it is because I stand on the shoulders of giants.' But all he did was figure out some obscure thing like gravity, so you can believe his statement or not.

"I see that you're all wriggling around in your seats, so we might as well take a short break. Anyone who is interested can hang around and I'll tell you what Plantagenet means, and when you come back after the break I'll let you know how the Bar exam is fixed."

That gets a lot of open-eyed looks from the group. Just like the television newscasters, I like to leave them with a 'teaser.' It acts as an inducement for them to stick around for the next portion of the lecture.

After the hangers-on get their Plantagenet answers, I take my own short break and check the voice-mail on my cell phone. Myra called to let me know that the grand jury returned an indictment of my John Doe and that as we had already arranged, she was sending her goon squad to transfer him to the County Jail. Why shouldn't this case be different from any other one I've had recently? Another client whose guilt can be proven up by countless witnesses, and I have absolutely no idea about what kind of defense to raise.

I told my client to be prepared for this occurrence. Myra's message also let me know that she informed my office, so Suzi could call Mister Doe and tell him to get ready for the transfer.

I better get my suit pressed, because I'll be making an appearance next week to try and get that indictment quashed. My break time is up, so it's back to the lecture circuit.

The last part of my lecture will be the analysis of previous Baby Bar questions and answers, so this brief segment I'll now be giving is the last of today's oratory.

"I'm glad you all came back so promptly. Maybe it's because of that inflammatory remark I made earlier about the Bar exam being fixed. Well it is, but it's completely unintentional. Let's say that you're in a small study group of three or four top students and you're all being tutored by a private instructor... some brilliant judge – if that's' not an oxymoron.

"Anyway, that judge happens to use the word Plantagenet in one of his examples while explaining how the common law comes into play. Let's also say that five years has gone by and one of the members of the study group is now a grader for the Bar exam. He or she now has been hired to grade about five hundred answers to a particular question and is now going through the last two of them. They're both about the same quality. Wobblers. They can go either way – pass or fail. The grader is prepared to throw one of them on each pile, so that one will pass and the other will fail.

"While skimming through both of the answers, the grader notices that one of them is talking about Henry, the first of the Plantagenet Kings, and how he started the common law system in his kingdom. Wow. What a coincidence. The grader can't help but think that one of these students attended a small study group that was coached by the same judge that he studied under. Now I ask you, which one of those papers do you think will be given the benefit of the doubt and tossed onto the 'pass' pile?

"Of course. It'll be the one that the grader thinks was written by the member of the judge's study group. That's not a crime or an intentional wrong. The grader is human and acts like it. The moral of the story? Realize that all the graders of Bar exams are in northern California, probably graduates of Berkeley or Stanford School of Law. So here's a tip: talk to someone up there and try to find out what casebooks and textbooks they use. Learn what outside reading is recommended for them. Try to be like them as much as you can. Do I think it'll help? Well, it couldn't hurt. Now, let's get on to the problem analysis.

I look around the room and fantasize that if it was proper, today's lecture would have gotten a nice round of applause. At least there is no one sleeping, and they seem to be exchanging looks of satisfaction at what they've heard today.

It's too bad that I don't have anything that satisfactory to say about John Doe's case because as they lead him away to the penitentiary after his trial I'm sure that no applause will be forthcoming... even in my own fantasy.

As the students file out of the room I notice that one of the older males is still straightening up his notes. I take a wild shot.

"Excuse me, but I noted on the class cards that we have students here with very diverse backgrounds and occupations. I was wondering if you would mind telling me what yours is."

"Not at all. I'm a doctor."

So far so good. If Suzi were here I'm sure she'd point out that copy of a medical journal sticking out of his briefcase as being a good enough clue. Now that I've found one of the doctors in the class, maybe I'll get lucky and he's the one that's the shrink.

"Oh, that's nice. Horses and people?"
"Ha, no, just people"
"Darn. Everyone's a specialist nowadays."

That seems to have broken the ice. Now for the final question.

"Any particular branch of medicine, doctor?"

"Yes, I'm a psychiatrist."

Bingo! The mother lode. We exchange some small talk and I ask him if he's having difficulty with any concepts we're covering in the review course. He tells me he's having a slight problem differentiating between the various crimes of larceny, theft by trick or device, and embezzlement. Good. Now, all I have to do is get him wrapped up in a conversation and lead him over to the nearby coffee shop where I can answer his questions and cross-examine him about mine.

After the coffee, sandwiches and half hour of discussing thievery, it's time for dessert and payback. I know that the court would never authorize the expense of my hiring a shrink to tutor me, so this is my chance to possibly learn something about my client.

"Doc, I wonder if you could answer a question or two for me... it's about a case that a friend of mine is handling. His client doesn't seem to remember anything about the accident. I think he's got some kind of amnesia. Is that a permanent condition?"

"That depends. Does your friend's client only have difficulty remembering the details of the accident that caused his physical trauma? If he does, that's called Lacunar Amnesia. If that's what he's got then it's usually only temporary, and he'll start to slowly remember things over time."

"No, that's not it, Doc. He doesn't even remember his name."

"Well in that case it's probably what we call Traumatic Amnesia, caused by a non-penetrative blow to the head, like in an automobile accident. It can result in anything from a loss of consciousness for a few seconds to a coma."

"Yes. That's right. He was in a coma for a while after the accident. That's interesting. I didn't know there was more than one type of memory loss."

"Mister Sharp, if you like surprises, you should know that those are only two of the many types. There's Fugue Amnesia, which is also known as Hysterical Amnesia. That's usually caused by some psychological trauma so terrible that the mind has difficulty dealing with it. And then there are also Anterograde and Retrograde Amnesias, where the patient cannot recall incidents either after the traumatic incident, or before it happened. And of course the ever-popular Korsakoff's Psychosis, which is caused over a period of time by alcohol abuse, plus Posthypnotic Amnesia, Disasscociative Fugue State, Transient Global Amnesia, Infantile Amnesia, and on and on. Need I continue?"

"No, no. That's quite all right. I get the idea. There are quite a few kinds of amnesia. But the bottom line is that most of the time it's temporary, right?"

"Yes, most of the time... unless the memory loss is being caused by a brain tumor, stroke, swelling of the brain, or some other non-psychological, strictly physical reason. But by using proper diagnostic procedures we can usually discover them, so it's not too hard to rule out those causes.

"Here's a tip. There are some things that are permanently burned into every person's memory. They may be the easiest ones for them to recall. If I was to speak to that patient, there are one or two questions I would ask him to maybe start the ball rolling. If he's an adult over sixty, I'd ask him where he was when he heard that President John F. Kennedy was shot. If he's an adult black male, I'd ask about the assassination of Reverend Martin Luther King Junior. If he's younger, I might try John Lennon's shooting, or ask about the tragic attack in New York on September 11th, the capture of Saddam Hussein, or any other huge memorable headline event. Even O.J. Simpson's or Michael Jackson's acquittals might do the trick and shake their memory, bringing them back to the present."

That was nice. A little more information than I needed, but at least I now know that John Doe's condition probably isn't permanent. I thank the doctor and make a mental note as to some of the questions I'll be asking John during my next visit. As we exit the coffee shop he hands me his business card.

"Here, Mister Sharp. I'm available to testify as an expert witness in the case but I'd like to at least examine your client before taking the stand."

6

My pre-trial motion to quash the indictment has been filed with the court and is set for a hearing this afternoon. The defendant's presence is not required for this hearing, and on his behalf I waive his right to be present. Both Myra and the judge feel that I'm doing the right thing by not having him brought in here from the jail hospital.

This is definitely not a high profile case and there will be no witnesses called to the hearing, so the judge decides to make it as informal as possible. He invites Myra and I into his chambers, where the court reporter has already set up her stenography device. He starts the ball rolling by calling the case and indictment number for the record. He then looks directly at me.

"Counsel, you're the moving party here, so you'll go first. I want you to know that I've already read your Motion and also the District Attorney's opposition paper. Do you have anything you'd like to add in the way of oral argument?"

This sounds like he's already made his mind up. I know the odds are against any judge setting aside an indictment.

"That depends Your Honor. If we could be given some hint as to which way you're leaning, my oral argument can be arranged to go from a brief thank-you, to about twenty minutes of impassioned pleading."

The judge picks up his phone and buzzes his clerk out in the courtroom. "Miss Hearn, please hold my calls for the next twenty minutes."

He has a subtle way about him. I start my plea, knowing that it's probably in vain.

"Your Honor, first I'd like to remind the court that in California, the felony murder rule has been reserved for deaths that occur during the commission of violent crimes. We're all familiar with a getaway driver being charged with the death caused by his partner inside the liquor store, but in the present case the only crime alleged is one against property, and not against a person. In fact the prosecution doesn't even have a complaining witness claiming loss of the personal property alleged to have been stolen."

I pause for a breath. The judge looks over to Myra and she takes the hint that it's her turn to respond.

"Your Honor, section 189 of the California Penal Code specifically adds Burglary as one of the crimes for which a defendant can be charged with felony murder if a death occurs during perpetration. In this particular instance, the underlying crime is burglary of property valued at more that the minimum required amount to classify it as a felony, instead of merely petty theft.

"Furthermore the court should realize that section 459 of our Penal Code expands the crime of burglary to include the breaking and entry into automobiles, which did not exist when the common law definition of it only included '…breaking and entry into the dwelling house' of another…"

I have to say something here so that I at least go down trying. "Your Honor, I can't argue against the District Attorney's statement of the law as it appears in our Penal Code, but we contend that the alleged crime, if there was one, was concluded at the time the defendant had possession of the property. The events that took place afterwards were not part of an ongoing crime or attempt to avoid capture... they were the result of an accident. The defendant lost his balance and fell backward into oncoming traffic.

"We must draw some line in the sand as to when what the District Attorney calls 'perpetration' concludes. Six months later, if there is a real owner of this laptop computer, he or she might discover that it's gone and drop dead of a heart attack. We admit that this is less than the one-year-and-a-day common law rule for a murder charge if injuries had been directly caused by a defendant, but it's certainly well past the 'perpetration' phase of the alleged underlying theft."

The judge asks Myra. "What about that Ms. Scot?"

"We'll go along with drawing the line at six months Your Honor, but not at six seconds, which is about the time between the theft and the accident causing the death. Furthermore, because the slim-jim burglary device was still in the car's door after defendant had appropriated the computer, we contend that the crime had not yet been completed. Our evidence indicates that the defendant was actually in the act of removing the burglary tool when he lost his balance. This is definitely a case of a death during the perpetration of the crime."

She scored big-time with that salvo. The judge was impressed.

"She's got a point there, Mister Sharp. How do you respond? Ready to call it a day?"

"Not quite, Your Honor. We would like to point out to the court that little by little, the law is chipping away at the felony murder rule. It originated in England, and even there it was abolished by the enactment of their Homicide Act of 1957. It has also been abolished in several states of this country, and the United States Commentary to the Model Penal Code finds the felony murder doctrine 'indefensible in principle.'

"In several other states not abolishing it completely, where the homicide is not intentional or foreseeable, it has been reduced to felony manslaughter. We would also like to cite one particular case of People versus Burroughs, where the defendant was convicted of 2nd degree felony murder because he was practicing medicine without a license and convinced a terminal cancer patient to not have a bone marrow transplant. The patient died at the defendant's residence as the result of a massive hemorrhage of the mesentery in his abdomen, brought about by massages performed by the defendant.

"In that case, the appellate court reversed the conviction and announced that they have held the felony murder rule in disfavor for some time. Their stated reason for the reversal was that the practice of medicine without a license in not inherently dangerous.

"In the present case before this court, we contend that the crime of larceny is not inherently dangerous, and a felony murder conviction for the theft of personal property as is here alleged stands a much better chance of being overturned than the unlicensed doctor's case.

"And we have one more recent case we'd like to cite, Your Honor. It's the matter of People versus Jones, which was decided in 2000 by the California Court of Appeal, 2nd District. In that matter, a defendant led the police on a high-speed automobile chase of a stolen vehicle through the streets of Long Beach, California. During the chase the defendant struck and killed a pedestrian. He was convicted of second-degree felony murder. Upon review the Appellate Court reversed that conviction, reasoning that a felony murder conviction requires proof that the defendant acted with the specific intent to commit the underlying felony. The underlying felony was only a felony because of the resultant death.

"In the present case there is no indication that the defendant knew the value of the stolen item and therefore it might not have been a felony, but only petty theft."

I think I'll stop while I'm not too far behind. They should both be able to see behind the feebleness of my argument, so I'll just sit here for a while and take it like a man.

Myra takes her final shot.

"Your Honor, all of the arguments presented here today seem to be dependent upon findings of fact. Whether or not there was a crime. Whether or not the defendant knew the value of the theft item. Whether or not the crime was complete or still in a stage of perpetration, and so on. We feel that the main purpose of a trial is to determine facts, so we would urge the court to not quash the indictment and let a court or jury find one way or the other. If they convict, then the defendant can appeal and let the higher court hear his arguments about the applicable law. In the meantime we don't think the defense has presented any valid legal argument against the indictment."

The silence in the room is deafening. The judge finally weighs in.

"Counsel, I believe that defense has raised some legal arguments against the indictment, but they just weren't enough. Unless you have something better Mister Sharp, I'm afraid that the indictment will stand. Do you have anything more to say at this time?"

"No further argument Your Honor, but we would like to place the prosecution and the court on notice that we intend to request a hearing on the defendant's competency to stand trial."

This brings Myra to her feet.

"Oh Peter, give me a break. I've never heard of a court in this jurisdiction holding that amnesia makes a defendant incompetent to stand trial."

The judge breaks in.

"Okay boys and girls, that's it for today. I can see there's still a spark between you two, so I'd appreciate it if you'd continue your legal bickering out in the hall, so that nothing gets ignited in here."

After the hearing is over I notice several photographers sitting around out in the hallway. They follow me to the elevator. I must be getting famous.

On the way back to the Marina I keep telling myself that today was an effort in futility and the motion to find him incompetent to stand trial will also be a waste of time. I'm going to lose this case.

There's no way to find someone else who really committed the crime. That lady is dead. My client has no memory, and the whole thing is on videotape, with two policemen as eyeball witnesses to the entire series of events.

Logic dictates that if you can't figure out a way to acquit the client of a crime or place the blame on someone else, then the only other possible solution is to prove that there was no crime committed. They have no complaining witness. Why is that? They know who the owner of the burglarized car is. Why isn't he complaining?

Shortly before Myra and I split up, when she decided to 'downsize' the household, a former law clerk of mine decided to 'borrow' my name to get an early start on his law practice. His efforts were helped along by a conspiracy he entered into with an unscrupulous attorney, an expression many people believe is a redundancy of words. Their efforts resulted in the State Bar politely requesting that I cease and desist the practice of law for a few years. The only good thing resulting from that experience was my getting back together with Melvin Braunstein, an old classmate of mine. Ultimately that also led to my living on this boat and being the legal guardian of his stepdaughter Suzi, so the experience wasn't totally for naught.

Thanks to the honest testimony of an employee at a private mailbox place where my former law clerk had his 'office' located, the Bar saw the error of their ways, punished the wrongdoer and reinstated my license to practice. That mailbox clerk is a fellow named Jack Bibberman, and since the first day that I started practicing again I've considered him a trusted assistant. He can think straight and does really good investigative work. If there's anyone who can find out what's going on with this John Doe case, it's Jack, so I call and give him instructions to pick up the video from my boat, get whatever other footage there is available from Myra's office, get copies of the police reports, and find the reluctant claimant who drove away after having the computer he denies owning stolen from the rear seat of his car.

Back at the boat I send a dog-mail to the 'front office,' requesting either a meeting or a report on any information that might have been gleaned from the laptop during the brief time we had a crack at it. I don't really expect to be honored with an in-person meeting, so I sit back and relax for while with a dog biscuit on the table in front of me, waiting for the maildog to appear with the report.

Sure enough, in less than fifteen minutes I hear the pitter-patter of huge paws.

The report is a brief note telling me that there wasn't enough time to go through the hard drive as thoroughly as we should have, but the serial number of the computer has been sent through various databases, and an attempt to trace the legal ownership of the unit is now under way. I guess that's about as much as she could have done. Too bad I didn't give her more time. Now that the laptop is evidence in a felony murder case we might not get another crack at it for a while. Another missed opportunity. Maybe Jack's snooping around can make up for the lost chance with the laptop's files.

Wait a minute. There's an indictment on the books now. We should be allowed to inspect the evidence. I'm calling Myra.

"Make it fast Peter. I'm on my way to City Hall for a meeting."

"The defense would like to have an opportunity to inspect the evidence."

"You had your chance. We sent it over to you, your office inspected it and then we picked it up again."

"Not quite. We had a brief look at a laptop, but it was not evidence at the time. Now it is, and we're entitled to have the opportunity to thoroughly inspect it. Information contained on the hard drive may give us some information as to our client's identity, which can help him to cooperate in his own defense."

Silence on the other end of the line.

"C'mon, Myra. You know we're entitled to it. Stop trying to play hardball like that. You've got a dead-bang case with my client's actions on multiple surveillance cameras and uniformed police officers as witnesses. What are you afraid of? Ah. That's it. You're worried that Suzi will find information in that computer that your high-priced technical experts missed. That's it, isn't it?"

"No way Jose. I've had the best computer techs in the country going over that thing for the past several days. Believe me, there's nothing on it that can help your case."

"Put your money where your mouth is Myra. Or better yet…"

"Don't try that crap with me on the phone Peter. This is my office. I'll tell you what. I'll have it sent back to you, but keep in mind that we've already made a duplicate back-up of the entire drive, recorded its serial number and etched some identification marks into it, so don't think you can pull some sort of switch on us."

"What about a little side bet on the case?"

"You're wasting your time Petey. You're going down on this one. What kind of bet do you have in mind?"

"Loser buys the other side's team dinner at Pollo Meshuga."

"Done."

I wish she wouldn't call me Petey, but if that's what I have to put up with to get that laptop back for the kid, it's worth it. I have faith in her. She'll find things that Myra's experts never knew existed.

True to her word, the laptop has arrived. The D.A.'s messenger is knocking on the hull. Looking over the rail, I see that it's not a messenger. She's having it delivered by two of her investigators. As they come aboard one of them is carrying a plastic bag that has one of those twist seals on the top of it, like the one that the electric company puts on a house's meter. That's probably so that they'll have positive proof that the evidence pouch has been opened. Through clear bag I can see that they've pasted a big label on top of the case. It contains serial numbers of both the computer and the hard drive, written with a large indelible marker pen. They present me with some paperwork to sign and while one of them hands me the sealed bag containing the laptop the other turns on a tiny video camera so they can tape me receiving the sealed pouch and signing for it. I don't know which one Myra would hate losing more – the criminal case or the dinner bet.

I leave the sealed bag on the navigation counter next to the ship's wheel. The kid has to walk right past there to go into her foreward stateroom, so she'll see it and get to work soon. I'm also sure she knows it just got delivered, because one of the portholes in her stateroom looks outside at the boarding ladder, and she doesn't miss the details of anyone coming or going around here.

The phone is ringing. It's probably my client John Doe. He's been calling me every day from jail and I can usually tell it's him calling because the jail's phone number is blocked out of my caller ID display. I guess they do that for some security reasons. We really don't have much to talk about. I ask him if he's started to remember anything, and he says 'no.' He asks me if there's anything new on the case and I say 'no.' The brief daily conversation then ends with me telling him to relax and try to remember, and him telling me to let him know if anything new comes up.

I feel sorry for the guy. All the other people in jail know why they're there. Not only does he not know why, he doesn't even know who he is. During one of our conversations I try asking him some of those key questions that the shrink in Bart's review class suggested, but they don't do any good. I guess it's just a matter of time before he starts to remember things. For his sake I hope it's before he gets convicted. At least then he'll know why he's going to the penitentiary.

The phone rings again. Jack Bibberman is calling.

"Tell me you found something good, Jack."

"I wish I could Mister Sharp. Suzi ran the plates for me and they came back registered to a car rental company in the Valley. I looked at the rental place's records and found the driver. He lives not far from the rental company and he used the car to go downtown to file a nuisance lawsuit against his neighbor for excessive noisemaking."

"Why did he rent a car? Doesn't he own one?"

"No. He's a young man named Neil Kaplan who is currently living in a 20-foot Airstream trailer parked in a relative's driveway and uses his bicycle to get around most of the time. He goes to college in the Valley and rents a car every once in a while when he has to go somewhere more than a couple of miles away. He says he doesn't know anything about any computer and that it must have been left in the car by the previous rental customer."

"I don't believe that. No laptop would survive a prior rental and car-cleaning process. Just to make sure, did you find out who rented that car last?"

"Yes sir."

"Who was it?"

"No one. It was in the shop for the past two weeks having a new transmission installed."

"Okay Jack. Some other small tasks. First, find out exactly what school he's going to and what he's studying there. And find out what you can about the relatives who are letting him live in that trailer."

"What's else Mister Sharp?"

"Offer him a gift."

The 'gift' remark made to Jack B. is a little code word we like to use. What it means is that Jack should use his fancy decorated metal tin box of cigars and candy. He hands it to the subject of our investigation, telling him it's a token of our appreciation for his cooperating with us and that he can help himself to anything in the box. After the subject opens the box, either takes something out or not and hands the box back to Jack, the box is sent directly over to Victor's place for fingerprint processing. Jack makes sure that the box is wiped clean of all prints before starting the routine and Victor knows exactly where Jack's fingerprints will be on the box because he always holds it the same way.

I feel in my bones that everyone involved in this case including me, Jack and the whole prosecution's staff know that young Mister Kaplan is lying about the laptop computer. I probably could have gotten his name, address and a copy of the statement he made from Myra, but then she'd know that I'm onto him. I'd rather let Jack B. handle it.

It never stops. This time it's Stuart's calling.
"What's up Stu?"
"I'm having some problems Pete. The auction service business is going fine, but I've been getting some fraudulent credit card charges that the cardholders are protesting, claiming they were not authorized. Whenever that happens, the credit card processing company takes the money back out of my bank account. It happens a month or so after I've already shipped the merchandise and paid my client, so it's a double loss for me on each chargeback."

"That's too bad. Don't you get an authorization or some kind of approval from the credit card processor before you ship?"

"Sure we do. But that's no guarantee the charge is authorized. It only lets us know that the card number is valid, active, and there is enough remaining credit on the card to cover our transaction."

"Okay, what about address verification? I've ordered expensive stuff on the Internet and was told that they can only ship it to the billing address of the credit card and not to my private mailbox place here in the marina. Can't you get that service too?"

"I have it. Every time we ship, we verify the billing and shipping address are the same before the package goes out."

"That sounds strange Stu. Are you telling me that for some strange reason people are deciding not to pay for the merchandise?"

"I don't know Pete. All that the credit card companies will tell me is that after a thorough investigation of each case they've determined that the charges weren't authorized by the card holders."

"So what are you going to do, go out of business? You can't let a couple of crooks force you to close up shop. There's got to be some way to fight this thing."

"Yeah, I know. I understand that Jack B. is doing some investigation work for your now. Do you think he'll be finished up soon? I could really use him to track down some leads we have about this fraud thing."

"I don't know Stu, I'll beep him and see where he is with my stuff. I didn't give him too much to do, so I'm sure he'll be available for you soon."

"Good. I emailed some info to Suzi earlier today, so maybe she can track down something for Jack to work with."

I'm sorry to hear that Stuart is having this problem with credit card fraud, but some of the things he's told me just don't add up. I have a friend who runs an internet business, and whenever someone contests a charge to his or her credit card, he gets a print-out of the UPS tracking page and sends it to the credit card company. Once he can show that the order was received and shipped the same day and then delivered to the customer, the credit card company usually notifies him that they have concluded their investigation and the charge will remain as it stands.

From what he tells me, his main problem is the name of his business, which is 'Magic Lamp,' from which he sells instructional videos on everything from Sign Language to Real Estate Appraisal. Evidently, when wives go through the family credit card statements at the end of each month, they see the name of his business and think that their husband has called some phone-sex outfit while away on his last business trip. This infuriates them, so they notify their credit card company that they're protesting the charge.

When he responds to the wife's protest with a copy of the order for the instructional materials, along with the UPS records, miss housewife discovers the stupid error she's made, and drops the protest. In Stuart's case, the name he operates under is 'Auction Specialties,' which is hardly the type of name one might confuse with a phone-sex company. I hope that Jack B. can do some good for him.

No report yet from Suzi about what she's found on the laptop's hard drive.

My last court appearance on John Doe's case was the motion to have his indictment quashed. At that time I put the court and prosecution on notice that we would be requesting a hearing on his competence to stand trial. The hearing has been scheduled, so I better get some points and authorities together. From what I've already researched on the matter it looks like this will be another losing effort for me, but it will accomplish one or two favorable things. First, it's a stall tactic that will give us more time. This is always desirable in criminal cases, because the more time between the alleged crime and the trial, the more time there is for witnesses to forget, or become unavailable. But that's not what time can do for us in this case. Here, more time means a better chance that John can start to remember things... things that might shed some light on this case, like why he took that computer, and how he knew it was there for the taking.
Secondly, the additional motion and hearing gives me the feeling that I'm trying everything I can to provide him with the best defense I'm capable of. And it also builds up my billable the hours on my time sheet, which will make my little partner very happy.

Jack Bibberman calls me back. He got all the important information on Neil Kaplan's family and also on the young man's studies at the local junior college. All the info is being sent directly from the school and credit reporting companies directly to Suzi's computer. I don't know how he arranged to have that done. I don't think I want to know. Jack is far from being in the Anthony Pellicano class of investigators, but I still think it's best for me to sustain some level of deniability. At the end of our conversation he lets me know that Stuart called him with an assignment. I tell him that anything else we have to do can wait and that he should go help Stuart out.

John Doe is calling.

"Hello John, how are you doing today? Any news on the memory front?"

"Not yet Mister Sharp. You mentioned that you were going to request a hearing to judge my competency to stand trial. Is that coming up soon?"

"Yes John, it is. Do you want to attend, or will you authorize me to waive your appearance right for this one too?"

"I'd rather not be there. If you're going to argue that I'm incompetent, I think I'd feel kind of uncomfortable sitting there and being the object of that type of argument. It's like you're saying I'm some kind of crazy person or something."

"It's not like that at all John. The main thrust of my argument will have nothing at all to do with your sanity... only with your memory loss making it impossible for you to effectively cooperate with counsel. But if that's the way you feel, then I respect your request to not be there. I'll let you know how it works out, but like I said last time, don't get your hopes up."

It's unanimous now. Everyone knows that this hearing will not be successful. But it's a legal step that must be taken to preserve his rights on appeal... after the conviction.

7

It's 'show-time' again. This time we'll be doing it out in the courtroom instead of in chambers, because both sides will be calling witnesses to the stand. I retained my shrink student doctor Sheldon Eidoch to testify as an expert. During our first conversation about it he said he wanted to personally examine John Doe. I told him that we couldn't afford all the time it would take for him to do it at the jail, so since this is only a hearing that will probably not be successful, he agreed to do it after only a telephone interview. I did promise him that if he testifies at the trial, we would definitely arrange for an in-person exam at the courthouse on the morning of his testimony.

I arranged to have John Doe call my cell phone at an appointed time when doctor Eidoch would be with me and available to talk to him. And to make matters even better, I got the court to pay for his exam and witness fee.

Myra has her own expert too. The district attorney's office has a female shrink on staff. She has a large rubber stamp in her office that says 'fit to stand trial,' and routinely uses it on every file sent to her office by the prosecution. The only time her standard finding ever got rebuked was the case of a cab driver charged with resisting arrest. He wouldn't talk to the police during the booking process, and his clever lawyer asked for a fitness hearing. The cab driver wouldn't talk to the shrink either. She spent about a half hour with him and then used the rubber stamp, noting in her report that he was lucid, alert and their conversation indicated he understood the charges against him.

At trial, it was discovered that he was one of those 'bandit' cab drivers who didn't understand or speak a word of English. He was able to interpret the customer's pointing of directions as he drove, but not a word anyone ever said to him.

Everyone in the legal community knows that no matter what your contention is, you can find an expert' to corroborate it for you. But you have to play the game because if you don't, the appellate record shows only one expert testifying, and no one to rebut that testimony. One good thing about having your own expert on the stand is that once a person's educational pedigree has been established, unlike other witnesses, an expert is allowed to offer opinions into evidence. This gives a creative lawyer the opportunity to raise many alternative theories as to the defendant's acts then and let the expert theorize to his heart's content. If you're lucky, you might also be able to sneak in some theoretical possibility that sounds logical, and maybe get one of the twelve jurors to latch onto a reasonable doubt that he or she can take into deliberations with them and argue for you.

The usual court choreography starts with the electronic buzzing between clerk and judge. Then the bailiff's announcement and the judge makes his perfectly timed entrance into the courtroom and up to his seat behind the bench. This is the closest I ever get to watching professional ballet.

Once the judge takes the bench he calls the case and both Myra and I stand to state our names and respective clients for the record. The judge duly notes that once again the defendant has waived his right to appear. The judge looks down at me.

"All right Mister Sharp. It's your party."

"Thank you Your Honor. We would like to begin by citing the federal case of Wilson versus the United States. It's been included in our points and authorities and provided to both the court and prosecution. In that case, the most well known that addresses this problem, the court established what became known the 'Functional Evaluation Approach' that looks into six factors to be considered in determining whether a defendant's amnesia impairs his ability to stand trial. As you can see by the attached documentation, number one on their list is 'the extent to which the amnesia affects the defendant's ability to consult with and assist defense counsel.'

"Just as important is factor number two, 'the extent to which amnesia affects the defendant's ability to testify on his own behalf.'

"We would like the court to especially note the fifth factor, which looks at the 'strength of the prosecution's case,' – most importantly, whether the government's case is such as to negate all reasonable hypotheses of innocence. The court then went on to hold that if there is any substantial possibility the accused could, but for his amnesia, establish an alibi or other defense, it should be presumed that he would have been able to do so.

"In this present case before the court Your Honor, the defendant has complete amnesia. As our expert witness will testify, it is not merely lacunar amnesia affecting the memory of a specific event, nor anterograde or retrograde amnesia, affecting memory after or shortly before an event. This defendant is suffering from complete traumatic amnesia. He doesn't even know his own name.

"The underlying crime establishing the felony upon which this felony murder charge is based is theft. As with other common law crimes, theft is composed of two elements – the act, or *actus reus*, and the *mens reas*, which we all know means the intent to deprive the rightful owner of possession and use of the subject property.

"The indictment lays out the crime of theft in generalities without mentioning the name or existence of a complaining witness supporting the alleged theft. Not only that, but the official police report, a copy of which is also included in our brief, shows that the driver of the car that the personal property was removed from denies ownership or possession of the item - a laptop computer.

"We intend to ask the court to consider that the defendant, without the ability to testify to any events leading up to or giving reason for his acts, is therefore incapable and unfit to provide necessary information, or to testify and otherwise cooperate in his own defense.

"Furthermore, the prosecution has failed to provide the defense with any information as to the history of the allegedly stolen item, which contains a serial number that should leave a perfectly good paper trail.

"At the present time our client is in custody. We are not asking for bail, nor are we asking for any type of release. We will stipulate to the continuation of his custody in the county jail's hospital ward pending his memory returning, or ownership documentation of the allegedly stolen property.

"Without either of the above two events taking place, we would ask the court to hold defendant temporarily unfit to stand trial and to stay any further proceeding in this matter pending a progress report hearing in thirty to sixty days, at which time the court can be provided with enough information to conclude its determination as to fitness or requirement thereof."

I call doctor Eidoch to the witness stand. Like a good soldier, he backs up everything I've said. I'm only concerned with one question that Myra might ask him on cross-examination. And she certainly doesn't forget to ask it when she gets the chance. In fact, it's her very first question to him.

"Doctor Eidoch, did you actually have an opportunity to examine the defendant, or is your entire opinion based solely on information provided to you by the defense attorney, Mister Sharp?"

I prepared him for that one and he comes through with flying colors.

"Miss prosecutor, I would never take the witness stand in any court proceeding without spending a minimum of an hour conversing with the subject of my testimony."

Myra bought it. She never asked if it was an interview in person. If push would ever come to shove, I told the doc to admit that it was only a lengthy telephone interview, but it never came up, so we avoided that bullet.

After Myra is through asking my doctor her standard questions I tell the judge that we're finished our main argument and I sit down. Whew! That was quite a mouthful. After the hearing is over I intend to ask the court reporter to prepare of transcript of that opening argument. I don't remember much of what I said because I must have been on autopilot for most of it. I'd like to read the words to see if any of it made sense. I don't hear any laughing in the courtroom, so I guess that at least part of it went well.

Myra's papers in opposition to my motion are replete with plenty of cases that hold completely the opposite of my argument. I don't know if this judge actually reads all the pages of junk he is presented with by both sides, but I know that if Myra really wants to, she's certainly got enough ammo to stand there and argue for the better part of an hour.

She stands up and starts. Nothing new here. She goes through all the well-known cases holding amnesia no reason to keep a defendant from standing trial. One by one she knocks down every point of my argument. She then calls her 'rubber-stamp doctor' to the stand and the testimony comes out just as expected. This shrink only spoke to my client for about ten minutes at the hospital, before Mister Doe was transferred to the jail ward.

When we're both through rebutting each other's arguments, we sit down and wait for the judge to earn his money. He looks down at Myra.

"I've read all the papers submitted in both your motions, and to be quite honest, I never thought I'd be going along with anything that Mister Sharp has said today, but he did bring up one important point. We have no idea in this case whether or not the defendant was in fact trying to recover an item that was previously stolen from him. I know that sounds strange, and many thieves have tried to use that defense in this courtroom over the years, but in this case the possibility does exist. We don't know anything about him, and it looks rather strange to me that he would appear out of nowhere on a downtown street in broad daylight and right in front of this Criminal Courts building, break into a vehicle and take a laptop computer.

"Although he didn't have any identification on him, which is strange in itself, he was well-dressed and didn't look a homeless person trying to steal something for wine money. Copies of the hospital records that defense provided us with do not indicate any narcotics in the defendant's system, so we can also rule out his being a drug addict stealing something to support his habit.

"No, I'm afraid we've got more here than meets the eye. I'm not ready to declare him unfit to stand trial, notwithstanding the extremely convincing argument Mister Sharp has made here. So as long as there's no request for bail or objection to continued custody, I'm going to go along with Mister Sharp's progress report request.

"This matter is being continued for forty-five days, until more information comes in. You can both check with the clerk for a date to come back here."

At first it looks like the judge has finished making his decision and we're through for the day. I'm wrong. He's got one final announcement to make.

"And counsel, I want you both to know that I don't intend to have this matter drag out indefinitely, so depending on the defendant's progress during the time between now and the next time I see you here we'll do either one of two things at our next meeting... either declare him unfit to stand trial, or hold the arraignment. Mister Sharp, depending on which way things turn out, you'd better be prepared to enter a plea at that time. And if his leg is still in a cast, I'll accept his waiver of appearance again."

That being said, the judge bangs down his gavel and leaves the bench. Myra and I look at each other in amazement. Neither one of us won, but we still can't complain. Her indictment is still intact, the defendant hasn't been declared unfit to stand trial, and we both have some additional time to do the things we need to do. Myra can use the time to make her case stronger and I can use the time to find out what the heck actually went on in this case and decide exactly what type of plea to enter, if necessary.

When leaving the courtroom I see the same group of photographers sitting out in the hallway and watching me. Previously, they were peering into the narrow windows of the courtroom doors, as if there was something in there to see. Maybe they're waiting for some celebrity to appear for an arraignment.

Driving back to the Marina, I call the kid to let her know what happened so she can tell John if he calls. One thing the judge said started me thinking. Where did John come from? I take out my little tape recorder and make a note reminding me to have Suzi start researching parking tickets and towed vehicles from the date of the incident to a week later, anywhere within a five-block radius of the Criminal Courts building.

If John drove a car downtown it wouldn't last for a week of overnight street or garage parking without being either ticketed, towed, or stolen. I also remind myself to take a picture of John and have Jack B. start it showing to every cab driver who delivered a fare to the building's location during two hours prior to the incident.

Those searches might turn something up if John drove downtown. I have a feeling that he didn't take a bus to the civic center, just to break into any car at random. Without prior knowledge of the fact that the car with the computer would be parked at that spot at that time, John most probably followed it… and that means he was in a vehicle too.

With a recent semi-successful court appearance under my belt and some new directions to look in, I'm a little sorry that Stuart has appropriated Jack's services because I could sure use him now to follow up on some things.

While it's so peaceful, I might as well take a shot at some leisure reading while the water I just put on the stove starts to boil. Tonight's gourmet treat will be pasta la marina, which contains exactly eight ounces of Anthony's large elbow macaroni cooked for exactly nine and one-half minutes and then drained – to which two squirts of Smartbeat transfat-free imitation butter is squeezed into and a jigger of Trader Joe's non-fat, cholesterol free imitation half-and-half is poured on. To the warm concoction a can of Campbell's 98% fat-free cream of mushroom soup it stirred in.

Once the project is complete, some non-fat imitation parmesan cheese will be sprinkled on, along with a little salt-free imitation garlic salt. This is the long version of the recipe. I'm glad I've got the time to spare because this is much better than the other mixture – the one that only requires the tossing in of some cottage cheese.

On an individual basis every one of the imitation ingredients I use really lacks any notable taste but strangely enough, when you put them all together the result isn't too bad.

The kid accuses me of having a juvenile palette but I really don't care, because the stuff tastes good to me. And no matter what I cook the dog will stay close by on 'crumb patrol.' There's nothing better in this world that a hot bowl of freshly cooked imitation food and something good to read - and tonight's reading selection is a classic.

I must have done something right with this batch because as I look toward the foreword stateroom I see two sets of eyes staring out at me through the partly open door. I reach up to the cupboard and get out two more bowls and a biscuit.

After our informal family dinner has concluded I do the dishes. Suzi gets a temporary pass on that detail because she still can't see over the kitchen counter top. We have a tacit agreement that once she's tall enough, she'll do that job for a couple of years straight. Fat chance that agreement will ever be fulfilled. By the time she's that tall in a couple of years, she'll probably be at Harvard Law School as either a student or a teacher.

As I sit down to browse through a book of collected 'locked-room' mystery short stories the phone rings. It's Stuart again, and from what he tells me, this is definitely a banner year for his business start-ups. He's proud to now be a certified Celebrant.

I have no idea of what that means, unless his pronunciation is a little off and for some strange reason he's telling me that he's given up sex, which I doubt.

He refers me to a website that explains his new services. He presides over ceremonies… everything from weddings to bar mitzvahs, circumcisions, funerals, business openings and divorces. His specialty is listed as 're-confirmations,' where people who have been married more than twenty years celebrate by renewing their wedding vows.

I was always under the impression that you had to be licensed by the state or have some type of official authorization before you could say the words "by the power vested in me by the state of California…." Evidently Stuart and the other celebrants get around that. It seems that as long as the parties have followed the standard approved procedures of getting a marriage license and blood test, anyone can perform the service and it will be fully recognized as a legal bond and not merely a common law marriage.

I'm told that he also officiates over the purchase and christening of new boats, so per his request I promise to call him should the need arise.

No report yet from Suzi about what she's found on the laptop's hard drive.

A couple of weeks have gone by and John Doe's progress hearing is still a month away. The flopping of large paws signals an incoming dog-mail. Tucked into his collar is the printout of an e-mail that was recently received.

Mister Sharp:
  I appreciate everything that you're doing for me and want to let you know that I'm getting little flashes of memory returning. I know that as an officer of the court you don't want to misrepresent my condition, so you hereby have my authority to move the progress report date up and request a trial date as soon as possible.
  It feels like my memory will return sufficiently by trial date and also realize that if it doesn't I'll stand a good chance of being convicted. Having this knowledge I still want you to set the trial date..
  I'm having difficulty getting to a telephone now that I've been moved to a different section, so from now on I'll be communicating with you by e-mail only. Unfortunately I can't receive it here, but I can send it out to you. If you have anything important to tell me, we can discuss it at the courthouse on the date of my trial. In the meantime, if I remember anything and can tell you some facts that might help my case, I'll be sure to get in touch with you.

Sincerely, your client – John Doe, at least for the time being.

8

This is an interesting twist. My pasta is still cooking so I might as well use the time to call Myra at home and let her know about my client's request. I'm sure she'll be pleased to know that the case will be moving forward once again.

"Hello Peter. To what do I owe this interruption? Did your usual pot of gruel go bad?"

"Be nice. I call bearing a gift. I heard from my client, and it seems that his memory is starting to slowly return. He thinks that it will be back completely by the time of the trial, so he's authorized me to have the progress report hearing moved up and a trial date set as soon as possible."

"All right Peter. I know you're up to something, so out with it. What trick have you got up your sleeve now?"

"I'm shocked."

"Yeah, right, just like Claude Raines was shocked in *Casablanca* when he found out there was gambling in Humphrey Bogart's café."

"No, really Myra. I'm disappointed in you. You've got what looks like a slam-dunk case here. I'm only a court-appointed attorney with no visible defense at this time, and you're suspicious of my motives? What more can I do for you, have him plead straight up to the murder charge? C'mon now, gimme a break, will ya? I just want to get this stinker of a case over with. You could at least make me an offer of some sort."

"What are you looking for here, man 1 or something?"

"No, we're really not interested in copping to any charge higher than the theft, but if you'll take a plea to the grand theft, maybe there's a little wiggle room in the amount of time he's willing to do."

"Sorry Petey. No can do. I've got real live relatives of a dead woman to deal with and I can't make any kind of deal that doesn't include her death in it. That would be too disrespectful to the family and I won't do it."

I hate to say it, but when she's right, she's right. There's no way to argue with that logic and I'd probably say the exact same thing if I was in her place. This surely is an awkward situation when a defense attorney agrees so wholeheartedly with a prosecutor. We didn't agree this much when we were married. I just wish she'd drop the Petey.

"Okay, mizz district attorney. I can't argue with your position. I guess we'll just have to let the jury sort it out."

"If it's okay with you Peter, we'd rather waive the jury and let the judge decide this case."

"I don't know. I think my guy would be more sympathetic as an amnesiac in front of a jury. If his memory has returned enough to testify on his own behalf and explain away his actions that will be fine. If the memory hasn't returned sufficiently, then I've got the sympathy card to play.

"Why don't you have your office contact the court and get us a new date for the progress report? My client won't be appearing at it anyway, so there's no sense waiting for his approval. You can email the date to Suzi and I'll see you there."

I'm almost through with my dinner and the dynamic duo are also obviously done because as I look up from my reading I see that they're both standing in front of me.

"Well, what a pleasant surprise. What can I do for you both? Some complaints about the dinner menu?"

I am now pleased to see that the little princess is about to actually address me, in person.

"Peter, we must file a civil lawsuit against Neil Kaplan."

She doesn't say very much to me, but boy, when she does, it packs a punch.

"Suzi, what are you talking about? We can't just go around filing lawsuits. For one thing, we don't have a client. And added to that, I can't think of a cause of action. Other than those two minor obstacles, I'm in complete agreement with you."

I know she'll have an answer to my objections and I can't wait to see what it is.

"Our client is John Doe and the cause of action will be an intentional tort."

"Great. We've got a client. Have you and the dog any suggestion as to exactly what intentional tort we should allege has been committed?"

"That's your job. You're the attorney here, and a law professor too. However, I might suggest that you tie it into the intentional infliction of mental distress due to Kaplan's willful failure to testify truthfully about the laptop computer that was removed from the back seat of his rental car. I'll start the pleadings and give you the paperwork to file it with the Superior Court when you go back there for the progress report."

"Suzi, this Kaplan is a kid. He's only about ten years older than you, but unlike you, he doesn't have a pot to do anything in. He lives in a trailer in his relatives' driveway. Even if we were successful with our civil suit, we'd never collect anything out of a judgment. This will be a waste of time, money and effort and probably won't get to court until after our client is already serving hard time in some penitentiary, which would make him less than a credible witness. What do any of us have to gain from a civil suit like this?"

Now she gives me one of those her eye-rolls, indicating frustration at my mental thickness and for not immediately realizing the genius of her suggestions. As they both walk toward her stateroom she leaves me with a closing remark that indicates the brilliance of her suggestion.

"Peter, in a civil suit, Mister Kaplan will have to testify. He can't avail himself of the Fifth Amendment like he could in a criminal prosecaution. I'll draw up the questions you should ask him in his deposition, which can be conducted before our client's trial. The answers will probably help with your defense of John Doe's criminal case."

Damn she's good. Of course... why didn't I think of that? Kaplan can refuse to give a statement to the district attorney and refuse to become a part of John Doe's criminal trial, but if he doesn't cooperate in a civil deposition, we can try to attach whatever assets he has and have him threatened with contempt.

I can't help but feel that Suzi knows some things that I don't know, but that's always the case. She's probably done quite a bit of work on that laptop computer that Myra's office delivered to us. I hope she lets me in on it soon, because at this point in time I've still got absolutely no defense for John Doe, or whoever he really is.

Another dog-mail lets me know that John's progress report has been set for a couple of days from now and that the civil suit against Neil Kaplan will ready by then for me to file with the court, while I'm downtown.

Stuart calls. He wants to thank me for letting him borrow Jack Bibberman for a while because Jack's come up with some fascinating information. It seems that each one of the unauthorized credit card purchases was put on the account of a customer who had recently notified the credit card company of a new billing address.

All of those new billing addresses are those private mailbox places that also has a street address and offers the service of receiving UPS packages for it's mailbox customers. One way or another, it looks like someone has been able to get their hands on a bunch of credit card numbers. Their next move was to notify the credit card companies of new billing addresses. This was no doubt done for two main reasons. First was to prevent the real credit card holder from getting a statement in the mail and noticing the unauthorized charges. The other reason is that it gave the crooks a shipping address identical with the new billing address, so they could receive the ordered merchandise.

I've got several credit cards myself, but the only thing I notice about the statements is that they keep coming every month. I don't think I'd notice it too much or complain if the statements didn't show up for a month or so.

Jack B. was a clerk in one of those private mailbox places when I first met him, so that probably explains why he was able to establish such an instant rapport with the clerks of those places. From what Stuart tells me, the clerks were cooperative, but wouldn't allow Jack to access the mail in the boxes. But they did let him come behind the counter, from where he could peek into the back of each mailbox and see that there was very little in each one. From return addresses on some mail that he was able to see, we learned that some of the P.O. boxes contained letters from credit card company collection centers, so we must be on the right track.

Their plan is clever. The billing address for local credit card holders is changed, and the complete credit limit of each card is then used up by unauthorized purchases of merchandise shipped to the new billing address of each card – a private mailbox place. Once each credit card is 'maxed out,' the crooks just toss it away and let the threatening collection letters collect in the private mailbox – all without the true credit card holder ever having the slightest idea of what's going on.... That is, until they try to use their credit card to make a truly authorized purchase, only to then discover that the card has been maxed out and cancelled for non-payment of previous statements.

I only have one or two questions to ask him.

"Stuart, if all this merchandise is being delivered to these private mailbox places, what happens to it? It's gotta be picked up sooner or later. No private mailbox place wants to act as a free warehouse. Is Jack following up on that?"

"Sure. From what his last report indicates, the crooks slip the mailbox place clerks an extra couple of bucks to not tell their bosses when the merchandise is starting to pile up into a noticeable heap. Every Thursday a van comes and picks it all up, leaving room for the next batch of stuff to come in."

"Great. What about some paper trail for the people who are renting those private mailboxes?"

"Jack says they're playing ping pong with contact addresses. They'll always pay cash to rent one private mailbox and then use it as a contact address when they go to the next private mailbox place. There's no way to trace them. No paper trail. They're too slippery."

"Don't worry Stuart. If anyone can find the trail, it's Jack. And you can do me a favor. I'm really curious about this, so please let me know when Jack finds anything interesting."

Wow, what a scam. Most decent credit card companies will let a customer with a good payment track record have at least a twenty thousand dollar credit limit. If the average consumer keeps a balance down to a thousand or so, there can be over fifteen grand of useable credit on each card. If this gang rips off only a dozen cards each month, they can wind up amassing a couple of million bucks a year. And that's only with a small operation.

All the merchandise has to wind up somewhere and there's probably too much of it for anything but a warehouse. All the various merchandise purchased with the cards is in so many different categories that they probably don't have one or two main buyers, so they're probably acting as 'power sellers' on eBay. This means they've got a complete storage, packing and shipping operation somewhere.

If all the private mailbox places Jack found so far are in the San Fernando Valley, then the warehouse is probably there too. I wouldn't be surprised if they also have some money stashed somewhere. The members of this ring are going to be good targets of civil suits and a RICO action, which is an acronym for a federal act the authorities use that stands for Racketeer Influenced Corrupt Organization. Once the authorities can establish that the bad guys are operating a criminal enterprise, by using the RICO Act they can seize all assets that are the result of ill-gotten gains, including the stolen merchandise and anything purchased with the profits from it. I hope Stuart can get to them before the authorities do.

Strangely enough, the auctions keep going on because that's how the feds and many local police agencies usually get rid of the RICO assets they seize. Most of the time it's expensive houses, jewelry and cars. Those are the toys that the bad boys go after. Come to think of it, so do I. I have a luxurious yacht, a Hummer and a Rolex. Well, the Rolex is actually a phony one that Stuart gave me, but it looks really nice and probably keeps better time than a real one because it's got a fine, cheap Chinese quartz movement.

Maybe that's why eBay's stock is such a good buy. The same merchandise can get auctioned off several times. The first owner sells it to the second and maybe even third owner before it gets into the credit card fraud ring's warehouse. They buy it from eBay and then turn around and sell it there too. If and when the authorities seize it, it probably winds up getting auctioned off on eBay again by the various police agencies, so the whole process can get started again.

The progress report hearing is scheduled for this afternoon and true to her word, Suzi has the civil lawsuit against Neil Kaplan all prepared for filing, including a check for the proper fee made out to the Superior Court. I see that there is another document included… it's a subpoena for Kaplan to appear at a deposition. The attached note tells me to have the Marshall's office serve the Summons, Complaint and Subpoena all at the same time and to make sure that I set John Doe's trial far enough in the future so that we have an opportunity to depose Neil Kaplan. She's the office manager, so I'll do as I'm told.

An old movie entitled *Meet John Doe* is shown occasionally on television. It was made way before my time, back in 1941, and was directed by the famous Frank Capra. It featured Barbara Stanwyck as a scheming newspaper reporter who concocts a story about a man so fed up with politics that he intends to commit suicide on a certain date. I think it was New Year's Eve. Of course the guy didn't really exist, but when her boss demanded that she produce him, she hired a down-and-out bum to pretend he was the guy she interviewed for her story. She named the homeless man John Doe, a part wonderfully played by Gary Cooper.

When all the other papers' reporters got wind of the story they went nuts trying to find out the identity of her John Doe. This is the exact type of situation I've been trying to avoid, and for that main reason have tried to keep my client out of the courtroom as much as possible.

After visiting the court's civil filing counter and Marshall's office, the Neil Kaplan suit is now filed, on the record, and being sent out to be served. Having completed that chore, I can now go upstairs for the hearing. The only real exercise I get nowadays is using the stairs in courthouse buildings and today is no different. As I make my way up the seven floors I notice that there are a few people who have the same idea. We're all using the stairwell instead of the elevator.

This afternoon the courtroom is packed with reporters, and camera crews are out in the hall waiting to get a picture of John Doe. Notwithstanding the crowd gathered, for some strange reason the clerk decides to ignore the case's popularity and calendar our matter as the last one of the day. While waiting for my case to be called, every reporter in the courthouse begs me for the opportunity to have an exclusive in-jail interview with John Doe. Frank Capra couldn't have staged this afternoon any better.

The case finally gets called and there are moans galore from the gallery when the judge states once again for the court's record that we've entered into a stipulation agreeing that my client has waived his right to be present today. The judge looks down at me.

"Mister Sharp, does the defense have anything to report today at this hearing?"

"Yes Your Honor. We are pleased to report that we are withdrawing our motion to have the defendant declared unfit to stand trial and at this time are offering a plea of not guilty on his behalf." The judge has his standard poker face, not displaying any emotion one way or the other.

"Very well Mister Sharp, the defendant's plea is duly noted. The clerk tells me that we're looking at about two months from now for the trial date, so check with her before you leave and pick a date mutually agreeable. And Mister Sharp.."

"Yes Your Honor?"

"I'll expect to see your client here for the trial, even if we have to bring the hospital bed in here with him."

I make it out of the courtroom without being attacked by the press, only to find out that the gaggle of reporters is waiting for me outside. There's no way out of it so I might as well give them something. Once the paparazzi flashbulbs die down and all the news cameras and microphones are ready, I begin.

"Ladies and gentlemen, I'm sorry, but I really have nothing to tell you. You've all probably seen the prosecution's videotapes, so you know as much about what happened as I do. As far as my client is concerned, it would be a complete waste of time for any of you to meet with him. He is in a total state of traumatic amnesia. He doesn't remember the incident. He doesn't remember anything before the incident. He doesn't remember anything after the incident. He doesn't even remember his own name.

"Both the prosecution and our office are doing everything we can to try to find out his real identity, from fingerprints to missing person reports to photos, and anything else we can think of. There was no identification on him at the time of the accident.

"We deeply regret the loss of that woman's life in the automobile accident that occurred when the police car struck my client. We have no intention to sue the police department for our client's injuries, which other than the amnesia consist of one broken leg.

"As for the case itself, we have entered a plea of not guilty and are still waiting to see if the prosecution can come up with anyone who will admit to being a victim of the alleged theft that is the underlying charge of their entire felony murder case."

Some of the reporters shout out the same questions that they usually do, about my ex-wife being the prosecutor and what my opinion of that is. I smile and ignore those questions and keep trying to make my way through the crowd towards the parking lot. One of them shouts out a question that gets a rise out of the crowd.

"Mister Sharp, are you going to bring in that cute little girl to solve this case for you, like you did last time?"

What a smart aleck. Sure, Suzi helps out quite a bit, but I'm the attorney. I'm the adult. I'm the one who really solves the cases.

They realize I'm leaving now. One last question is shouted out.

"Mister Sharp, when you went to the filing room and Marshall's office, what papers were you filing?"

That question tips me off to the fact that not only are they surrounding me here, but they started following me as soon as I entered the building.

"I also handle other matters. John Doe isn't our office's only client."

I finally get to my Hummer in the underground parking area, where one or two more reporters have staked out my car and are waiting for me. They get the same answer as the others. No interviews with my client and no further comment from me.

The wait for our turn in the courtroom causes me to get back to the boat just in time for dinner, and upon arriving I see that Suzi has arranged for the Asian Boys to deliver and serve us a gourmet Chinese dinner from the restaurant around the corner. This is very nice of her. I also see that she's been considerate enough to put out the evening's newspaper for me to read. The television is on and as I'm sitting here watching myself on the early evening news and getting ready to start reading the paper, the phone rings. My caller ID display shows a number I don't recognize. It's been forwarded to us from our listed office answering service.

"This is attorney Peter Sharp. Can I help you?"

"Yes Mister Sharp. I saw your ad in the newspapers."

"Would that be today's paper?"

"Yes, it's on page four."

Before I can get to the page she mentions, she lets me know the purpose of her call.

"I am the wife of your client John Doe."

9

This is a surprise. I tell her to hold on for a minute while I try to find this 'ad' she claims that I put in the paper. It's not an ad. It's a featured article by a modern-day Barbara Stanwyck. There it is – a large picture of my client, Mister John Doe. It's a blurry black-and-white. One of the reporters must have dressed up like an intern and snuck into his hospital room before the transfer to county jail. It looks like the picture was shot while he was sleeping.

They've put our phone number in their tabloid-style news story, re-hashing the old Gary Cooper movie and asking the public to please provide any information that might provide a clue to my amnesiac client's identity.

One of the articles even goes so far as to offer a reward for the correct identity info. This must be what my caller has dimwittedly understood to be my 'ad.' At least the paper spelled my name right.

"Madam, I did not place what you think is an ad and I am not offering any reward. If you are interested in money I suggest that you contact the newspaper."

Her silence tells me she now realizes I will not pay her. I politely end the conversation.

"Thank you very much for calling, and I'm glad that you've found your husband."

Immediately after hanging up the phone I call the answering service and tell them that under no circumstances are they to forward any more calls to my private number for at least another thirty days, and to refer any reward-seekers to the newspaper's telephone number.

I see that Stuart is joining us for dinner. He's brought his law books so he's probably here for a study session with Suzi. I wouldn't be surprised if she takes my place at Bart Levin's review course in a couple of years. Maybe even sooner than that.

Suzi and the beast join us for dinner, but she rarely joins in the conversation. She's too busy analyzing everything that Stuart and I say. The dog is on constant crumb patrol.

Stuart fills me in on Jack B.'s progress so far. He's a thorough investigator but he can only do so much without some help from the people he interviews. The clerks he's encountering all over the San Fernando Valley are cooperative, but they can only go so far in helping him out, because none of them want to violate their boss' strict company rules about customers' privacy.

Stuart asks me if I have any suggestions that might help Jack out. I think about it for a short while and then tell him what I think might be a successful approach.

"I've learned that when everything else fails, as a last resort for gathering information, sometimes truth can work. This investigation is about violation of state and federal crimes involving interstate credit card fraud, so it should behoove any person in the custody chain of this merchandise to bend over backward with cooperation. Any effort less than one-hundred and ten percent might be an indication of complicity in the crimes and could possibly result in prosecution for being an accessory with the active conspirators."

Stuart agrees my suggestion might work and promises to get the word about it to Jack. I also suggest that he have Jack try to find out anything he can about the van that comes to pick up the merchandise. I seem to remember hearing that the van usually comes on Thursday, so I suggest that he stake out one of the places and if he sees the van, to follow it for the rest of the day. Maybe he can find out where all their incoming stuff is received and stored.

No report yet from Suzi about what she's found on the laptop's hard drive. This is not normal. She should be done with it by now.

The phone rings. It's a number I haven't heard from in a while... the Uniman Insurance Company, and it's old man Uniman himself calling.

"Hello Peter, how are you doing? Do you know who this is?"

I don't want to deflate his ego by letting him know that both his name and number appeared on my called ID display when the phone was ringing.

"What a pleasant surprise. Of course I know who it is. I could never forget your voice. It's nice to hear from you Mister Uniman. I'm doing fine, thanks. To what do I owe the pleasure of this call?"

"I understand from the news reports that you're representing that John Doe fellow."

"That's right. You don't insure him do you?"

This gets a chuckle out of the old man.

"No, I can't say I do. But he's been a co-defendant of mine in many lawsuits."

Clever. Many times when a civil lawsuit is filed, plaintiff's attorney will make allowances for additional defendants to be discovered at a later date. This is done by including in the caption of the lawsuit not only the known defendant's name, but by also adding 'and John Doe I through X.'

"Peter, in addition to our carrying the personal automobile insurance policy of the police officer who was driving the vehicle that the woman crashed her car into, we also have a life insurance policy on the deceased woman who crashed into the police car. The deceased woman's family is suing the city claiming that the sudden stop of the police car was not necessary to prevent a crime because the crime had already taken place. That it was done to stop an escape. Therefore, they say that both the city and the police officer are jointly liable.

"The woman's family has also put in a claim to collect under the double indemnity clause of her one million dollar life insurance policy."

"I understand what you're saying Mister Uniman and know what it would take to help you save a million or two, but once again you've put me in the middle. I can't possibly help both you and my criminal client at the same time, because the interests are diametrically opposed. In order for your company to get off the hook, my client must get convicted.

"I admit that we've worked well together several times and I'd certainly like to help you out here too, but I'm afraid there's nothing I can do for you on this case without causing a tremendous conflict of interest."

"I understand Peter, but as in the past, I'll make you the same offer. If for any reason you can figure out how to help me get off of the two million dollar liability hook that I'm on, there's the usual ten percent bonus in it for you. And while we're talking about it, I don't want that bleeding-heart conscience of yours to hold you back. If we don't have to pay out on the double-indemnity clause the family will still get their one million dollars life insurance benefit.

"During your thorough investigation, if you should happen to discover that the dear woman was in violation of any particular law, like driving too fast for conditions or following too close, or something like that, please let us know. A back door escape clause in our double indemnity policy provisions allows for us to get off of paying the second half if the insured was in any way contributory to the accident that caused her death."

"Okay Mister Uniman, I'll keep my eyes open for anything that might help you, as long as it doesn't conflict with my client's defense."

This old man is one smart cookie. I hope he isn't hinting that I throw John Doe's criminal case, because there's no way that's going to happen. What will really take place is that I'll lose the case because I have no defense to offer for him... and then old man Uniman will not pay me any bonus because he'll claim I lost the case on its merits without doing anything special to protect him. This whole matter is a lose-lose situation for everyone involved.

A dog-mail brings me an email from Suzi's incoming folder. It's the retainer agreement from Uniman Insurance that promises me a ten-percent fee for providing information to his company that results in them saving money on the claim payments to the deceased woman's estate. I turn on my terminal to send him a response to our conversation, locate Uniman's e-mail and see that Suzi has added a small paragraph to the end of the agreement. She wants the ten percent fee to apply to *all savings* of liability and financial exposure arising out of the John Doe matter, with an additional amount added on to cover reasonable expenses we incur in investigation.

I have don't know what other *savings* the kid has in mind, but there must be some reason she added the paragraph. There usually is. I add a side note letting Uniman know that our law firm accepts the agreement with the additional paragraph, and that if he agrees to the revised fee agreement to send us a snail mail printout of the document with his signature on it.

The classic case of psychological suggestion in a sporting event is exemplified by a boxer's manager who knows that his fighter can knock out the opponent in the first few rounds, and goes into the dressing room before the fight to give his boy some words of encouragement. "Listen Slugger. I know you're going to win tonight, but I want you to know that if you knock this palooka out in the first couple of rounds, you'll not only retain your title, but his career will be finished and you'll have really earned that five million bucks you're making tonight.

"On the other hand, if by any strange stroke of luck he manages to hang on for the whole ten rounds and you win by a decision, not only will you get the same victory and the same five million, but there'll be a re-match next year, at which time you'll win again, and walk away with at least eight million. Now I want you to go in there and do your best."

This is the same mind-trick that Uniman is pulling on me. If I knock out the opponent, there'll be no re-match, which in this case is spelled r-e-w-a-r-d. Well that's too bad. Everyone has to draw a line in the sand over which they won't cross, and mine is drawn. I've got to give my client the best possible representation I can. I just wish I had something to work with. A recent email from John Doe says that there's been no further improvement in his memory situation. That means there'll probably be no help from him at all in explaining or justifying his actions in removing that laptop from Kaplan's car.

More than twenty years ago, as a naïve undergraduate college student, I allowed a sadistic counselor to talk me into signing up for a calculus class. One day our professor tried to explain the concept of something he called a 'limit.' He said we should imagine that we want to walk closer to a wall, but each time we would be restricted to stepping only half of the distance between us and the wall. As he explained it, we could take as many steps toward the wall as we want to, but because we could never move more than half way to the wall with each step, we would never really get there. That, he said is a 'limit.'

I never got around to using any of my math courses in real life after college and law school, but trying to figure out a defense for John Doe looks like trying to take steps toward that wall.

No report yet from Suzi about what she's found on the laptop's hard drive. This is starting to concern me.

The phone rings. It's Myra calling.

"Peter, I'm sending someone over to retrieve that laptop. We've got a trial date now and you guys have certainly had enough time to inspect that evidence."

"Sure, send someone over. It doesn't make any difference. His memory hasn't come back yet and you're going to win anyway, so please, be my guest. I'll tell Suzi to get it ready for you."

"Fine. And you can also let her know that we'll be sending over the other videotapes she requested, along with the police traffic accident report. I have no idea what you want it for, but the messenger will bring it."

Somewhere in the back of my mind I get the same old feeling I've had before. The kid has something up her sleeve. I shake the biscuit box and give Bernie a message to deliver, letting her know that the laptop is being picked up within the hour. This whole case is frustrating me. I think I'll take a quick nap.

It seems like I just closed my eyes and the D.A. investigators are already here knocking on the hull. I invite them aboard and see they've brought their little video camera along this time too. I certainly hope that Suzi has gone through that hard drive thoroughly, because this is probably the last time we'll have the opportunity. She must be aware that Myra's crew is aboard because I hear the paws of her advance party.

There's nothing like a dramatic entrance and she definitely knows how to make one. This time it consists of sending the dog out first and then letting us all stand for a minute or so while we look toward the open door of her stateroom until she slowly appears carrying the plastic evidence bag that contains the computer. While this scenario is taking place I'm bent over the table signing the paperwork for the new group of videotapes they've brought to us.

Behind me I hear the investigators thank Suzi for handing them the evidence. Once she goes back to her stateroom I hear their confused conversation. In hushed tones they're discussing the evidence.

"What the hell is going on here? Why did the boss have us make this trip two times if they weren't even going to do something?"

I turn around and see what they're talking about. It's hard for me to understand it, but I try to keep my cool and pretend to know what's going on. The thing that surprises them and amazes me is the fact that the seal of the evidence bag that the computer is in has not been broken. No wonder there wasn't any report as to what she found on the laptop's hard drive. She never opened the seal and hasn't touched that computer at all.

10

The only way that the bag could have remained sealed like that is that she either managed to open and close it without disturbing the evidence seal, or that somehow she used a wireless device to access that hard drive through the bag. I can't possibly believe she completely ignored the opportunity to go through that computer. She's always been a very responsible person when it comes to the matters of a client.

Ordinarily I never get the chance to find out what's really going on in that brilliant little mind of hers, but this time I'm going to have to ask. She should be coming out here shortly to retrieve those videotapes that Myra sent over. Ah, here she comes now.

"Suzi, I couldn't help but notice that the evidence bag we sent back to Myra didn't look like it had been opened."

At first she just ignores me. I'll try again.

"Didn't you want to thoroughly inspect it and see what's on the hard drive?"

As she struts back to her stateroom, I get my answer.

"No."

I've always known that even if I live to be a hundred I'll never learn to understand the female thinking process. I now know that their process starts confusing us men even before they're teenagers.

It looks like her entire focus has shifted from the John Doe computer to the videotapes. I've already seen the five or six minutes of security camera footage that shows the most important stuff… the theft and the accident. By the looks of the package they delivered today there must be about seven or eight tapes. I don't know what she hopes to gain from looking at the same thing from multiple cameras angles, but I guess it's best to just let her do her thing.

I'm going for a ride up the coast toward Malibu. That usually clears my head a little and gives me some isolation time to think things over. I check my wristwatch and do my daily comparison with the radio-controlled clock we have on the boat's navigation station. It gets a signal from some atomic clock in Colorado and is never more than a millionth of a second off. I see that the phony Rolex Stuart gave me is working fine. It only gains about five seconds a month, so being just after the first and having recently been reset, it's right on time.

I check my cell phone to see if the battery has a full charge and notice that the time is slightly different from the atomic clock. After waiting until the nav station's clock changes from one minute to another, I watch the time on my cell phone and see that it's time indicator changes to the next minute when the atomic clock says it's already seven seconds past the minute. Even without getting anything higher that a 'D' in my last math class, I know that means the cell phone's clock is seven seconds slow.

As I drive my Hummer on Pacific Coast Highway I doodle mentally by thinking about the time difference I noticed earlier. Unlike a computer, the cell phone doesn't have an internal clock. Whatever date and time appears on a cell phone display is being sent to it from the nearest cell on land, which gets its signal from the cell phone company's headquarters.

My wrist watch is set to the same time as the boat's clock, so I pull into a parking space overlooking the Pacific Ocean and while watching the California blondes frolicking on the beach, I continue with my timing experience and discover that the cell phone time can be anywhere from 1 second to 49 seconds behind the actual time.

This is strange, because I've never imagined a clock could fluctuate like that. I finally realize what may be causing the fluctuation. The cell phone company's clock is probably also set to the atomic clock in Colorado. The fluctuation in the time indicated on portable cell phones is caused by the fact that the time isn't 'streaming' from the base station to the individual cell phones. By not flowing in a continuous stream, each cell phone gets a time update only when it checks with the base station for an update.

I would imagine that depending on the manufacturer's specifications, the cell phones probably are set to request an update in periods that might range anywhere from five to fifty seconds. This periodic setting might be a battery-saving effort.

At one time I was playing with the settings on my computer and discovered that a user can instruct the computer to check for incoming mail at different intervals. Mine is set to check once every minute.

Up to now I've been thinking that this thought process about telling time was just a form of daydreaming to take my mind off of the fact that I'm on a losing case, but something I once learned in a college psychology class has just come to mind also. Maybe I'm not just daydreaming about the time... and that one girl in the string bikini that I've been noticing quite a bit down there as she bounces around playing volleyball.

For some strange reason an old pop tune is going through my mind. Something with words that go like "she wore an itsy bitsy teeny weenie yellow polka-dot bikini..."

Everything we do is supposed to be controlled by our subconscious, so what got me thinking about the time? Let's see... the only event that occurred shortly before those thoughts was the appearance of Myra's goon squad. Wait a minute. Those tapes they delivered all probably had the same indicators burned into them as the other one that Myra sent over to me. It's called 'time-code' and it appears on the bottom of the screen as an indicator of the hour, minute, second, and video frame as the tape is running. The numbers run by like those on a digital stopwatch, so you always know exactly where you are on the tape with respect to running time or actual time.

Okay. That's logical. The combination of the time-coded videotapes delivered and me checking my wristwatch with the boat's clock may have started the whole time daydream, but why? I think I finally may have been able to keep up with the kid. That's it. She's on to something that has to do with the time.

She's going to time everything and find some inconsistency somewhere.

So what? It doesn't make any difference what the time is. The continual set of actions contained on the videotape I saw support Myra's underlying theft charge, no matter what the time was. It's the same series of events whether it took 53 seconds or 54 seconds. The kid's succeeding in confusing me again. My only consolation is that her request for those additional tapes has probably got Myra confused too.

My cell phone is vibrating. A text message just came in from Jack B. The only time he sends a text message instead of calling is when he's in a situation where it's not convenient to be seen talking on the phone, so I won't blow his cover by calling him back. His message lets me know that he's found the van.

Come to think of it, today is Thursday. Jack must have staked out one of the private mailbox places and lucked out by being in the right place when the van arrived to pick up the merchandise purchased by those unauthorized transactions. On second thought, luck probably didn't have anything to do with it. If I know Jack he probably had that mailbox place staked out from six in the morning, just waiting for a van to pull up. He probably paid a couple of bucks to the clerk inside for a phone tip to verify that the merchandise was being picked up inside, so he knew he had the correct van.

I start my return trip to the marina and wave a mental goodbye the volleyball girl. On the way back my phone rings. It's Jack B. calling.

"Hello Jack. I got your text message. What have you got?"

"I've got the van Mister Sharp. I waited for it at one of the mailbox places and watched it load up some merchandise. I then followed it to two of the other mailbox places and watched it pick up stuff there too. It's now unloading."

"That's great Jack. You've found their warehouse. Where is it?"

"Sorry Mister Sharp. It's not a warehouse. It's another one of those mailbox centers."

"I don't understand, Jack. If they use the van to pick up merchandise at the mailbox places, why are they delivering it to another mailbox place?"

"This one is a really big place Mister Sharp. It also offers other services other than just private mail boxes."

"So what? They've still got to get all the stuff to some central location where they can pack it and have it shipped out."

"This is it Mister Sharp. That's one of the services this location offers… they pack and ship."

Clever. These guys don't even have a warehouse. They pick up their merchandise every seven days after it's already spent up to seven days in transit to them. That means they can offer the items on eBay the instant they buy them, and still have almost two weeks for the seven-day auctions to be completed, and collect from each of the new buyers. Instead of bringing the merchandise to a warehouse, they just bring it to a place that packs and ships. In most cases the items are probably sold before the crooks even receive them. The exact same pictures and descriptions that appeared on the web pages where they bought the merchandise can be copied and put onto their own eBay websites for sales purposes.

"Okay Jack, we're still in the game. You follow the van after it's unloaded, and see where it ends up. That'll tell us something about the people involved."

"I did Mister Sharp."

"Already? That van guy must live really close by."

"He doesn't have to Mister Sharp. One of the other services that this large mailbox place offers is van rentals. Once the van was offloaded, the guy walked across the street and hopped onto a bus. There's a divider in the middle of this street, so I couldn't get to the other side of the street in time to follow it. If I took the time to go around the block I would've caught up with the bus, but would have missed one or two stops that he might have gotten off at without my knowing."

"Well Jack, I suppose you know where you're going to be at about this time next Thursday, don't you?"

"Yes sir, Mister Sharp. I'll be standing across the street at the bus stop. I'll give you a report next Thursday evening when I see you at the boat."

"You're coming to the boat next Thursday?"

"Yes, I have to deliver some papers to Suzi. They won't be ready for me to pick up for a couple of days, so I'll give you my report when I bring those papers over for her."

"Do those papers have anything to do with my criminal case or this fraud thing you're working on?"

"I don't think so Mister Sharp. Suzi said that it was on another matter."

I can't keep up with her. Of course she has the right to work on whatever things she wants to, but if it has anything to do with the practice of law I'd sure like to know about it, because it's my license on the line if she screws anything up.

The week hasn't gone by fast enough for me because I'm anxiously awaiting Jack to get here and fill me in on what he learned about the van driver today.

Now that dinnertime is finally approaching Suzi asks me to reach up into the cupboard and bring down dinner service for five.

"We're having guests this evening?"

No answer. The mere fact that 'service for five' is more than the two of us obviously answers the question for me, so she doesn't have to.

Once the table is all set up very nicely she instructs me to get the tea set out. I dutifully obey. The dog has just quietly whined a relaxed warning that someone is approaching the boat. It must be a 'friendly' because he isn't even getting up. I look over the rail and see that Jack B. is bouncing up the boarding ladder. Once he enters the boat he hands Suzi an envelope that looks like it's from the telephone company. Then Jack and I retire to the main saloon to discuss his activities.

I used to think that the parlor area of a boat was referred to as a 'salon,' but an older guy who is a boat neighbor of ours on the dock corrected me. I now refer to it as the 'saloon.' He's the friend with an internet marketing business that was advising me on the credit card issues for online sales. Because a lot of the DVDs he sells are boating related, our other neighbors look him upon as the most knowledgeable person on the dock with respect to all matters nautical. There's a rumor going around that at one time he used to practice law, but if he never volunteers any information about that. I'll respect his right to privacy and not mention it to him in future conversations.

"Okay Jack, what did you find out today?"

"First of all I started from the beginning, waiting for him to appear at the mailbox place to pick up the van. As expected, he got off the bus right in front of the place, walked in to pick up the keys and then drove off, with me tailing behind him.

"One by one, he made the rounds and stopped at each of the mailbox places they use to receive their loot. I even discovered several more places than I already knew about. At the end of the afternoon he made his last pick-up and then headed back to return the van. As soon as he pulled into the parking lot I got out of my car and peeked in to see what he was doing.

"He had a pile of UPS shipping labels already printed out and one-by-one was pasting them onto the packages. This means that all the merchandise was already sold and he was putting new labels on so they could be shipped to the new owners. When he finished with his labeling work he started bringing the packages all inside. At that time I walked across the street and waited for him by the bus stop.

"In about fifteen minutes he came across the street and we both boarded an eastbound bus. Just three stops later he got off the bus and I followed him as he walked down the street about a half block, got into a car and drove away, leaving me standing there with no car to follow him with.

"I got the license plate number and called it in to Suzi. She ran it through and told me that it was from a car-rental place. I walked back to the main street and took a cab back to my car and then drove to the rental place. Their office was already closed for the evening, so I had to call it a day. Next Thursday morning I'll be there bright and early to see how our van driver arrives at the rental place. He must leave his own car there, and I should be able to get the plates and some more information about him."

I don't see Suzi anywhere near us, but I'm sure she heard every word of Jack's report. The dog is up and wagging his tail. This means that a new first-time visitor must be arriving. Because there is no snarl, it also means that Suzi has told him that this new guest is to be treated as a 'friendly.'

To my surprise our guests are a mother and daughter combination, both Asian. Mrs. Chang and her daughter, Lotus. The mother is in her late thirties to early forties, but still looks extremely nice. The daughter is a little taller than Suzi, but I don't think she's that much older. She's not cuter than Suzi, but she's still a pretty little girl.

I was never told who these people are, so I assume they're some friends the kid has made at the restaurant. The mother is very attractive and speaks fluent English with only a slight bit of a British accent. They're obviously a couple of high-class people and the mother seems well-read and educated too.

Just before dinner Jack and I have a nice conversation with the mother, during which she tells us some very interesting stories about Hong Kong and life there before it was given back to China to be governed. The two small girls are having their own conversation in Chinese. This is the first time I've ever seen her with another person her own age, and it's nice to see that her usual anti-social behavior is reserved only for me.

Suzi walks over to the dog and whispers something in his ear. The dog suddenly gets up and dashes off the boat like he really has something important to do. Looking out the window, I see that Stuart is walking down the dock towards the boat. He probably heard that Jack B. would be here with some information about the fraud ring.

I see the dog rush toward Stuart and jump up to greet him, placing one large paw on each of Stuart's shoulders. This is a pleasant surprise for Stuart, who always gets along fine with Bernie, but it also stops him in his tracks, because there's no forward motion possible with that dog standing up in front of you.

Suzi then walks over to Jack and says something to him in a language that I don't believe is Asian. It sounds European. Jack nods in agreement, excuses himself for a minute and then steps off the boat and walks over to Stuart. Looking out the window, I see that as soon as Jack reaches the point where Bernie and Stuart are standing the dog lowers himself from Stuart's shoulders and returns to the boat.

Jack tells Stuart a few words and then Stuart turns white, turns around and hastily leaves the dock.

He walks over to his car and drives away. I don't know what just went on, but because I have two other humans to ask other than the kid, there's a good chance that this time I may eventually get some explanation as to what actually happened... and why.

Jack isn't the type to sit around and schmooze, so he leaves shortly after dinner is over while the Asian Boys are clearing the table. The kids are both in the foreward stateroom and because the door is open I can see them playing with the computer. What ever happened to dolls?

With Jack gone and the kids busy the beautiful mother and I decide that it would be nice to take a brief walking tour of the marina, so we put the leash on Bernie and leave the boat. I have to admit that she is a very nice 'arm lady,' and that's exactly what she is this evening as we casually stroll through the marina with her arm around mine. I enjoy taking strangers on this tour because it gives me an opportunity to point out all the big yachts that are owned by the rich and famous. Strangely enough Mrs. Chang isn't the slightest bit interested in who owns any of the boats... she wants to know all about me.

About an hour passes before we get back to the boat and when we step aboard I see that the kids are still wrapped around the computer, probably bidding on some stuff at eBay.

Mother tells daughter that it's getting late, so they both get ready to depart. The girl is trying to make the visit last another few minutes, so I offer to walk Mrs. Chang to her car. She tells her daughter that she is expected to be up at the car in no more than five minutes.

Our last few minutes before the daughter gets here is very pleasant and we're standing very close. When we see the daughter walking up the dock, escorted by the dog, Mrs. Chang tells me she enjoyed herself very much, says goodbye and plants a very nice platonic kiss on my cheek. As she does, I glance down at her windshield and notice the parking sticker decal placed inside the glass. It sends a slight shiver down my spine while I stand there waving goodbye to them both as they drive away.

Once they're out of sight I make a beeline back to the boat. Suzi is still supervising the Asian Boys as they complete their clean-up operation. Bowing their heads to me, they depart.

After she nods goodnight to me and goes to her stateroom I pick up the phone and call Stuart.

"Hello Peter, what can I do for you?"

"Just one question Stuart. What's the name of that I.R.S. auditor who requested you to come to their offices?"

There's a slight hesitation before Stuart answers.

"Uh, she was Asian. I think it was Chang."

11

I knew it. Somewhere deep in my bones I had a feeling that Stuart didn't hire an accountant to go with him to that I.R.S. audit. Suzi must have noticed the name of 'Chang' on the audit letter and figured she could handle the situation. Stuart probably drove her there and waited outside while Suzi was inside working her magic.

It's no wonder she was able to wrap Mrs. Chang around her little finger, especially since Mrs. Chang has one like her at home and Suzi probably spotted Lotus' picture on the auditor's desk. I also feel pretty sure that Suzi dangled the dinner invitation to mother and daughter as an extra psychological incentive for a favorable result of the audit.

It worked. Stuart got off the hook and Suzi got a new friend to play with. As much as it rubs me the wrong way to see Stuart get away with his tax scam and phony marriage, I feel a lot better seeing this kid find someone else her age to communicate with. I'm sure that this mother-daughter team will make a return appearance here, and to tell the truth I'm looking forward to seeing the older one again. I never asked her about her husband, but if she had one, he probably would have come along with them.

Now that I've learned what that routine was with Bernie going out to stop Stuart from getting to the boat until Jack could warn him away, the only remaining question in my mind is the origin of the language Suzi used to instruct Jack. I can't resist any more, so I call Jack B.

"Jack, it's Peter Sharp. I have one question to ask you. When you were on the boat and Suzi wanted you to head off Stuart so that he wouldn't bump into his I.R.S auditor, what language did she speak to you in?"

Jack laughs a little. This is the first time I've heard him do this.

"It was Yiddish. That's the language Jewish people used to speak in the old country. I didn't know she was aware of the fact that I spoke the language… that's the only way I was able to communicate with my grandparents. They never learned to speak English. From what I've heard, her stepfather Melvin used to speak Yiddish when kibitzing with some of his older Jewish friends. I guess she picked it up from him."

Amazing. A young little Yiddish-speaking Chinese girl is running my law firm. She'll do just fine when the Red Army gets here.

"Oh by the way Jack, did you ever get any information on that fellow Neil Kaplan's family? The people who are letting him stay in that trailer in their driveway?"

"I wrote down the license plate on that trailer and Suzi ran it to get the registered owner's name. It matches the person who owns the house there. I also contacted a friend of mine at a credit reporting company who ran the guy through and found out that when he works, it's usually for a janitorial company that cleans offices nearby. It doesn't look like he's doing very well. He's driving an old beat-up car and his credit report shows that he's got a charge account at K-Mart. Definitely not in the upper middle class, if you know what I mean."

"Let's keep digging Jack. And if you're wondering why it looks like I'm butting in on the fraudulent credit card assignment that Stuart gave you, it's because Suzi tells me that he's retained us to find out who is behind it and go after them for punitive damages. And you know that we're a little freer when it comes to spending his money than Stuart is, so don't hesitate to do whatever it takes to get some results. Just try to keep the billing separate between the John Doe investigation and the stuff you're doing on Stuart's case"

With John Doe's arraignment now taken care of and Jack B. doing all the grunt work on several cases we're working on, I'm going to waste time my favorite way other than by reading, which is surfing the internet. I'm not a compulsive shopper but I hate to walk through malls and visit stores. I used to buy every item of clothing but shoes on the Internet, but I just saved about $60 on a $149 pair of Ecco walking shoes by getting them through a Yahoo store. These particular shoes use the European sizing method and to my pleasant surprise they fit perfectly.

Because we have a high-speed broadband cable modem internet connection coming into the boat, we leave the computers on all the time. This gives the unsolicited emails a chance to build up in our incoming folders, notwithstanding the 'spam' filters that the kid installed. I see that one of them is from American Express.

They are pleased to announce that they have completely upgraded their security system and are now offering me instant access to my account on the Internet. If I will sign up for this new service and allow them to eliminate the need to print out a statement each month and mail it to me, they will give me 25,000 air miles as a bonus. All I have to do is verify my American Express credit card information and I will not only get the free air miles, but also get an American Express carry-on bag.

Wow. This is very inviting. The picture of the premium they're offering looks good too. It resembles a gym bag, is made of leather and has the distinctive American Express logo silk-screened on each side. And I certainly could use the additional air miles because they'll come in handy on my next trip over to Maui.

The form that appears on this attractive and well laid-out page has just a few blanks that require filling out. They ask for my current American Express card number plus the same information that was presented at the time the card was applied for, including address, mother's maiden name and social security number. Once this information is filled in, I'm instructed to create a user name and password for future access to my account. As an added feature, if I provide them with my bank and checking account information, I can receive an additional 25,000 air miles by authorizing them to automatically deduct the monthly balance from my checking account to pay the credit card bill.

Not meaning any pun, I really must give them credit. They've designed a beautiful website that offers all the features that their card-holders will appreciate. The company will save time and money by eliminating the paper statements and the card-holders will save time and money by accessing their accounts online and having them automatically paid.

In addition, the thousands of air miles and handy carry-on bag go together perfectly. There's only one slight problem with the entire program. The website is phony. I don't have an American Express card.

I also now notice that the email wasn't addressed directly to me. It was in our office's incoming folder, and was specifically addressed to the member of our office staff for whom a special email folder was created to receive personal correspondence between our closely-knit organization. Mail coming to this folder must be specifically addressed to that particular staff member, a Mister Bernard Braunstein: the canine member of our staff.

This verifies my theory about the website's authenticity. The message is not from American Express. From what I've experienced in the past, they run a pretty sophisticated operation. It's bad enough that they could possibly send out a message like this to someone who doesn't even have an American Express card, but sending it to a dog is the type of error I don't believe that company would ever make.

I get in touch American Express through their official company website and after contacting their fraud department, forward them the e-mail we received. The investigator calls me personally to offer the company's thanks and tells me that they've received quite a few inquiries about the authenticity of that website. They are now preparing a warning notice to be posted on their company's official website.

From what he tells me, there is a new activity on the Internet called 'phishing,' whereby a counterfeit website is created and designed to look exactly like the credit card company's, complete with logos and corporate information. The emails are sent out at random to millions of people, in a 'phishing' expedition to get a small percentage of the recipients to jump at a chance for free air miles and a nice leather carry-on bag.

When unsuspecting people fill in the blanks and submit the form, the crooks have enough information to start a shopping spree using the American Express cards of some unsuspecting victims.

Most American Express card bills are paid in full at the end of each monthly billing cycle, so the thieves use their ill-gotten information to change the billing address so that the actual credit card holder never receives the statement. American Express users are a prime target for this fraud ring because it's the toughest credit card to get, and only people with the best credit ratings and highest credit limits have them.

I've gotten about as much information as this security guy wants to give me, so I politely thank him and end the telephone conversation. My next move is to arrange for some re-enforcements. I'm calling the FBI

Over the past year or so I've established a sort of working relationship with a Special Agent named Snell who runs the Los Angeles FBI office from his plushly furnished suite in the West Los Angeles Federal Building on Wilshire Boulevard, just off the San Diego Freeway.

Our working relationship usually goes like this: I do all the work and he gets all the credit. His getting all the credit is the downside, but the upside is that on rare occasions when he thinks it will benefit the government, I get his cooperation and full resources of the FBI. This arrangement has worked out quite well in the past and we've cooperated on the breaking up of two illegal operations. One was a bank-robbing team and the other was a motion picture piracy gang.

After being on hold for about five minutes I finally get through to him.

"Hello Sharp. What is it this time?"

Same old Snell. I think that the FBI trains them to not be friendly.

"I'm fine Special Agent Snell. Thanks for asking."

"Cut the crap Peter. Things have changed a lot around here and I don't have time for chit chat."

Okay, that's a good sign. He's using my first name.

"Agent Snell, I think it's about time I made you famous again and took you out of your current routine of sneaking around mosques and writing down license plate numbers."

"That's not funny Sharp. We're fighting a serious enemy now and the last thing we need is your wise cracking about our efforts."

"You're right Agent Snell, and to help you with your efforts I'd like to offer my assistance in breaking up a ring of people who may be practicing wire fraud and identity theft to raise money for funding terrorists."

I have no idea if there's any connection with our credit-card fraud people and terrorists, but that seems to be the best way nowadays to get the government's attention, and by using the "T" word it looks like I did. All you have to do is hint that some activity is connected to Osama's gang, and you can get whatever you want.

"Okay counselor. I'm listening. What've you got?"

"I've got a phony scam to get people thinking they're receiving emails from their credit card companies. They're promised bonuses like free air miles and other small premiums for signing up to access their accounts on line and are tricked into revealing their personal information, including bank accounts, credit card number and social security card number."

Silence on the other end of the line. I'll try to close the deal now.

"That's what I've got. Are you interested?"

"Not really."

"What do you mean 'not really?' I'm offering you a criminal fraud ring on a silver platter and all you've got to do is have your gang track down some emails and a couple of internet service providers. My crew will do all the work and your guys will get all the credit. You know what I mean. That press conference bit you do so well."

"You heard me Sharp. I'm not interested. We've got bigger fish to fry. Anything else you want today?"

Now I've heard everything. From what I've seen, the FBI relishes the opportunity to show off their prowess at press conferences where they can 'be pleased to announce' that once again they've come to the rescue of us citizens. For some strange reason Snell says he's not interested. I don't believe him.

This only gives me more motivation to crack this ring on my own and rub it in his face at my own press conference.

I go back to the phony American Express website and fill in what belongs on any phony website: phony information. As of now, Mister Bernie Braunstein now has an American Express card number, social security number and a mother – complete with a maiden name.

Now that Snell has cut me adrift, to break up this gang of crooks for Stuart's sake and to spite Snell, I compose a new e-mail instruction for Jack B.

Jack:
You won't be watching for the Van driver until next Thursday, so in the meantime I'd like you to utilize the downtime by going to each of those mailbox places where they receive the merchandise. If you do it Wednesday afternoon, you should be able to see all of the packages that UPS has delivered for them. The UPS trucks leave their garages full of packages that all get delivered in the morning. This empties out the trucks so that there's room for the packages they pick up all afternoon.
If you start hitting those mailbox places around one in the afternoon, it'll be after they've already received the day's deliveries from UPS and you should be able to see a full week's stolen inventory and also see who shipped each package. A return address should appear on each carton. Enter all the information into your laptop computer right at each mailbox place. Then go to a Starbuck's that offers wireless Internet access and email the package

info to me. I want to contact each of these people. They're all prospective clients in a lawsuit against this ring, and if any of them are local you'll probably be interviewing them to get statements.

Jack must have been sitting at his computer just as I sent the email to him because an answer came back in less than a minute

Mr. Sharp:
If I'm going to be in a Starbuck's using their internet access I should look like a customer, so will your office cover my expenses incurred ordering up the goodies they offer there?

There's nothing I enjoy more than a hot cup of freshly brewed coffee, but I'll never understand why people wait in long lines at those Starbuck places begging to pay up to five bucks for a cup of hot flavored water.

Jack:
No problem covering the expenses to make you look like a customer. I understand that McDonald's also offers wireless access. As long as it's a going to be a working lunch, you might as well visit the Golden Arches and get something a little more substantial. I understand they offer salads now, and their milkshakes are made with low-fat milk.

If Snell isn't interested in putting these people in jail, then I've done my duty. I told him what I was investigating and he decided not to get involved. That leaves the crooks for me to go after and as long as they're not in jail or arrested by Snell, I'll have a better chance to get at their assets and get some money back for the people they've defrauded.

I now feel that I've got this case pretty much solved. The crooks use what that guy from American Express calls 'brand spoofing' to fool people into giving their personal information. Somehow I get the impression that there are some people who think that Suzi is really the brains behind our law firm. That may have been true when Melvin was still allegedly running things, but I actually go to court, take cases to trial, deal with the prosecution, give instructions to our investigative staff and generally make sure that everything is going along smoothly.

We have a pretty good track record so far, never having lost a major case. Sure, the kid's a great help and provides a wonderful service with her computer skills, but I want to prove once and for all that I'm the real star around here. She does have one other tremendous skill that makes me jealous. Because of her cupie-doll face and expression, she has the ability to mesmerize people. I don't know how she does it, but once someone looks into her face and she gives off that special expression, it's all over. The subject doesn't have a chance.

I've seen her do this to everyone from Myra to superior court judges, and it's uncanny. Franz Mesmer would have been proud of her, and I think she'll do a lot better than he did. In 1778 the Viennese Empress' god-daughter was a gifted pianist who suffered from hysterical blindness. Good old Franz was asked to try and cure her, which he did. Unfortunately when she became sighted again, the inundation of visual stimuli ruined her nerves and destroyed her ability to play piano. The empress was not amused, so Franz wisely left the country and moved to Paris where he ultimately wound up broke, mainly because some American guy named Benjamin Franklin helped to de-bunk most of Mesmer's hypnotism tricks.

Fortunately, she can't work that magic on me because she rarely speaks to me in person, and when she does, it's usually just to bawl me out for doing something wrong. She must have noticed that I'm playing with my computer because I now see that she's decided to join my little chat group.

To Peter:

If it's okay with you, we've been invited to spend the night sleeping over at Michelle's house. Any evening this week would be good for me.

To Suzi:

No problem. I enjoy sleeping on land once in a while. Only one question: who is Michelle?

To Peter:

She's Lotus' mother, Mrs. Chang. You met them on the boat recently. I know you're getting older but didn't realize your short term memory was starting to go.

To Suzi:

All right Miss Einstein, it would have helped a lot if you would have mentioned her first name at least once after she left. What are the sleeping arrangements over there?

To Peter:

She has a very nice two bedroom home. I will be sharing Lotus' room, sleeping in the upper bunk.

To Suzi:

That's good for you, but what about me? I don't do floors.

To Peter:

You're not going to be there. The phrase 'we've been invited' referred only to me and the friendly, more dependable big male beast on board.

It's not exactly the type of communicating I was hoping our relationship would lead to, but at least it's communicating. Further messages inform me that Michelle will be sending her aunt to pick Suzi and the other large male animal up at the restaurant tomorrow afternoon. Michelle will be out of town on business when Suzi's sleeping over and the aunt will be the adult in charge. Little does the aunt know who will no doubt really be in charge that evening.

Other than an occasional sleep-over at Myra's this will be one of the few times that the kid hasn't slept on the boat. I'm glad her friendship with Mrs. Chang's daughter is coming along so well. When they were here on the boat together sitting at Suzi's computer, it sounded like their chatter didn't stop for the entire visit. It looks like she'll talk freely to just about anyone but me.

I'll use another box of wine as bait to attract Laverne's attention tomorrow evening. I'm sure she'll feel sorry for me because little Suzi is gone for the night. Somehow I've got to figure out some nice way to tell her not to bother with that greasy French toast the next morning. In the past I always had difficulty in getting it down, but after the dog refused it, I don't even want to look at it anymore.

Jack Bibberman is a good man. It's now Wednesday and he's just emailed me the list of people who sent items to the fraud gang. Suzi's in an especially good mood since her sleep-over at Michelle's house last week, so I instruct her to send out an announcement to each person who shipped something to the crooks. It's just a plain and simple notice that they may have been paid by the unauthorized use of a credit card, and to contact a special agent named Snell at the West Los Angeles FBI office, who is anxious to receive their complaints. They should also consider hiring an attorney to help them recover damages.

I specifically instruct her to add a sentence letting the people know that the notice is definitely not a solicitation of their legal business, and that under no circumstances would we handle their cases. If they need a lawyer, they are instructed to contact the referral division of the local bar association in their community.

My next move is to contact eBay's fraud department. I let them know all about the investigation we're now conducting and ask them to inform all of the sellers conducting auctions on eBay sites to be particularly careful when any winning bidder gives them a shipping address that is one of the seven mailbox places our fraud gang uses to receive merchandise.

Now I'm really on a roll. Tomorrow morning Jack will be at the car rental place waiting for the van driver to pick up the car that he leaves near Ventura Boulevard before taking a bus to the large mailbox place where the rental van is waiting for him. In the meantime maybe I've single-handedly put a crimp in their operation by having the eBay sellers alerted about the gang's receiving stations. If they try to get new places to receive the goods, Jack will be right on their tail by spending each Thursday following the pick-up van, and I can easily update the list of addresses sent to eBay's fraud department.

This feels good. Most of the time I rely on Suzi's computer research to give me a lead as to which direction to turn. This time it's all my brainpower and Jack B.'s legwork. I hope the kid doesn't feel too bad at the end when I crack this case without her help. Maybe it'll take her down a peg or two and she'll start to show a little more respect for me around here.

The Return of Service has come in, letting us know that the Marshall's office successfully served Neil Kaplan with our civil suit. This means he's also been notified that his deposition has been set, so I instruct our office to arrange for us to depose him in the court reporting agency's conference room.

Whenever we take someone's deposition we'd much rather use their conference room than invite opposing strangers to the boat. Another reason we like this place is that they have a special room set aside for children. So many depositions take place in divorce cases that this particular court-reporting agency prepared a special playroom to attract new business. The lawyers like it because the women involved in divorce proceedings don't have to worry about arranging for childcare while their depositions are being taken.

Suzi also likes this arrangement because whatever lucky kids happen to be in the playroom when we're there on business get a big new furry playmate for a while.

We tried bringing the dog into a deposition with us once, but the court reporter balked. It's not that she was afraid of dogs or anything, it's just that part of any transcript she prepares must state who is present during the deposition, and she was concerned that her including the name and description of a Saint Bernard being present would detract from the demeanor of the proceeding and be confusing, should the transcript be read any time in the future by an appellate court.

I've never seen Neil Kaplan other than from his driver's license photo, but I think that's him sitting across the waiting room from us, conferring with his attorney. I've also never seen his attorney before but I would say that he's an 'office' lawyer. That's one of those guys who sounds like a fighter for your cause when discussing the case in his office, but once they get into a courtroom where there's another side shooting back at them, they usually crumble.

Kaplan's lawyer is at least as old as I am. When we finally meet in the middle of the room he hands me his card and I notice that his office is located in Sherman Oaks. I've never seen him in court once during the past twenty years, so I expect him to be especially combative during the deposition because 'office' lawyers usually know how to put up a big fight everywhere but inside a trial court.

We're escorted into the conference room. The court reporter is all set up waiting for us and I've got my usual opening statement ready. Attorneys usually do a pretty good job of preparing their clients for a deposition, but I never like to give a deponent the opportunity to later claim that he said something during the deposition because his attorney didn't prep him properly. The court reporter swears Neil Kaplan in and then nods for me to start.

"My name is Peter Sharp, State Bar number 0476763 and I represent the plaintiff in this matter, filed as Superior Court Case number 8279123. We are here to take the defendant Neil Kaplan's deposition. Mister Kaplan is present and being represented by his attorney, who will properly identify himself prior to asking any questions of the deponent.

"Mister Kaplan I don't know if you've ever had your deposition taken before, so I want to remind you that everything you say here is under oath and will be taken down by the court reporter. When this deposition is over the court reporter will type up everything that was said here today and bind it into what we call a transcript, which you will have an opportunity to read before signing in front of a notary public.

"Whatever you say here today is also under penalty of perjury, which means that if you don't tell the truth, it is a felony in the State of California. If you subsequently change your testimony so that it is different from what you say here today, your credibility will be suspect.

"I'm not here to trick you. All we want is direct and truthful answers to our questions. If you don't understand the question, please don't hesitate to let me know and I'll make every effort to restate it for you.

"Do you understand what I've just told you?"

Kaplan nods in the affirmative.

"Mister Kaplan, I appreciate your nodding in agreement, but the court reporter can't take down nods, so you'll have to give us an audible yes or no answer."

Kaplan responds with a meek yes answer and I continue. Shortly before the deposition I took a brief look at the questions that Suzi prepared. They don't look very thorough, but since this whole civil case is her idea, I'm just going to follow the program and if it doesn't work out, we'll know who to blame.

I start the questioning. The first series usually pertain to identity, like date of birth, place of birth, education, employment, residence address history and so on. His attorney objects to my asking Kaplan's social security number. We argue about this for a minute or so and then I back down. I just wanted to see that attorney's reaction and how he handles himself during a dispute. He did okay. Now I get to the real meat of this depo by informing him that the next group of questions all are applicable to a certain date – the day that our client was injured downtown in front of the Los Angeles Criminal Courts Building in.

First I get him to admit that he was there that day and that he saw our client being struck by the police car. Under further questioning he explains that he wanted to get his car out of the way to make room for the emergency vehicles arriving soon, and because he didn't see our client touch his car, he had absolutely no involvement with the accident, so he drove away.

With Stuart's assistance we were able to get another laptop computer that is the exact same model as the one that John Doe is supposed to have removed from Neil Kaplan's car that day. I put the computer on the conference table right in front of Kaplan as I continue my questioning. I don't say anything about this not being the same computer allegedly removed from his car, hoping that maybe this will rattle him a little. He's the only one in the room who is under oath now, so I feel free to take a little liberty with my conversation.

"Mister Kaplan, before asking you my next few questions, I'd like you to know that we have your fingerprints on file. We also have given this computer to a laboratory that specializes in fingerprint acquisition and analysis, and they have thoroughly examined this computer inside and out, dusting all the components, the case, the display and every key. The lab has also examined the fiber content of the back seat of the vehicle you were driving that day and compared it to some microscopic fibers found on the computer. Their results are conclusive and will be offered in court during our client's criminal trial.

"Your statement to the district attorney's office was to the effect that you did not have a laptop computer in your vehicle and therefore no computer was stolen from you. This type of testimony helps our client, so we want to make sure that it is in fact truthful. You also told the authorities that if there was a computer in the back seat of your vehicle that day, it was probably left there by the previous rental customer for that vehicle, so we want you to know that for two weeks prior to your renting that particular sedan, it was in the repair shop having a new transmission installed.

"We also have traced the serial number of this computer and have found no record or paper trail that leads it to being owned by you. So I now ask you to answer this question under oath, being reminded of the penalty for perjury: was there a computer in the back seat of your vehicle when you went inside the Criminal Courts Building?"

This is where the rubber meets the road. I may be playing a little game by using this duplicate computer as a prop, but Kaplan now knows that it's time to 'fess up,' because he's been led to believe that we've got the scientific evidence to nail him for perjury if he lies now. After some whispers are exchanged between them, his lawyer speaks up. He looks over to the court reporter.

"Can we please go off the record for a minute?"

The court reporter looks to me for a decision. I nod that it's okay to stop the record. Now off the record, the lawyer goes on.

"Up to now, all Mister Kaplan has done is answer some questions for one of the district attorney's investigators. If his testimony here today is any different than what he may have said before, then his prior statement may possibly be construed as a mere false statement to a sworn peace officer and possibly excusable because of confusion."

I agree with him wholeheartedly. He looks over at his client with an expression of success, like he just scored a game-winning point in the super bowl. His nod lets Kaplan know that it's okay to continue, so I tell the court reporter that we're back on the record.

"I may have been mistaken when I talked to those officers. Some people from school were with me in the car earlier that day and one of them may have left a computer in the car."

"Thank you for your candid response Mister Kaplan, but that doesn't quite explain the fingerprints we found on it."

"Well, we all study together, so maybe I used it a little at one time or another. I watch those crime shows on television, and I don't think you guys can tell when fingerprints were put on it, right?"

Yeah, right. I give him the impression that this clears up a lot for me.

"By the way Mister Kaplan, that uncle who lets you stay in his trailer... what does he do for a living?"

"He works nights for the Markle Janitorial Service."

"What about you. Do you have any kind of job?"

"Yeah. Sometimes my uncle gets me hired part-time to fill in when one of the other members of his clean-up crew doesn't show up for work."

I get information as to the location of that Markle Janitorial Company and inform Kaplan and his attorney that we have no further questions. Kaplan's lawyer feels no need to rehabilitate his client by cross-examining him, so we both stipulate that any notary can be used and tell the court reporter that we're through for the day.

At this point I realize that not only is Kaplan less sophisticated then I thought he might be, but his attorney is a complete idiot. The basis of our lawsuit against Kaplan was Suzi's trumped-up contention that Kaplan caused our client mental distress by not admitting that he had a computer in his possession that our client may have been trying to retrieve because it was stolen from him.

At no time during the deposition did I ask one question about the other people that were supposed to have been in the car with Kaplan. Any attorney with half a brain should have been able to see that this civil lawsuit is just a back-door attempt to depose a potential witness for a criminal trial. Kaplan's lawyer didn't say one word about it. He probably was too involved in savoring his victory at keeping Kaplan's social security number out of the record… a number Jack already got off of Kaplan's school records.

I hope the kid is happy now. About the only information we got out of this entire waste of time and money is the name of the janitorial service that Kaplan's relative works for. On the way out I try to cut our losses a little by informing the court reporting agency that we won't be requiring any transcript of today's deposition. Unfortunately that doesn't work. I'm informed that there's a minimum requirement of our purchasing the original and at least one copy. Fine. Suzi can keep it as a souvenir. The only question remaining in my mind now is why the heck would Kaplan lie to the investigators?

The laptop computer didn't show up on any hot list. The only thing I can imagine is that there must be something incriminating on its hard drive. Too bad for us, because now we may never know what that is. Myra's experts went through it and didn't find anything and Suzi didn't even open the evidence bag when we were given a second shot at it. Nothing computes in this case so far. It's just not coming together for me.

Thursday morning Jack calls in. The van driver didn't drive to the rental place to pick up a car today. He walked. From what Jack tells me, it's impossible to tell where he walked from. He may have even taken a bus and got off down the street and then walked to the car rental place. This part of the assignment is going to be harder than Jack thought. He did succeed in getting some good photographs of the guy and we'll be using Suzi's facial recognition software to see if we can get a match with any headshot in California's Department of Motor Vehicle's drivers license database.

Several years ago California gave drivers an option. Your driver's license could display either a photo or your thumbprint. Because my drivers license picture always comes out looking so terrible, one time I decided to opt for the thumbprint. Everything was going along fine until I got stopped for a traffic violation one afternoon. The motorcycle cop looked at my driver's license and then asked me a question.

"Is this your license, Mister Sharp?"

In one of the stupidest acts of my career, I smugly held my thumb up to him and said. "Sure, don't you recognize me?"

By that action I immediately failed the 'attitude test' and in order to avoid the moving violation from appearing on my driving record, I was forced to sit all day in a 'traffic school,' which is an alternative that California traffic violators are offered. You can only attend the school once every twelve months, and avoid having the ticket on your record.

Because insurance rates are so high, everyone wants to keep moving violations off their record, so the schools are doing a big business. They even have 'comedy traffic schools,' which is the kind that I chose to attend back then. It wasn't the least bit funny. The only reason they call it that is because the teacher is an out-of-work stand-up comedian who isn't funny at all... that's why he's out of work.

And on the subject of not being amused, Jack B. definitely isn't We didn't get any hit on the van driver's photo and his address on the driver's license given to the rental company is an empty lot in North Hollywood. When Jack points this fact out to the car and van rental places they don't seem to care, responding that this customer always pays cash, leaves a nice big deposit and buys the highest amount of insurance available. Also, there's always the possibility that the place he was living in when he got his drivers license was recently demolished for new construction. The rented vehicles are always returned promptly with full gas tanks, and all they care about is their bottom line. Another dead end. People believe whatever they find convenient to believe.

Jack spends each successive Thursday morning watching a different street for the driver to appear from at the rental cal place, but the route varies and Jack can't find out where the guy comes from. When the car is returned each Thursday evening the guy walks away in a different direction every time and takes shortcuts that Jack can't follow with his car. He says that next time maybe he's going to borrow an old friend's tricycle and load the rear basket up with some groceries. He plans to pass by the car rental place at the same time the driver is walking away and then follow him. I wish him luck.

While the time is going by, John Doe's trial date is approaching. He calls the office once in a while and talks to Suzi and also sends me an occasional email, but there hasn't been any improvement in his memory, so there's no help there either.

Myra refuses to talk about dropping the homicide portion of her complaint, so there's nothing to talk about in the 'copping a plea' department. I might as well get used to the fact that I'm going to lose this case. John Doe is going to do some hard time for a crime that he doesn't even remember committing.

I'll bring Suzi along to the trial so she can see for herself that notwithstanding how hard we try, sometimes we'll still lose. We're not infallible.

THE TRIAL

I rarely have this feeling, but with no case, no facts and no defense, I've got a knot in my stomach. In an effort to avoid being ambushed by the press, I've put our old plan into effect. Jack Bibberman drives us to court in the Hummer and waits outside with the dog for my call so he'll know when to pull around to the exit and pick us up.

It's not too bad facing the press after you win a trial. It's terrible after you lose. The only questions they seem to ask after a loss is what you think went wrong to cause your loss and whether or not you'll be filing an appeal. If you try to avoid their questions completely it looks like you're so ashamed of losing that you're hiding from them. I'd rather just sneak out of a side exit and avoid them completely. I wouldn't mind if they asked some questions that displayed the slightest bit of legal knowledge, but what can you expect from a group of reporters who developed their entire law backgrounds by watching television re-runs of *Judge Judy*?

It shouldn't be too hard escaping without being noticed. Once the trial concludes Myra and John Doe will be the centers of attraction - not the losing attorney.

Our arrival in the Yellow Hummer with air ace Snoopy's goggled furry head sticking up out of the sunroof is a photographer's delight. Every camera in the area is covering us as we pull up in front of the courthouse. I hear a round of applause but I'm sure it's not for me. After Suzi and I step out of the back seat, Jack and Bernie speed away to await my pick-up call.

While walking that short distance to the building, most of the questions are being shouted at Suzi. They've all seen her in action before. In some previous cases she made court appearances to present the solutions to some mysteries that she somehow figured out. The press wants to know if she'll be saving my rear end this time too. Whenever the press is around she usually starts her mass-mesmerizing routine by holding my hand as we walk and innocently gaping at the reporters like they're intimidating her. Hah! Fat chance of that ever being true. I can see she's already got them wrapped around her finger. I notice some satellite trucks from foreign newsgroups parked there too, so not only am I going to lose locally, my reputation as a loser will now be distributed all over the world.

The presiding judge must have been reading the papers and realized that this John Doe case has been attracting a tremendous amount of publicity over the past weeks, so he wisely scheduled the trial in the building's largest courtroom, to accommodate the press. After this is all over they may want her and the dog to make guest appearances, but I doubt if I'll get any requests.

The only good thing about this morning is that the kid is not trying to bring the dog into the building with her. She's tried that a couple of times in the past, and I don't think the bailiffs appreciated its presence in the courtroom.

Reporters surround us as we walk through the courthouse corridors. They're all shouting questions, but like outside, they're all directed at Suzi. They want to know why she hasn't brought the dog to court this time. She loves being the center of attention and I get the impression that if she wasn't holding my hand so tightly, the crowd would whisk her away to an all-day press conference.

Ordinarily my ego would suffer a bit with the spotlight directed away from me on this day of battle, but in this case I don't mind much at all. I really don't have anything to say to the reporters. For that matter, I don't have much to say today in court either. I just want this case to be over soon.

The presiding judge made a smart decision picking this courtroom. Looking at the size of it, I wouldn't be surprised if it's the one used on Monday mornings for the large amount of defendants brought in for week-end drunk driving arraignments. It must have seating capacity for almost two hundred people, and today it's packed with reporters from all over the world, waiting to get a look at our Mister John Doe. Frank Capra must be turning in his grave.

For criminal cases, the front row seats are usually reserved for relatives of the victim and the defendant. In this case there are only two people here from the deceased lady's family, along with their lawyer. None of the horde of wannabee relatives of John Doe who called in seem to have made it today, so there are plenty of extra seats available for reporters. I see that Myra had the bailiff save one front row seat for Suzi to sit in.

The main purpose of our being here today is to pick a jury. The prosecution was happy to try this case with a judge alone, but I thought we'd have a better chance of playing the sympathy card with a jury, so today's the day for juror selections. The judge left word with his clerk that because jury selection might take a day or two, there was no need to have the defendant brought here in his hospital bed. We all agreed, so no one but the press seems to mind his not being here this morning.

Picking the jury is going a lot faster than usual. There are no special types of issues to use in disqualifying jurors. Both sides couldn't care less if some juror has a relative on the police force or working in the insurance industry, or if anyone has issues with the police. The judge announces that now the jury is seated, we'll start the trial first thing after lunch. Myra tells one of her assistants to arrange for the defendant to be brought over from the jail and she then joins Suzi and I for lunch upstairs at the cafeteria.

Ordinarily a prosecutor and defense attorney don't want to appear too friendly during a criminal trial, but Suzi arranged for this lunch and Myra didn't seem to mind. She knows she's going to win today, so there's no chance of anyone accusing her of giving the defense any special treatment in this case.

The cafeteria allows us to sit in the section usually reserved for police officers and judges. This will give us an opportunity to eat in peace, which would not be possible if we were forced to sit with the general public. On the other side of the dining room I see flashbulbs going off every second as the reporters get their pictures of the three of us trying to nonchalantly have lunch. Even though Myra and I are slightly on edge because of the constant press coverage, the kid happily ignores it and scarfs down her sandwich like she's the only one in the room. I don't know how she does it. Myra and I exchange looks of amazement at this kid's nerves of steel. But then again, what's she got to be nervous about? She goes home a winner no matter what happens today.

With the gourmet cafeteria lunch now history, we use the back hallway to get downstairs. Myra has a key to the private elevator reserved for judges and other special people, so we can get back to the courtroom without being forced to fight through the throng of reporters. At first I was a little surprised she had this access until I remembered that being District Attorney of Los Angeles County, she's the top prosecutor and one of those 'special' people.

Suzi seems to like being able to use the special eating area, special back corridor and private elevator. It wouldn't surprise me to learn she just decided that some day soon she expects to be one of the special people these perks are designed for. I like the treatment too, but I'm just not as ambitious as the little one is.

We enter the courtroom through the back door reserved for the judge. The front doors haven't been unlocked yet, so aside from the clerk, court reporter and bailiffs, we're the only ones here. I see that there are many faces peering at us through the small glass windows in the courtroom doors. When those doors open, it's going to be like a half-off sale at Wal-Mart the way they run in and try to get good seats.

Once the horde of reporters and victim's family and lawyer are seated, the usual courtroom choreography takes place with the buzzing, announcement, and grand entrance. When the judge takes the bench he motions for the bailiff to bring in the fourteen jurors, of which two are alternates, saved for any emergency that incapacitates one of the main twelve.

Nothing is happening. There is silence in the courtroom. A soft murmur of the crowd can be heard in the background as everyone seems to be whispering the same question. "Where is John Doe?"

The judge looks down at me, and then over to Myra.

"Mister Sharp, where is your client?"

"Habeas Corpus, Your Honor."

"Yes Mister Sharp, I realize that we have the body, he is not out on bail. I want to know where he is."

He looks over to Myra.

"What about it Miss prosecutor. Where is the defendant?"

Myra looks at her assistant, who then runs out to the hall to use her cell phone. Myra tries to stall a little. "He should be here very shortly Your Honor. They probably had some difficulty in arranging for transportation because he's still in a cast with that broken leg. I'm sure they'll be rolling the hospital bed in here any minute now."

The judge is not a happy camper. Judges don't like to be kept waiting. They're the ones who usually keep everyone else waiting. This judge is no different. He decides he's not going to sit up there on the bench and wait. "Miss Scot, I'm going to take a fifteen minute recess. When I come back out here I expect to see a defendant sitting over there."

He points over to the defense side of the courtroom as he gives his warning. I'm glad it's Myra on the hot seat and not me. As long as the court's not in session I might as well participate in a little photo op, so I invite Suzi to come over to the counsel table and sit with me. I may lose this case big time, but until the guilty verdict comes in I'm going to get as much favorable press coverage as possible… and some free shots for our family album.

Suzi sees me motion to her and in no time at all she's up on the counsel chair next to me, her feet dangling above the floor. At this rate, there will definitely soon be a shortage of whatever it is that creates those flashes in the news cameras. I'm pretty sure that they stopped using flashbulbs when I was a teen-ager. The kid does her best to make sure she's sitting facing me instead of to the front of the room. This gives the photographers a better chance at her profile. I don't know where she ever learned to romance cameras like that. Myra does a good job of it too. I guess it comes naturally to women.

Looking over to Myra's table I see that she's not in the room. I never noticed her leaving. The judge will be back on the bench shortly and here comes Myra and her assistant back in through the regular doors. There's confusion on their faces.

The bailiff makes his announcement, the crowd simmers down and the judge comes back in and takes the bench. I look down to my side and see that Suzi is still sitting there. That little ham has decided to be second chair in this trial. I can feel my face starting to turn red as the judge looks down at us. He can't resist making a comment.

"Well Mister Sharp, I see you've got one of your office staff assisting you here today. I also see that the prosecutor has one of her office staff assisting her today. I guess if the prosecutor is entitled to some help, you are too. Young lady, you may remain seated right where you are."

I don't believe it. In less than a few minutes she's managed to get the judge under her control. Myra isn't so lucky. The judge looks down at her now.

"Miss Scot, I've been looking over at the defense table, and for some strange reason I don't see a defendant. Would you care to comment on that?"

Myra stands up to address the judge. I can tell she's nervous. She almost stammers. I can't remember ever seeing her like this before. Not even at our wedding.

"Your Honor, there seems to be some difficulty in locating the defendant. We called the county jail and spoke to the captain and the chief of the hospital ward. They are looking for him right now."

The judge is no different than the rest of us in this courtroom.

"I don't understand Miss Scot. I've heard of prisoners escaping from jail before but I've never heard of one doing it with one broken leg in a cast and taking a hospital bed with him too."

The background conversation gets a little louder, making the judge feel that a few bangs of his gavel are required. Once order is restored he asks Myra to approach the bench. Normally when one side goes for a sidebar with the judge the other side joins in. This is one that I'm not interested in taking part in, so I'm glad the judge understands my wave as I signal that it's okay with me if he speaks to the prosecution only.

I feel a tug at my sleeve. My second chair person is trying to get my attention. I look down at her. "What?"

She whispers to me. "Can you do the trial without him being here? I think that would be a good idea."

What is she talking about? Is she trying to tell me that she knows something I don't know? That's impossible. I've been spearheading this case from the beginning and the most noticeable thing she did was to not even open up the evidence bag and inspect John Doe's computer hard drive.

This may give me a wonderful opportunity. I'm going to lose this case anyway. I can feel it in my bones. If I take her advice and not object to trying my client *in absentia*, then when I lose I can try to make her think that it was her fault. This is good. Losing is bad, but losing with an excuse takes the edge off of it a little.

The judge is still boring a new one for Myra. He asks her some questions, like the exact date that she ordered him transferred from the private hospital to the jail infirmary, and who she gave the transfer assignment to. He then tells us that the court will once again be in recess while Myra is being given a half hour to get some people into the courtroom so that the judge can hold a quick hearing to try and find out what happened to defendant John Doe.

He sends the jury home, telling them that they will each receive a telephone call from his clerk by the end of the day, telling them whether or not to report for duty tomorrow.

As soon as the judge leaves the bench again the courtroom erupts into many frantic conversations as each reporter in the room is shouting some story into his or her cell phone. Myra and her assistant are both in the jury room also desperately making phone calls to round up people the judge wants to question.

The half hour has gone by much faster than I thought. Suzi has been sitting next to me taking the whole series of events in. I try to find out what she thinks of this mess.

"Well, how does it feel to sit here during an actual trial."

"This is no trial. You haven't even cross-examined one witness yet."

"I know that. But you have to admit that what's going on here today is quite interesting. I've never seen anything like this before."

Try as I can, there's no getting a rise out of her. I hope she never decides to play poker because it's impossible to read her expression. I once read in some entertainment magazine that our alleged dock neighbor George Clooney used to have some famous friends over once a week for a poker game. If he still does that on his boat, I'd like to see this kid worm her way into the game. We'd probably wind up with his boat.

I try one more time.

"Do you think our client will show up here today?"

She gives me another one of her cryptic answers.

"He's not going to be here. You'll have to do the trial without him."

For some strange reason the noise level in the courtroom goes down quite a bit. Some new players have walked in and approached Myra's table. She tells them to sit down in the row of chairs behind her table and then signals the clerk to start the buzzing routine that gets the judge back out into the courtroom. It works, and in less than a minute the judge is back on the bench talking to Myra.

"All right Miss Scot, have you brought your friends to court like I asked?"

Myra stands up and gives him a feeble "Yes, Your Honor. They're all here."

The judge takes over.

173

"Miss Scot, please call to the witness stand your lead investigator. The one who was responsible for transferring the defendant to county jail."

Myra calls her guy to the stand. The judge starts to question him.

"Investigator, I've been led to understand that you were assigned to get the defendant in this case transferred from his private hospital room to the infirmary at the county jail. Is that correct?"

"Yes it is Your Honor."

"Did you go to the hospital to carry out your assignment?"

"Yes sir. I went there with two other investigators. We went to his room, identified ourselves to the uniformed guard outside his room and then went inside."

"Good. Now please tell me what you did next."

"Yes sir. We all went into the room. There was no one in there. He was gone. The bed was there, but he wasn't in it. There was no one else in the room."

"Did you ask the guard if he happened to notice anything unusual that day – like someone carrying the defendant out of that room?"

"Yes we did Your Honor. In fact he's in the courtroom right now. He's the uniformed police officer sitting behind the prosecutor's table."

"Thank you, Investigator. You may step down. Miss Scot, would you please direct that officer to the stand?"

Myra tells the cop that it's his turn. He walks over and sits down in the witness chair. The judge starts to question him.

"Officer I've been told that you were on guard duty outside the defendant's hospital room from eight that morning until ten thirty. Were you in fact on duty during that two and one-half hours? And was that duty continuous?"

"Yes it was Your Honor. I didn't leave my chair the entire time. If I would have felt the need to take a restroom break, my instructions were to ask a hospital security person to fill in for me for a few minutes. But that didn't happen."

"And during that period of time, did anyone enter that hospital room?"

"Yes sir. I reviewed my notes and see that I wrote down the fact that at nine that morning a nurse went in and came out about a minute later. Then at approximately ten-fifteen in the morning a couple of plain-clothes detectives arrived with a gurney. They told me there were there to transfer the patient to a jail hospital ward. It took them about five minutes to get the patient out of there on the gurney. After they left I still sat there until the investigator who just testified arrived. He and his men went into the room. When they came out I told him what happened and he said that there must have been some crossed signals and the sheriff's department already did the transfer."

There is another round of murmurs in the courtroom. One bang of the judge's gavel brings it to an end.

Next to the witness stand is the deputy sheriff in charge of all incoming prisoners at the county jail. He testifies to the fact that the private hospital is only about a ten minute ride from county jail and that from ten in the morning to twelve noon not one incoming prisoner was booked in with a broken leg. Furthermore, of the nineteen new inmates that entire day, ten were Black, six were Hispanic and three were Asian. Not one Caucasian inmate was admitted that day, and especially no one with a broken leg. Every prisoner brought to the jail that day was escorted by uniformed peace officers from various police agencies in the county, also bringing proper paperwork. They all had names. Not one John Doe that day. Our client has disappeared into thin air.

12

The judge has finished his hearing into the John Doe transfer. I can't help but think about Jacques Futrelle's Professor Van Dusen. If he could get out of prison cell 13 without being caught, I guess it's not too much to believe that John Doe could have gotten out of his hospital room somehow.

The judge doesn't like to leave loose ends. He excuses all of the witnesses that testified and then directs his attention to Myra.

"It looks like you've misplaced something Miss Scot. One defendant, to be exact. I don't know how this happened and I can't really blame you for it, but this case has been called and a jury has been sworn in. We can't all go home now and forget about this just because the defendant isn't here. From what I've heard, it looks to me like his absence is his own doing, so I'm not blaming either side here." He looks over to me.

"What about it Mister Sharp? Have you got any idea about where the defendant is? And more importantly, did you have anything to do with his disappearance?"

I'm shocked by his question, but I know that for the record he must ask it.

"No sir Your Honor. This is as much a surprise and a mystery to me as it is to the court and the prosecution. I have no idea where he is or what happened to him."

The courtroom is almost silent once again while the judge is deep in thought. Everyone here is sitting on the edge of his or her seat waiting to see what's coming next. The judge finally brings it to a head.

"All right, I'll tell you what I'm going to do. I'm going to continue this case for one week, during which time I expect the prosecution to conduct a thorough examination into what happened to the defendant. In the meantime, I want both sides to prepare points and authorities for a hearing as to whether or not this trial should proceed without the defendant being present.

"My conclusion in this matter is that his being absent from this trial is not the doings of either prosecution or defense. That leaves only one other possibility, which means that he has fled to avoid prosecution. Take that holding into consideration when you do your research. I'll expect to see you both here at this time next week. My clerk will inform the jurors accordingly."

The gavel bangs down, the judge leaves the bench and everyone in the courtroom sits there looking at each other. No one here has ever seen this happen before. Sure, plenty of defendants have failed to show up for their court dates, but this is a little different. Here we have an allegedly amnesiac defendant with a broken leg who disappeared from a hospital room, with the help of some 'mystery' men.

What's more distressing is the fact that after his disappearance, he kept on calling me and sending emails, leading us to believe that he was in fact transferred to the county jail. I didn't mention that to Myra or the court because I wasn't asked, but it's bound to come out sooner or later.

Suzi walks over to Myra's table. They talk for a minute or so and then Myra comes over to tell me that she'll escort the two of us out through the back hallway and the judges' elevator. I call Jack to arrange for our pickup.

The local evening news is having a field day. As I sit here and watch the reports, one broadcast after another shows us arriving in the Hummer. Every time Baron von Bernie is shown sticking up out of the sunroof I hear a giggle from the foreward stateroom.

Then the usual group of television legal experts take their turns, each espousing one theory or another about what happened to the mysterious John Doe, who was in on the alleged conspiracy to keep his identity from being discovered, and the points of law involved in having him tried *in absentia*.

These guys are all supposed to be actively practicing lawyers. Don't they have anything better to do than try to sound smart on some crummy local news show?

I thought the news frenzy would die down after a while, but when the network news comes on, each one of them has a brief item about the case too. Amazingly my face doesn't appear in any report. The only shot they seem to find newsworthy is our arrival in the Hummer. So much for accurate reporting. News has finally made the transformation complete. It is now purely entertainment, and with those giggling sounds coming from the foreward stateroom, it's been a successful transformation.

Myra should be home by now. I'm calling her to discuss this matter.

"What is it Peter?"

"I'm fine thanks, how about yourself?"

"Please don't start with me. I've had enough aggravation today."

"Any luck finding my client?"

"No, and if I didn't know better I'd think you were behind his disappearance."

"Listen Myra, I'm court appointed on this case. I'll do my best to defend this guy but that doesn't include helping him escape. If it isn't an item I can put on my timesheet and get paid for, the kid won't let me do it. Besides, that's not the reason I'm calling you. I'd like to make a trade."

"I know what I've got to offer Petey, but I can't think of anything you've got that I'd trade it for."

"We filed a civil suit against that Neil Kaplan guy... the one who didn't have a computer taken from his car. During his deposition I got him to admit that there might have been a computer in his backseat. He says that one of his friends probably left it there."

"Sure, that sounds reasonable Peter. He rents a car in Van Nuys and twenty-three minutes later parks it in front of our building, where someone breaks into it. The Criminal Courts Building is about a twenty-minute freeway ride from the car rental place, so I guess that left plenty of time for him to stop and meet with his friends. He's a liar and we both know it."

"Wow. What a show of appreciation. I just sealed up the last loose end in your case. You now have a witness who will testify to the fact that there was a theft. I've finally put that computer in the car for you. Now you don't have to rely completely on the videotape evidence. Don't I get some little bit of thanks?"

"Oh all right. So you've given me another part of the jigsaw puzzle that was almost complete without it anyway. What do you want? There's still not going to be any kind of deal on the table."

"Not to worry Miss prosecutor, I've already given up on that. It's just that now I know for sure that Kaplan was lying, I want to know why. The answer can't be the computer itself, because refurbished models like that are going for just a couple of hundred dollars on eBay. It's gotta be something inside the computer. Some data on the hard drive.

"I know you've had your people go through it. Suzi had a crack at it too, but she hasn't reported any findings to me. I'm hoping for a miracle… that the kid missed something your experts may have found. I'd like a copy of their report, and quite honestly I think the defense is entitled to it."

"You're wasting your time Peter. I'll be glad to send you a copy of the report, but if you want to save us both some time I can read it to you over the phone. It was only one sentence. It said that there was absolutely no information on the hard drive... it had obviously been re-formatted. There wasn't even an operating system on it."

"Well the least you could do is have dinner with me tonight as consideration for that useless information I just gave you."

"Suzi put you up to this didn't she?"

"Not at all. In fact, she's not even going to be here tonight. She's found a new friend her own age. A Chinese girl named Lotus, and Suzi informs me that she'll be sleeping over there again tonight."

Myra is happy to hear that Suzi has someone her own age to play with and also turns me down flat on the dinner invite. As for what she told me about that report from her experts, I believe her. From what Stuart tells me, that's the way he receives computers when he buys large quantities of lease returns. The lessees usually re-format the hard drive before returning it to the leasing company so that no sensitive company information is left on there and accidentally disclosed.

The only positive result of our conversation is finding out that her experts didn't find anything out that we don't know about. Other than that, we both agree that if the judge is amenable, both sides will stipulate to trying Mister Doe *in absentia*.

Now the nagging question is this: if there was nothing at all on the hard drive and the computer wasn't hot, then what reason could Kaplan possibly have for lying about having possession of it? This is worse than a limit. At least with a limit you can at least step half way towards your goal, but with this case it's one step forward and two steps backward each time.

The phone is ringing. It's Jack Bibberman calling.

"Hi Jack. What's up? You got something new for me?"

"Oh, hello Mister Sharp. I must have dialed your number by mistake. I'm trying to reach Suzi's private line."

Why on earth would Jack be calling the kid? Could she have him running down some leads that I don't know about? No, that's impossible. I've been on top of this case from the beginning. It must be something else he's doing for her. I accept Jack's apology and remind him of the kid's private number.

I hear large paws. They're both standing by the door, which means it's time for me to drive them over to Mrs. Chang's house for their sleepover.

She must do pretty well with the I.R.S. because the house is a recent one of four built on a cul-de-sac in Culver City. It's a two-story job with a nice big attached garage.

Michelle Chang and Lotus both greet us as we approach the front door and we both get kisses on the cheek from our same-sized counterparts. The kids disappear immediately to somewhere upstairs while Michelle gives me the tour of her immaculate home.

Suzi told me that it is a two-bedroom house but it actually has three bedrooms, one of which was converted into an office where both Michelle's and Lotus' computers are located. The Changs can't stop complimenting the job that Suzi did last time she slept over. They show me the wireless equipment she installed, making their entire home a network. Now by using a laptop with built in wireless capability, they can surf the internet and send emails from anywhere in the house.

I bid them all a pleasant goodbye and promise to return for Suzi by noon tomorrow. I'm getting some vibes from Michelle. I think she'd like to spend some more time alone with me, but I can't do it just yet. This is too complicated a situation for me. I know that Suzi has a master plan to get Myra and I back together again and I'm afraid that letting Michelle Chang have her way with me will upset the applecart. I think I'll wait until I've had a chance to think a little more about this before making any move on Lotus' mother.

Michelle looks disappointed, but I explain that I've got a trial to prepare for.

At this point in time I've got several important matters going. First and foremost is John Doe's criminal trial, which I am surely going to lose. I'm not worried about disappointing him because he's escaped from custody and is probably now in another country. Another is the case against Neil Kaplan, which I'm also going to lose because there really isn't any case there. We filed against him just to take his deposition and find out that really was a computer stolen from his car, putting a final nail in the John Doe coffin.

Third is another one that Suzi insisted we handle, which is trying to recover the money that Stuart lost to that fraud ring. Jack B. hit the wall on that one and we have absolutely no idea of who runs that operation, aside from my brilliant theory of how they obtain the credit card numbers.

My losing the criminal case will most certainly mean that the police were in fact stopping a crime when they slammed on their brakes, so Mister Uniman will be forced to pay out an extra million dollars on the deceased woman's double indemnity clause and I'll probably lose Uniman's Insurance Company as a client. And that's the only good civil defense account I've ever had. All in all, this court-appointed John Doe case has probably cost me most of my career. The only minor benefit is that after losing John's case, I get to buy Myra dinner. That was our bet.

The most disappointing aspect of it all is Suzi's lack of support. Usually she digs into our cases and works hard. She even gets lucky once in a while and finds things out for us. But not this time. The final blow was when she didn't even take the time to open up that evidence bag the computer was in. I believe Myra when she says that there was nothing on the hard drive, but I still would have appreciated Suzi's at least making an effort to check it out.

No sense complaining. John Doe's trial is coming up in another day or so. Myra's office has already notified the court that she has been unable to locate the defendant and that both sides have stipulated to have him tried *in absentia*. I'll be back in court on this case soon, and the jury will have the opportunity to convict a person they've never laid eyes on.

The press has been eating this case up. There's been more coverage of John Doe than there would have been if he was available for trial. Every reporter has a theory about who Mister Doe is. Some tabloid magazines have published interviews with people who have shielded their identities but claim to be either a wife, child, business partner, partner in crime, or CIA operative. The list goes on. One report even has John identified as being from another planet, having come to earth specifically to obtain computer evidence about human intelligence on earth. Good luck with that one.

Somewhere deep in my bones I'm troubled by John Doe's escape from the hospital. We know he didn't do it alone, because the uniformed guard says that some police-type guys came to take him away. The only thing that comes to my mind now is the possibility that our John Doe is in the witness protection program. Unfortunately that's one database even Suzi can't hack into, and no matter what I tell Special Agent Snell he would never confirm or deny my suspicion about it.

My only possible defense becomes an attack on the theft of the computer. Without the defendant present, maybe I can convince at least one juror to give him the benefit of the doubt as to the ownership of the computer. No person in his right mind would ever take the chance of breaking into a vehicle parked in front of the downtown courthouse, with police walking around all over and a squad car coming down the street unless he had a good reason. If I can get just one juror to go along with my argument that the defendant may have possibly been retrieving his own property, then the theft goes away and so does the felony murder. Reasonable doubt is my only chance.

I remember talking to a pit-boss in Las Vegas some years back. When asking him about the chances that someone might actually create a 'system' for winning that was legal and successful, he gave me an answer that also applies to my defense. "Slim or none - and Slim's out of town."

The phone is ringing. It's Stuart calling.

"Cheer me up Stu. I'm going down in defeat tomorrow."

"That John Doe case? Boy, are they covering that one. Every paper has pages on it, and those tabloid television shows are eating it up. You know, we've been friends for a long time, and you know you can trust me. What's the real story there? I can't believe you're going to a jury trial on this case without knowing more than you're telling."

"Stuart, you've got to believe me. I haven't the slightest idea who this guy is or where he went to. He came out of nowhere on the day of that accident downtown and now it looks like he's gone back to where he came from."

"But he was in the hospital with a broken leg. From what the news reports say, the judge held a hearing and found out that some guys beat Myra's crew to the hospital and got him out of there. Who were they?"

"I don't know, Stuart. I don't know any-thing. The court appointed me to represent this guy and that's it. I'm going to trial tomorrow with no client, no evidence, no witnesses, no defense and no chance of winning."

"Peter, I know you're going to come out okay on this. Between you and Suzi, there'll be some way for you to get your client off."

"Don't remind me about Suzi. I think she really slacked off on this one. I guess she realized early on that it was a loser and just didn't want to waste any of her valuable time on it."

"I don't know about that Pete. I've been trying to get Jack B. to do some work for me and he says he can't until tomorrow because Suzi's got him working almost full time. And it's been going on like that for the last week or so."

"Are you sure about that? Because I haven't given him any assignments, and he certainly hasn't been calling me with any reports."

"Peter, all I can do is tell you what Jack told me. The rest is between you guys. Good luck with your trial. I'll be watching for you on the news tomorrow evening."

This is interesting. I don't think Jack would lie to Stuart. Jack's not that kind of guy. But what could he be doing for us? Jack's hourly rate is about thirty-five bucks plus expenses and mileage. When he's out running around it can cost us between one and two thousand dollars for a whole week. Usually Suzi and I discuss the firm spending any amount over a couple of hundred dollars. She must have some things she's working on that she doesn't want to bother me with, knowing that I'm preparing to go to trial tomorrow. I'm sure she'll let me know about it soon. She's pretty tight with a buck, so whatever she's spending our money on must be worth it.

I call Jack to make arrangements for him to drive us to court tomorrow. I really want to sneak away from that building fast tomorrow. It's bad enough being mobbed by the press after winning a case... I don't want to go through it as a loser.

Jack's answering machine picks up the phone and gives an outgoing announcement. "This is Jack Bibberman. I'm quite busy today and tomorrow, so please leave your name and number and I'll get back to you."

Hmmmn. Interesting. I'll call Vinnie and have him to the driving.

There's a crowd around the courthouse waiting for us to arrive. I promised Suzi that she could sit second chair at the trial today. The judge didn't seem to mind last week, so I think it'll be okay today too. The press hopes Suzi is coming today too because several of them called yesterday to ask her. I honestly think that the coverage of our arrival is more because of the goggled dog and Suzi. By now it's a foregone conclusion that I'll be losing this case, so they're probably leaving me alone out of sympathy.

We make our way to the courthouse door and Suzi is definitely the center of attention. She does her 'vulnerable little girl routine,' holding onto my hand tightly and looking intimidated. Vinnie knows the pick-up routine, so he and the dog are all set to aid and abet in our escape after the loss.

Two bailiffs meet us downstairs by the elevators and escort us around to the private judge's entrance and allow us to go up to the courtroom floor in the private elevator. Suzi is not the least bit surprised by this. That means she probably talked

Myra into arranging it. And if Myra wouldn't, I'm sure the kid could have talked the judge into it.

We enter the empty courtroom from the judge's private back door and see that they've got several extra bailiffs on duty. One of them mentions to me that they're expecting a much large crowd today. The press has gotten the judge to allow standing room only along the rear of the large courtroom I've been told that Court TV will have its three remote-controlled camera activated, so the trial can be broadcast live.

I've never performed before such a large crowd before. Too bad I'll be going in the dumpster with this one. This place is starting to feel more like an exclusive nightclub, with everyone who is anyone trying to get a seat to watch. Two bailiffs have a list of people with reserved seats, so they go outside into the hall to invite the elite in first.

To my surprise I see several familiar faces being escorted in. Special Agent Snell from the FBI's West Los Angeles office is here and I haven't the slightest idea why. Maybe it's morbid curiosity and my feeble defense of this defendant is being likened to the automobile accident that everyone slows down to get a look at. Several men accompany Snell. FBI guys are a lot like nuns. You rarely see them outside alone.

Also filing into the room is none other than Mister Uniman. I guess that if he's going to be forced to spend another million dollars on a claim, he wants to see why.

The next two are a surprise to me. One of them is Neil Kaplan; the other is our own Jack

Bibberman. No wonder he's busy today. He's busy being a spectator.

I haven't the slightest idea what these people are doing here today, but I hope it's not to see one of Suzi's stunts. She's done that in the past with great success. I hope she doesn't try it again today because I'm not in the mood for any excitement. If I'm going to lose I want it to be as smoothly as possible, without any of the kid's surprises.

Several Asian reporters come up and whisper in Suzi's ear. Next they're posing next to her while someone else takes a picture. She's now become a photo-op celebrity.

The judge's private door opens and in comes Myra with her assistant. There are also several uniformed police officers with them, probably the ones involved in the accident and subsequent investigation. The medical examiner is here too.

I haven't been keeping score, but I'd estimate that Myra has a dozen people on her side. On our side it's just me and the kid, who probably thinks it's about even.

Now the bailiffs have opened the doors to the public, which in this case consists of one hundred percent reporters from all over the world. For the life of me, I don't know what the big interest in a John Doe case is, but it must be selling papers, so here they all are en masse.

The deceased woman's family and attorney are conspicuous by their absence. That's okay with me. I really hate it when survivors of a victim are sitting there glaring at me for having the audacity to defend a person they are convinced is guilty of causing their loved one's death.

Myra and Suzi talk for a minute or two as they stand midway between the counsel tables. I guess this is to avoid the press seeing either one of them going all the way over that full five feet to the other side's table.

Once the girls are seated the clerk starts the overture by buzzing the judge. The usual choreography is performed flawlessly and the judge is now banging his gavel down while calling the case.

As soon as the official record starts, the judge tells the bailiffs to bring in the jury. When they're all seated, the judge addresses them.

"Ladies and gentlemen of the jury, I want to apologize for any inconvenience you may have been caused by the one-week delay, and thank you for your patience and cooperation. Outside of your presence, both sides have stipulated to allow this trial to go on without the defendant present. At this time we do not yet know reason for his absence, so I want to caution you to not allow that to cause you to come to conclusions about his innocence or guilt."

He then looks down to Myra. "Are the People ready to proceed?"

Myra says that she is and will not be making an opening statement. The Judge tells her to call her first witness. I don't even waste my time asking that any prospective witnesses be asked to wait outside the courtroom. It won't make any difference today.

Normally I would be sitting on the edge of my seat at this part of a trial, listening carefully to every bit of testimony and making notes on my legal pad for points to attack on cross-examination. This trial is different because I don't have a lot to say, so now

I'm just a spectator. I see that Suzi has a legal pad in front of her and she's also brought her laptop computer in. Lawyers do that a lot now because so much information can be stored there for instant retrieval.

I'm not wearing my Sunday goin'-to-church suit today. Maybe the jury will show a little sympathy for this poor defenseless defense attorney.

Myra starts to present her case. She's very thorough and offers testimony in the same order as the events unfolded at the scene of the accident.

Her first witnesses are the two police officers who were driving the squad car that struck John Doe. In addition to their testimony, Myra shows footage from the outside security cameras and the jury sees John Doe break into the car and then get hit by the squad car as he loses his balance while forcefully trying to remove his jammed burglary device from the cars' door.

Next to the witness stand is a detective who headed up the accident investigation. As Myra finishes up her direct examination of the detective, Suzi slips me a note telling me to ask a question. I don't know why she wants me to do this, but what the hell, I might as well go along with her program.

"Detective, when you investigated the crash of the Plymouth Acclaim into the rear of the police squad car, did you see any skid marks that could have been left by the Plymouth?"

To my surprise, he says that there were absolutely no skid marks under the path that the Plymouth traveled before rear-ending the squad car. I'm starting to realize that Suzi may have a plan, but I can't figure out what it is.

Now Myra calls the paramedics to the stand and one-by-one they testify to the fact that four people were transported to the hospital: Both police officers, the defendant, and the woman who was driving the Plymouth.

Her next step is to establish the death of the woman, and for this purpose she calls the medical examiner. First he must be qualified as an expert. To save us the boring details of his college education and all the autopsies he's conducted I decide to save everyone a lot of time, so I stipulate to his expertise. This allows Myra to get right to the questions. She elicits testimony that the decedent did in fact have an existing heart condition that was aggravated by the accident. Her time of death is estimated to be about two days later, while she was still in the hospital. The cause of death is allegedly due to aggravation of the heart condition caused by the accident and the shock of her airbag being activated.

Once she feels that the whole case is sewed up, Myra calls Neil Kaplan to the witness stand. After showing that video footage in which Kaplan is seen getting into the vehicle and driving away, the jury would definitely question why the victim didn't testify. Myra dances around the issue of ownership of the computer, trying only to establish that the car was in fact broken into and the computer was removed... and that Kaplan did not give anyone permission to do this act.

When it's my turn to cross-exam Kaplan, I've got to make some kind of showing, or the jury might think I'm sleeping through this trial. If I'm going to create any reasonable doubt in this case it'll be as the result of tearing poor Neil Kaplan apart. He knows who I am. He remembers me from his deposition.

"Mister Kaplan, would you please tell the court what type of computer was taken from your vehicle?"

"Uh, it was a laptop."

"What was the brand name?"

"I think it was a Toshiba."

I know that it's a Compaq, so I go over to the evidence table and pick up the computer. Unlike what you see on television shows, you can't approach a witness without the judge's permission.

"Your Honor, may I approach the witness to show him some evidence?"

I get his permission and walk in front of the counsel table to hold the computer up for Kaplan to get a good look at it."

"Mister Kaplan, would you please tell the court the brand name of this computer, as displayed on its label?"

"Uh, yeah... it's a Compaq."

I walk the evidence back to the table, trying to look as smug as possible, as if I've just caught an important witness in a lie. I glance over to Myra and she looks disgusted, as usual.

"Mister Kaplan, would you please tell the court the size of that computer's hard drive and how what type of storage and memory it has?"

"I'm not really sure of how many gigs the drive is. It might be forty. It probably has about 256k of memory."

"Mister Kaplan, this really isn't your computer, is it?"

He hesitates for a second and then admits that it isn't. There's a slight murmur in the courtroom.

"Mister Kaplan, isn't it a fact that when the district attorney's investigators first interviewed you, you denied having a computer in your vehicle?"

Before he has a chance to give some feeble answer, I push ahead.

"And Mister Kaplan, isn't it also a fact that during a civil deposition you mentioned that the computer may have belonged to a friend of yours? And didn't you also tell an independent investigator that if there was a computer in your rental car, it was probably left there by a previous rental customer, notwithstanding the fact that the rental car had been in a transmission shop for at least a week before you rented it?"

By this time Myra is jumping up out of her chair and loudly objecting to the fact that the witness is being asked a compound question and that the defense attorney is offering testimony by trying to introduce facts in the questioning that haven't yet been offered as evidence.

All three of us know that Myra is right, so I save the judge from being forced to rule on her objection. I tell him that I withdraw the last two questions. I really don't care if those questions are on the record or not. It's the jury that was supposed to be convinced of the fact that Kaplan was a flake. If I'm going to attack the underlying theft that supports the felony-murder here, I've got to shake the jury's confidence in Kaplan's credibility.

In further questions to Kaplan he fails to remember the names of his friends who may have left a computer in his car. He also can't explain how his friends were able to get into his car to leave a computer during the twenty-three minutes from his picking up the car at the rental place, to the time it was parked downtown, where it was allegedly broken into.

It might not mean very much, but I feel like I got the job done. The jury doesn't believe a word that Kaplan says. I'm sure of it. My last question is the final thrust of my epee.

"In fact, Mister Kaplan, since you have no idea of who the real owner of that computer is, isn't it possible that the defendant was actually trying to retrieve his own property?"

The courtroom is filled with conversation, as each reporter present is stunned at my theory. Naturally Myra is up again like a Jack-in-the-box. I know that her objection will be sustained. I don't even wait for the ruling. Using an age-old dramatic courtroom tactic, I toss my pen down onto our counsel table and with disgust say to the judge in a derogatory manner, "no more questions for this witness Your Honor, but we reserve the right to recall him again and would request that he be ordered to return."

I sit down and glance toward Suzi. She seems surprised that I can be as phony as she can be.

It's now a little after four in the afternoon and my drawn out cross-examination of Kaplan seems to have worked. The judge is going to call it a day and the last thing the jury heard was something that could be construed as damaging to the prosecution's case. I call Vinnie and we make our escape without stopping to visit with Snell, Uniman or Jack.

Back at the boat I call for a meeting. Once the three of us are seated in the boat's main saloon I start out with Suzi.

"Okay, what's going on? Stuart tells me that Jack Bibberman has been busy almost full time for the past week or so, and when I called to arrange for his driving services today his answer machine said he wasn't available. And then he mysteriously appeared in court. Is he working for us? And if he is, which case is his fee being charged to, and what the heck is he doing?

"And what was that little meeting with Myra today before the trial started. That's not done. There's no associating with the enemy before a trial starts. It's just not done. You have to put your game face on. The people expect to see it or they won't think you're serious about your case.

"And while we're at it, what's the big deal about there being no skid marks under that lady's car… and who the heck is this additional witness that the clerk says has been added to our list? I never heard of this guy before. Am I supposed to call him to the stand? And if I do, what can he do for us?

"Don't think of walking away young lady, I'm not through yet. Do you know anything about why Snell and Uniman were in the courtroom today? And are we paying Jack to be spectator there too?"

No answer from either her or the dog. After a few seconds she prepares to make her exit and gives me one of her one-line exit answers. "You're just going to have to trust me."

Trust her? What does that mean? They two of them have now gone to her stateroom and this meeting is over without me getting one answer to my questions. Why am I not surprised? That's usually the way it is around here.

We're back in court again and today I see that not only have all the spectators from yesterday returned, there are two new ones I recognize. The lovely Michelle Chang and her daughter Lotus. Wonderful. Not only are we going to go down in flames losing this case, the kid has invited her new friends to come and watch. Now I can make a nice losing impression on Michelle.

The judge has some other court business to attend to so he tells us not to come back in until two this afternoon.

When the afternoon trial session starts Myra doesn't call Kaplan back to the stand to try and rehabilitate him. She knows he's not that important a witness to her case, so she's willing to let me win that tiny little battle. She knows she's going to win the war.

Her next witness is a criminal procedure expert witness who spends too long of a time answering her questions about theft and felony murder. She wants the jury to have a lecture on the concept of the felony-murder rule.

On cross-examination I question her professor about all the cases we found where the felony-murder rule wasn't applied. My procedure is to submit some hypothetical facts to him, get his expected opinion that the rule does apply in that situation, and then sucker punch him by offering the actual case citation into evidence where the court said that the felony-murder rule didn't apply.

It's now getting later in the afternoon and I'm tired of sparring with this legal egghead, so I end my questioning and sit down.

Myra tells the judge that the prosecution rests its case. The judge looks over to me. I notice out of the side of my eye that the kid has slid a slip of paper over to me. I glance down at it and see that it tells me to call Karl Shaeffer to the stand. This must be the extra witness that was added to our list.

I don't like this. No trial lawyer asks a question in court that he doesn't already know the answer to, let alone call a witness he doesn't even know about. The only reason I'm going to take a chance and call this guy is because it's almost four in the afternoon and I can always tell the court that this will be a lengthy examination that I'd rather start tomorrow morning. Judges are no different than other people and if this one can get out of work early today, I'm sure he'll grant my request. That'll give me time to get together with this new witness and see what he's got to offer for our side. And if things go bad for us I can fake a heart attack and let the kid finish this case for me. She'd love to do that.

"Your Honor, the defense calls Karl Schaeffer to the stand."

There's another round of murmurs in the courtroom. This is a new player that no one has heard about. I don't even know who he is, and he's my witness. After the bailiff calls his name there are a few seconds when no one gets up to take the witness stand. Looking to the back of the room I see some motion. A guy is removing his sunglasses and beard and walking slowly toward the witness stand with a slight limp. Who the hell is this guy, and why did he come in that costume? He's using a cane to steady himself as he walks.

The soft murmur of the reporters is gradually building in volume. The judge brings everyone back to order with a few bangs of his gavel. This guy looks strangely familiar to me. He sits down in the witness chair and gets sworn in by the court reporter. His voice sounds familiar too. Well, I've called him to the stand, so now I have to go through with it.

"Mister Shaeffer, you look very familiar to me. Have we met before?"

"Yes we have, counselor."

This is an embarrassing position to be in. I'm a trial lawyer and this is my witness. Now I'm forced into a position of making it look like I don't even know who my own witness is. Very amateurish. I've got to try a wild shot here and hope it doesn't backfire on me.

"Mister Shaeffer, please tell the court where you know me from."

"You're my attorney. You came to visit me in the hospital where I was checked in under the name of John Doe."

13

If the judge bangs his gavel down any harder, the business end of it will fly off of its handle and hurt someone. The courtroom is going crazy. There are even some photographers out in the hallway trying to take some pictures through the small glass window in the rear door of the courtroom.

The judge has given up trying to restore order in the court. Everyone here including me is astonished. We've all been taken completely by surprise. We all just sit for a few minutes until the noise subsides by itself. It finally reaches a point where the spectators' curiosity has kicked in and they realize they're not going to learn what's really going on until they shut up and give us a chance to continue.

With over twenty years of trial experience under my belt I was somehow able to keep my cool, so I'm sure that they all think I orchestrated this whole show. Little do they know.

Now that my client is on the witness stand I feel that I owe the court some explanation. I also owe Karl Shaeffer some instant legal advice. The judge realizes the need for an admonishment too. He looks down at me.

"Mister Sharp, I'm going to give you the benefit of the doubt here and assume that you are as surprised as the rest of us are about this witness' testimony. So I ask you Mister Sharp. Is this your client? Is this the man who you met at the hospital as John Doe? And have you been aware of his whereabouts? Because the clerk informed me that your firm added his name to the witness list, so you're a suspect here until proven otherwise."

"Your Honor I hereby represent as a sworn officer of the court, under penalty of perjury, that I had no idea up to this moment the true identity of this witness and have had absolutely no knowledge as to his whereabouts."

"All right Mister Sharp, I'll take your word on that, but I want you to know that as of this moment you're on dangerous ground here. This is a criminal trial for a serious matter and you have just called your own client, the defendant, to the witness stand. Would you like to admonish him or should I? And do you want him to stay on the stand right now, because if he does, he'll be subject to cross-examination by you-know-who."

I get his drift, so I start my monologue.

"Mister Shaeffer, as the defendant in this criminal case, you have the right to not take the witness stand at all. You have a right not to testify against yourself and cannot be forced to incriminate yourself in this trial.

"As you know, I wasn't aware of your true identity as the defendant when asking the court to call you as a witness. Now that you're on the stand, I don't believe it's too late for you to get off and sit down next to me at the counsel table, where you belong. So having been advised of your rights, do you still wish to be on the witness stand?"

"Yes I do Mister Sharp. I insist on being able to testify on my own behalf."

That's too bad. I was hoping he'd want to get off the hot seat, but now that he's on it for good, I'm along for the ride too. And I'm sure Myra's going to make it a bumpy one. Now that I know who he is I've got to get out of questioning him today. There are too many questions I have to learn the answers to before making a presentation to the jury and a court full or reporters.

"Your Honor, due to it being nearly the end of the day, at this time we would like to request an early adjournment of the court so that we might have an opportunity to meet with our client, who has obviously regained enough of his memory to now start cooperating with his defense. I'm sure that the People would also like to have a chance to speak to him.

"So with those thoughts in mind, we respectfully ask the court for a one week continuance in this matter."

The judge calls both sides up to the bench for a sidebar conference, out of earshot of the jury and spectators. I see that my second chair person is getting up to join us there. I give her one of those 'don't press your luck' stares and she sits back down in her chair with a disappointed pouting look. Myra is already up at the bench. I join her for the judge's sage advice.

"Counsel, this is a new ball game. No longer do we have an amnesiac defendant on the lam. He's here and he brought his memory with him. So talk to me. What's your pleasure today?"

I beat Myra to the punch. "Your Honor, if the district attorney will not object to my continuance request, then I would be more than happy to make my client available to her for questioning, as long as I'm present. And my presence would not be merely to tell him to keep his mouth shut, because the theft of the computer is already out of the bag, so he has nothing to lose and everything to gain by now explaining his actions."

Myra can't really argue with my logic. She tells the judge it's okay with her if we get our continuance. The judge doesn't mind either, but he doesn't want to leave the jury hanging, so he says he'll do it only on the condition that every one of the jurors agrees that they can come back one week from today. This shouldn't be problem for them because their jury duty is now broken up so that it's only a day or so at a time, instead of the usual solid week or two during a trial.

The judge polls the jury and we get our final approval for the continuance. The judge has something to say about custody.

"Mister Sharp, until I hear evidence to the contrary, I'm going to presume that this defendant willfully failed to appear for appearances before this court and he is now under the purview of the bench warrant that this court has had issued for his arrest.

"I'm sure you'd like to have him not in custody to make it easier for you to get together, but I'm afraid I don't trust him to not disappear again, so I'm going to remand him to the Sheriff's custody, where he will stay until next week when he's brought back here for the continued trial."

The judge bangs his gavel down and steps off the bench. Three bailiffs instantly appear and whisk Karl Shaeffer out the back door and to the lock-up.

All of the reporters have already run out into the hall to file their 'late breaking news' stories by cell phone. Several are being videotaped by camera crews who I am sure will rush out to their vans and send the footage to the stations via satellite uplink. I call Vinnie and we get out with no problems. The press realizes that we don't know anything more than they do.

Back at the boat I attempt another meeting. "Suzi, who is Karl Shaeffer, where did he come from, and how did you know who he was to tell me to call him to the witness stand?"

"I don't know who he is."

"How can you stand there and say that? You're the one who handed me that slip of paper with his name on it and told me to call him. And the clerk told me that you're the one who added his name to the witness list. If you don't know anything about him, why did you add his name and tell me to call him as a witness?"

Aha. I've got her now. Let's see her try to wriggle off this hook. She starts to try.

"I received an anonymous email saying that a Karl Shaeffer might be able to help us, so I had the clerk add his name to our witness list. Then while we were sitting in court I noticed that we were also in a hot spot where the wireless internet connection on my laptop would work. Because you wouldn't let me do anything important, I decided to check my e-mail. There was another anonymous message telling me that this Karl Shaeffer would be in the courtroom today and that it would help our case if you called him to the stand, so I passed you that note."

Having made her statement, she does an about-face and the two of them march to her stateroom. She did it again. She got off the hook. The phone is ringing. The caller identifies himself as Karl.

"Hello Mister Sharp. First of all, I'd like to apologize to you for misleading you in the past. Unfortunately, I can't talk to you for the next few days. I know that you promised to also make me available to the district attorney, but I can't speak to her for a few days either.

"I have to go now, so please understand that I'm not trying to do anything that hurts you or the case, but there are reasons I can't talk to you now. I hope to be able to explain myself before the trial resumes. I'll see you there."

He hangs up on me. What nerve. This guy's got stones of steel. I'm his lawyer. I'm the one who's trying to get him off the hook on a murder charge, and he's telling me he's too busy to talk to me now. Who the hell does he think he is? If I go to the county jail and bring Myra with me, she swings enough weight to have him brought down to the interview room whether he wants to come or not. Once Myra and I both gang up on him in a small room he won't have a chance. I'm going to find out what's going on and that's that. Too busy to talk to me, is he?"

I call Myra at home.

"Yes Peter, I know you're surprised. Don't worry, I believe you. There's no way on earth that you're smart enough to have pulled off this stunt on your own, so I have no intention of prosecuting you for obstruction of justice."

"Oh gee, that's sweet of you. Thank you, but the reason I'm calling is to invite you to join me for a no-holds-barred conference with Mister Doe on your home turf... the county jail. That arrogant jerk just called me and apologized for his actions to date, but said that he just can't talk to me for a couple of days... like he's got something more important to do.

"I've just about had it with this guy, so I'm going to do a terrible thing to him."

"And what would that be, Peter? You're already his lawyer. I would think that's enough punishment."

"Very cute, but it's not bad enough for him. I'm going to give him the ultimate punishment. I'm going to turn you loose on him."

We discuss going to the jail to interview my client. Coincidentally, Myra can't make it for a couple of days. That's okay. Karl said he couldn't talk to me for a few days, so by the time we'll get there he'll have no more excuses left.

Suzi has never visited the county jail and she knows that if she can wrangle an invitation to go with us, it'll be another occasion where Myra and I are together and the kid can temporarily have her imaginary family intact. That's okay with me and I'm sure she'll be able to talk Myra into it.

We drive to the county jail together in my Hummer and it isn't until we pull up in the private parking area that we realize we haven't brought anyone along to watch the kid and dog while we're in the visiting area. She knows she won't be allowed in with us.

Suzi assures us that it's okay and that she'll be happy to wait for us in the jail's outer lobby. She'll probably bump into several cop friends of hers, so we agree. Just to play it safe we notify one of the guards that under no circumstances should she be allowed to leave the waiting room.

I identify myself to the gate-keeper. Myra doesn't have to. She's got that badge that says 'District Attorney' on it, and it's badge number '1.' We're led back to the area where the lawyer interview room is. Myra tells the jailer which client we'd like to have brought down. A few minutes later a guard tells us that it will be a few minutes, so we should go back out to the waiting area and they'll send someone for us when the prisoner is ready.

When we get back to the waiting area Suzi and the dog are gone. I go to the reception desk and ask what happened to her. She tells me that the little girl and her dog are in the captain's office.

Myra and I are escorted behind the counter and back to the private office area. Walking down the hall to the captain's office, we hear laughter. When we get there we see that a mini party is going on, with Suzi and Bernie the centers of attraction. The captain, several of his officers and some of the jail staff are all crowded around the dynamic duo and they're having a grand time.

We stand there in amazement, seeing how she's managed to take control of the entire jail in less than ten minutes. There's no sense going in there and spoiling the party, so we go back out to the waiting area and discuss how we're both going to surgically take this guy apart for what he's done to us.

The captain comes out from his office and motions for us to please join him. We go to his private conference room and he tells us the news.

"I'm sorry, but we have no prisoner with the name you gave us. We checked the computer to locate him and see that the person you want to interview was never brought here from the courthouse.

14

Myra is fuming. She's the top prosecutor of Los Angeles County and she can't get the police authorities under her jurisdiction to keep track of this one prisoner. She's now in the process of starting a full-blown investigation into what happened at the courthouse and where the defendant may be.

This guy may be the greatest escape artist since Houdini. Not only did he manage to get out of the hospital, but he even succeeded in disappearing from the courthouse' private lock-up. On top of that, he called me that same evening and told me not to come and visit him. This was obviously an attempt to avoid my finding out that he's disappeared again.

We finally succeed in extracting Suzi from the jail staff, and all the way back to Myra's office there is not one word spoken in the car. Myra is dropped off and I've now got another chance to talk to Suzi. We're in the car now and she can't just turn around and walk away from me.

"Okay kid. Out with it. The last time we had a conversation like this, you told me to trust you. I did trust you, and where did it get me? If you have any desire to keep this law firm from going directly into the dumper, you'd better talk to me. Unlike you, I don't have a couple of million dollars in the bank, so if I don't work of a living, I don't eat. The way this case is going, it's making a fool out of me, and that affects my career as a trial lawyer and it also affects the amount of money our law firm can take in.

"So if you've got anything to say, you'd better come out with it, because not only am I getting tired of being embarrassed, but Myra's fed up with it too. From what I see, Myra and I are the closest things you've got to family, and if we don't get some answers, you're irritating your closest relatives."

There's silence for minute or so. I can tell she understood what I've told her, and that bit about antagonizing her own family must have gotten to her. She finally starts. Quietly.

"When Victor went with you to the hospital to fingerprint John Doe, I told him to get you out of the room and then to take a DNA swab."

"Why didn't you want me to know about that?"

"Because I wanted to do some investigation on my own, and if I got a good hit on his DNA, I thought I could be an important person in court again."

Gee whiz. Why didn't she tell me that? I don't mind her being a little star. I didn't know it meant so much to her.

"Well? Did you get a hit? Did you find out who he was?"

"No, but I found out who he isn't."

"I don't get it. I don't even know what that means. Who isn't he?"

"He isn't a member of the general public. For some reason his DNA results were blocked. Fingerprint evidence can be kept out of the system. They do that all the time for people like protected witnesses and law enforcement personnel. But once DNA gets into the system, it's out of the authorities' control. There are too many databases in the civilian sector. His DNA was in there, but the identity was blocked. When I saw that, I knew he was someone other than John Doe."

"What about his amnesia? Do you think that was real, or was it faked?"

"He didn't have complete amnesia."

"Suzi, how the heck can you know that? You never met him."

"You told me."

"What do you mean 'I told you?' I never said anything like that. I told you I didn't know whether it was real or not. I even said I was starting to feel sorry for the guy."

"Yes, but you also wrote in your report what the two of you talked about, and you said that he knew who the *RoadRunner* was in those cartoons. When Doctor Eidoch called to make arrangements to pick up his check for the expert witness fee, I told him about my suspicions and he agreed with me. Either you don't remember anything, or you do. In John's case, once he admitted to remembering that cartoon character and almost gave himself away by working that computer for a minute or so, I knew he didn't have amnesia."

"Do you think it was faked right from the start?"

"No, he probably did have a memory loss right after the accident, but it came back soon enough for him to make arrangements to get out of there."

"I suppose you know how he got out of the hospital too. How about getting out of the court's lock-up facility. You got that one figured out too?"

"Oh Peter, that was so easy. I'm surprised you didn't get it."

Two things really steam me. One of them is Myra calling me 'Petey.' The other is this kid being surprised how poorly my large brain functions in comparison to her small one. I don't want to start an argument with her now because I really want to find out what she knows. Besides, I secretly think she's right. She's a lot smarter than I am – but I'll never admit it to her. Her head is big enough as it is. Even Myra is in awe of her intelligence, logic ability and computer skills.

"Okay, I've got a theory. Let's hear yours and we'll see how close it is to mine."

I think she realizes I'm bluffing, but she does me the favor of not calling me on it.

"I had Jack Bibberman pull the hospital's phone records. The police report didn't show a cell phone in his property, so if he called out he'd have to use the hospital room's phone. I did a reverse number check on where he called on his second day in the hospital. He only called two numbers. One was yours. The other one came back as being installed on the seventeenth floor of a building at 11000 Wilshire Boulevard in West Los Angeles."

"Wait a minute. That's the federal building."

"And who is on the seventeenth floor of that building?"

I knew it. That's the FBI's executive offices floor. It took him over a day to realize what had happened to him and where he was. He must have called Snell.

The FBI has fifty-six field offices located in major cities throughout the states. A Special Agent in Charge oversees each one of those offices, except for their three largest ones in Washington, D.C., New

York and Los Angeles. An Assistant Director in Charge manages those main offices, and they are assisted by Special Agents in Charge. Bob Snell is one of those Special Agents in Charge, and if anyone could have gotten our John Doe out of that hospital, he's the guy.

Now I know why he was there in court. He knew that when his guy Karl Shaeffer stepped forward and came out of the amnesia closet, the judge would order him remanded to custody. Snell and his boys were there to save the day. And now that we have the answer to that set of questions, we now have to ask the big follow-up one.

"Okay, Suzi. That sounds about right. And Snell's being in court verifies what we figured was going on. But now we have to know why someone connected with the FBI was going after the computer in Kaplan's car. Any theories?"

"I'm working on some leads, but I'd rather not say anything until some results come in."

"I'll tell you what, kid... you keep me advised of what's going on so I don't get embarrassed in court, and I'll let you be the star again."

I don't believe it. Looking in the rear view mirror I think I actually see her blushing. That may have been caused by her embarrassment, or by her shock at having such a long conversation with me. That's the most amount of talking to me she's ever done. I suppose she'll clam up again as soon as we get back to the boat, figuring that I've been blessed with enough words to last for another couple of months.

The fact that we don't know what the FBI wanted with Kaplan's computer doesn't give us one answer, but it does give us another. Kaplan is involved in something that's against federal law.

With a name like Kaplan, it doesn't look like he' some kind of anti-Israel or Islamic terrorist, but we'll wait and see. The past few years have shown us all that you can't judge that kind of book by its cover.

When we get back to the boat I decide to make a phone call to do a little fishing for information. I inform the kid that because she's finally decided to be forthcoming with me I'm going to let her listen in on this phone call and see how we adults get something done without the use of a computer.

I call the West Los Angeles office of the FBI. They answer and I start my little routine.

"Hi, I'd like to speak to Special Agent Karl Shaeffer, and if he hasn't been promoted above GS-11 yet, he should take my call."

There's a slight giggle on the other end of the phone. The receptionist realizes that I know about the pay grades of special agents. When they get hired, they start out at GS-10, and after their first four-year field assignment they have the opportunity to be promoted as high as GS-13. I figured by Shaeffer's age that he's probably been with the Bureau for at least five years, so I'm taking a shot that he's either a 10 or an 11.

"I don't know if we have an agent here by that name."

"Oh yeah, I know. He told me about that assignment. Tell him it's his big brother and if he doesn't take my call he's in line for some serious nuggies."

The receptionist probably doesn't know what I mean by that, but that's okay. I don't know what it means either, but it sounds like some private little joke that might be shared by brothers. She puts me on hold for a minute. After a while, someone picks up the phone and I get lucky.

"Hey, bro. I didn't know you were going to be in town until next week. And for your information I'm still a GS-10, so you're going to have to pay for dinner."

"My pleasure, bro. This Peter Sharp your attorney, and the good news is I've got you booked into the Magic Castle in Hollywood. They're willing to pay top dollar for an escape act like yours."

Silence on the other end and success on our boat. As Suzi and the beast leave the room she gives me the 'thumbs-up' sign, which means I'm now highly enough respected around here to play in her league.

"I'm sorry about the role-playing, but we've really got to talk. And listen, you can ask your boss Special Agent in Charge Snell about me. I can be trusted to keep my mouth shut, but only if I know what not to say.

"And I'm willing to buy that dinner if you'll meet with me. How about it?"

"We knew you'd wind up snooping around here soon enough. I've already talked to Agent Snell and he says you can be trusted, but only so far. At this point we don't want the district attorney involved in our investigation. Your history with her is public record and there's a strong possibility you're still carrying a torch for your ex-wife. That's what worries us now."

"Listen Shaeffer, I've got a bet with Myra about this case. If I win, she has to buy me dinner. If you think you know how I feel about her then you'll know how important it is for me to win that bet, so I'll keep any information from her that I have to in order to spend that evening with her."

I can tell he's thinking about it. I'm also sure that as soon as he found out it was me on the phone, Snell was in there listening to our conversation.

"Agent Snell will be in contact with your office."

"You mean he's going to call me?"

"That's not what I said. He'll be in contact with your office."

Wow. She's got them wrapped up too. He must mean that Snell will be calling Suzi. Boy, I'm glad she's on my side.

The phone is ringing. It's Myra.

"Hello beautiful. What can I do for you tonight? That sleep-over perhaps?"

"I'm not going to dignify questions like that with an answer. I just want you to know that we're starting an investigation tomorrow. By this time tomorrow evening we'll know exactly where your client is and I expect to get him back, no matter what it takes."

"I love it when you talk tough."

"This is a courtesy call. You invited me to join you for an interview with him at the jail. It's not your fault he wasn't there, so I'm returning the favor. When we get our hands on him again we know he's being represented, so we'll give you a heads-up and you can be present at the interrogation."

That's it. The conversation is over. She didn't ask me any questions so I didn't have to lie to her. I'm straight with her and straight with the FBI. Even the kid thinks I'm okay now. Things are good.

Now that a lot of my stress has been relieved, maybe it's time to walk over to the liquor store to pick up a box of wine.

I can't eat this grease any more. As much as I try, it just won't go down. I won't say anything to Laverne about it, but I just can't eat it. Maybe I could suggest we switch to eggs. How badly can she screw up eggs? The bed is made. Just as I'm finishing the dish, a dog-mail arrives. Jack B. has called and he's on hold waiting for me to get back to the boat.

"Hello Mister Sharp. I want to apologize for not being able to drive for you."

"No apology necessary Jack. I know Suzi had you real busy. And you did a good job. We're on the way to winning the criminal case. Do you have anything new for me today?"

"No, I just wanted to make sure that we're okay and to let you know that I'm available to drive you next week when your trial starts again."

"Okay Jack I appreciate that and I'll look forward to seeing you then."

"Oh, you'll probably see me before then. I've got some more stuff for Suzi that I'll be dropping off at the boat."

I knew it. She's got a lot more she's not telling me. That's okay. I'm not going to fight it. Now that she knows I'm not going to prevent her from taking some credit, she's probably working her tail off trying to solve stuff for us. I don't know what other things need solving, because we've probably won the John Doe case. If the FBI was involved, then they probably had a warrant to grab that computer out of Kaplan's car and took the opportunity to do it while he was in the court building that day.

If there was a warrant, then there was no theft. If there was no theft there was no crime and therefore no felony-murder. Once I get all the stuff together and have Shaeffer testify in court I'm sure I'll get an outright dismissal. That makes our civil case against Kaplan a moot point, so that case will probably be dismissed too.

The only loose ends still out there now are the ones that lead to the gang that is ripping off people on the internet with their unauthorized credit card purchases. That's more of a crime-solving thing than a case, so I guess we'll just keep at it for a while because our friend Stuart is a victim. Sort of a multi-millionaire victim, but I guess his losing a couple of hundred dollars still entitles him to representation, so I'll keep Jack B. working on it.

Now that things have calmed down a bit maybe I can take a little time to read the newspaper. I haven't been keeping up with the news lately. Amazing. I'm sitting here reading and there've been no interruptions for the past half hour. I'm almost at the end of the paper and have nothing to do for the rest of the day. It's times like this when I usually start to read every word on the last few pages in an effort to keep the reading going on longer. Now I'm at the obituaries.

I have a friend who says that every morning he gets up out of bed, picks up the paper and goes right to the obituary section, where he goes through all the names of people who have just died. He says that if he doesn't see his own name there, he gets dressed and goes to work.

I don't see my name there, but I do recognize a name that sounds familiar. There's an obit for one Priscilla Schwarzman. What a coincidence. Just as I'm thinking how strange this sounds I read that the late Priscilla left behind her dear husband Stuart.

This is too much for me. The phone is ringing. It's Stuart calling.

"Hello Stuart. I have a feeling I know what you're calling about."

"Oh, you saw it, huh?"

"Yes, Stuart, and I'm sorry for your loss. Will there be a service. Maybe at PetLand Acres?"

"C'mon Peter. I was just following your advice."

"My advice? Are you crazy? I never told you to kill that cat. Don't ever accuse me of something like that."

"No, no. You told me that I shouldn't keep that marriage thing going because it wasn't in my best legal interest. I figured that after I got off the hook with the IRS, I should quit while I'm ahead.

"Priscilla was killed by a passing motorist. It was a terrible thing to happen, but she was getting up in years and I think she was in a lot of pain most of the time. Maybe it was for the best. Anyway, when it happened I figured why not? This can be my way of going straight and taking my best friend's advice. The only other way was a divorce, and I didn't want to go through with something like that.

"This way I have the obituary to prove that I'm a widower, and I can start filing my taxes again as a sole individual."

"Stuart, I'm happy you finally decided to be on the up-and-up, and I apologize for my smart-aleck remark before. I know you were fond of that cat. Is there anything else I can do for you in your time of need?"

"Yes, as a matter of fact there is. We're having a wake at my office next week, and I know Priscilla would have wanted you to be there. And no flowers, please. If you like, you can make a donation in her name to the A.S.P.C.A."

This conversation is over and once again I here some giggles coming from somewhere near the foreward stateroom.

When logging online I see that the kid's been surfing for cruise websites and seems to have spent some time on a particular one that offers special rates once a year for their 'widowed spouses' three-day trip to Ensenada. I guess that Stuart will be getting a nice gift certificate in the mail soon.

15

The kid hasn't been out of her stateroom for the last two days, but she seems to have no needs that aren't met. The Asian Boys are continuously delivering food, I've been walking the dog and Jack

Bibberman is always popping in with an envelope that's probably got investigative results in it.

Our conversation in the Hummer a few days ago when we returned from court was obviously all the words she intended to waste on me for the rest of this month. I'm now just sitting around reading the paper and waiting for some word that our client Karl Shaeffer has agreed to meet with me.

I hear the sound of paws approaching. It's either an incoming dog-mail or time for my afternoon walk. I don't see him carrying the leash he makes me wear in my hand while he holds the other end with his neck, so it must be a message. It is.

Peter:
The judge is expecting you in chambers at three this afternoon. There will be a meeting.
Please report fully afterwards.

Short and sweet. She sure has a knack for saying a lot with very few words. It would have been nice to receive some sort of clue as to what this meeting is about, but I'm getting used to flying by the seat of my pants, so I'll just follow instructions and show up.

The courtroom is not in use today, so the bailiff hasn't unlocked the doors. I see him sitting at his desk, so I gently rap on the little window. He sees that it's me and I get welcomed in and escorted through the private back door to the judge's chambers.

Sitting and waiting for me is a small but select group of people that includes the judge, Myra, the court reporter and Special Agent in Charge Bob Snell. Every time I see him I keep wondering why the most formal people seem to want to use the most informal names. President Carter was 'Jimmy,' President Clinton liked 'Bill,' and Vice President Cheney used 'Dick.'

There is no exchange of small talk. The judge motions towards a chair and I sit down. He speaks to the court reporter.

"This is a meeting in chambers with regard to the People versus John Doe, Superior Court case number 8222985. FBI Special Agent in Charge Bob Snell has brought to the attention of this court certain evidence which is now being admitted without any objection by the prosecution or defense counsel."

At this point the judge looks over at me again with one of those 'I'm sure you don't object' looks. I shrug my shoulders as if to indicate that anything that's okay with him is okay with me. He continues.

"I have admitted into evidence a sealed affidavit executed by two FBI Special Agents. It requests that a federal judge issue a search warrant for any premises occupied by a certain person. This warrant was being acted upon at the time of the accident which is the subject of this current prosecution.

"Because the defendant in this present case is an authorized agent of the federal government who was acting on behalf of a valid search warrant, I find that there was no crime committed by the defendant.

"Furthermore, upon finding that there was no underlying theft committed, this court also finds that there is no support for the felony murder charge. Therefore, upon receiving assurances from both prosecution and defense counsel that they agree to abide by the gag order this court is now issuing, this criminal case is hereby dismissed."

Both Myra and I tell the judge that there is no objection from our respective sides. I feel that a question should be answered.

"Your Honor, Miss Scot is the county's top prosecutor. It's not too hard for her to simply refuse to comment. I on the other hand am a private citizen, subject to the onslaught of the press. Do you have any suggestion as to how I should handle myself when attacked by the reporters?"

"No problem Mister Sharp. First of all, they don't know anything about this meeting, and my gag order means that it will stay that way. Secondly, because you and Miss Scot were stood up once again by the defendant a few days ago, the word has already leaked out that he's pulled off another successful escape. Watch the news headlines tonight. They'll do your job for you. Case dismissed. Any questions?

"Good. Now – everyone out. I can still get in a round at the club today."

Out in the hall there's not much conversation. Myra informs me that she's going to examine the situation more closely to determine whether or not I've won the dinner bet. She says she'll get back to me with an answer and takes the private elevator up to her office floor.

Snell and I use the regular exit. There's no conversation between us until we leave the building. Just before he gets into his waiting car, he finally speaks to me.

"I'll be sending one of my people to your boat this evening to pick up what you owe me."

I haven't the slightest idea what he means but I know that somehow the kid is involved. I know it can't be money he's talking about. Suzi has something else he wants and I'm starting to get the feeling that it's being traded as consideration for his appearance today and the dismissal of John Doe's case.

After parking my car I walk to our dock's entrance gate and notice the evening edition in the newspaper rack. Under the headlines is an article with big bold letters in the lead. 'Mysterious John Doe escapes again. Case continued indefinitely until he is captured.' I guess that's what the judge was talking about.

Inside the boat I see a small wrapped package on the table. It has 'for Snell' written on it. This must be what he was referring to when he said I owed him something. Suzi just came out of her stateroom and is opening up one of the galley's lower cabinets to get a dog treat out. I take a chance, hoping she's got a few words left for me this month.

"Suzi, Agent Snell said he'd be sending someone by to pick up a package. I see that this one has his name on it. Should I give it to his messenger?"

She nods affirmatively. I try my luck once again.

"Uh, any chance you might like to give me some hint as to what's in the package?"

Silence. As she heads for her stateroom I get an answer.

"The original hard drive."

"Wait a minute, young lady. What do you mean the 'original' hard drive. Is this supposed to be the one from John Doe's computer? And if it is, what are we doing with it. We might have violated the law here. If you figured out some way to get it out of that evidence bag without breaking the seal, we've been concealing evidence. We could both go to jail for this. I'm responsible for whatever you do and I'd like some explanation."

She looks up at me with one of those aggravated expressions and gives me the usual eye roll, as if to let me know that once again I just don't get it.

"Oh stop worrying. I didn't touch that evidence bag."

"Well if you didn't touch the bag, how come we've got this hard drive here? You know you can't just palm off any old hard drive on the FBI."

"It's the real one."

"Okay, I give up. You've got me. How did you get it out of the computer while it was sealed up in that bag?"

"I didn't. I got it out the first time you had it on the boat. Before the criminal indictment came down and before it was evidence."

"But when we gave the computer back, it had a hard drive in it. Where did that come from?"

"It came from one of Stuart's used laptops that was the same make and model as John's was. I switched the hard drives and gave Stuart a brand new one in exchange. He didn't mind at all."

Ah, so that's what that empty package from CompUSA I saw in our wastebasket contained. She did the switch right at the beginning.

"Okay, so we weren't hiding evidence. Now I know why you didn't touch that evidence bag when they returned the computer to us."

"No. That wasn't the reason I didn't touch it. I didn't touch it because I didn't want my fingerprints on the bag or the computer. I was afraid that Myra would do what she did last time, when she hauled me into court as a witness after finding my fingerprints on our client's property."

Wow. I didn't know she was so traumatized by that last court battle. We had a dock neighbor who was teaching Suzi how to re-load ammunition for use at a firing range. When he was charged with a crime, Myra's CSI unit found Suzi's prints on one of the defendant's shell casings and she got subpoenaed as a witness. The case worked out okay in the end, but I don't blame her for not wanting the same experience again. It's one thing to go into court voluntarily as a lawyer. It's another thing to be hauled in as a witness, subject to cross-examination by one of your best friends.

"All right. I understand your feelings. Does that mean Myra's experts were examining the switched hard drive? The one taken from one of Stuart's used computers? Oh yes. Of course. No wonder Myra complained that there was nothing on it. If it was a lease return, the hard drive would have been re-formatted to erase all information that a company employee would have had on it.

"And if it was a computer that the FBI was after, then they'd be just as disappointed as Myra was. That's it, isn't it? You made a deal with Snell. If he produced our John Doe and had the charges dropped, you'd give him the hard drive, right?"

With a smirk on her face, she speaks again. "By George, he's got it."

"Well little miss genius, if you really had the original hard drive and went through it the way I know you surely did, what was the information it contained that was important to the FBI?"

This conversation is now ended, because she's entering her stateroom. I get one last answer from her.

"I'd tell you, but it's on a need-to-know basis."

"Damn. She did it again. Not only did she solve the criminal case, she's promoted herself. No longer content to be associated with our local police agencies, she's now a junior G-Man. I still don't know how she knew that the FBI was involved in this case, but it looks like I'm not going to get any more information out of her today. I'm going to have to ask Myra's help with this. The kid desperately wants Myra's approval too, so maybe she'll give some answers to her.

I feel good that the criminal case is over. I'll prepare my time-sheet and present it to the court. Unfortunately, the one-step-forward, two-steps-backwards principle is still in operation. John Doe, or Karl Shaeffer, or whoever he is has been cleared, but the computer they were after was in the possession of Neil Kaplan. That means he's involved in something and we've still got a civil suit going against him.

The phone is ringing. It's Jack Bibberman calling and for once he's got some good news. He tells me that he's still working on the fraud ring that made Stuart lose out on a couple of transactions. Jack succeeded in getting the car rental place clerk to give him one of the Xerox copies they keep on file of customers' driver's license photos. He's now got a picture of the guy who drives the van that picks up all the loot from the mailbox places. Jack will be bringing it over to the boat so that Suzi can run it through her facial recognition software and see if we can find a match.

Several years ago there was one of those tabloid television magazine shows that exposed an illegal business some people were running in Los Angeles. If you drove down to a corner near Eighth and Vermont Streets, you could make contact with someone who would provide you with a phony drivers license, social security card and green card, which is the nickname given to the certificate of permanent residence that allows aliens to work legally in this country. According to the television show, the federal authorities swooped in and supposedly cleaned up the illegal ID business and thanks to their efforts the world is a safer place now.

About a month or two after the area had been cleaned up, Stuart asked me to do him a favor. His maid needed to buy some cooking supplies and he pleaded with me to give her a ride down to that area so that she could go to a store she was familiar with to gets some pots and pans. Stuart's a good friend, so because he had a dentist appointment and couldn't take her that day, I agreed to help out. There was no parking space available in front of the store where she wanted to shop, so I decided to drive around the block looking for one.

At the time I was driving an older car from Rent-a-Wreck, an economical car rental place on Pico Boulevard. I was a steady customer there because my Jaguar was in the shop getting repaired so often. Not too long ago the British attempted to land a robot on the planet Mars. It failed. Why am I not surprised? They should have made Mars wait until they could have made a car that works. But it's a good thing the Jag wasn't working that day, because the appearance of an old jalopy containing a Latino maid was too much to resist and the hustlers came out of doorways, running up to the car shouting "ID, ID." All you need is an old car and a Hispanic person, and there's no problem in being solicited by one of the many gangs that the government had allegedly 'cleaned up.' All you have to give the runner who approaches your car is a small photo of yourself and a couple of real twenty-dollar bills.

If I could have gotten a fake drivers license just a month or two after the government cleaned things up, it's probably gotten much easier in the past several years, and the gang's van driver probably availed himself of these services to get a new drivers license with a fictitious name and residence address of some vacant lot in North Hollywood... but if the face on the license is real, then Suzi will find him.

This is good because it means that piece-by-piece, we're putting together the jigsaw puzzle and when it's completed we'll be in a position to bust up the gang and possibly get Stuart's money back. More important is the fact that we'll probably stop a good percentage of internet fraud and identity theft. I'd like to rub Snell's upturned nose in it. He told me not to waste my time on this stuff because the Bureau wasn't interested. It was too small of a matter. We'll see what he thinks when we break the case. I'm sure he'll be first in line when it comes to taking all the credit.

Out of curiosity I log on to the internet learn that the FBI has partnered with another Department of Justice creation, the Internet Fraud Complaint Center, to receive information from the general public about the frauds that are floating around out there in cyberspace. Statistics from the IFCC show that there are six main areas that the crooks concentrate on including Auction Fraud, Non-Delivery of Merchandise, Credit Card Scams, Investment Fraud, Business Fraud and last but not least, the ever-popular Nigerian Bank Letter.

Being currently involved with Stuart's problems I'm now quite familiar with credit card fraud, and I've also received quite a few letters from various public officials in Nigeria who have solicited my cooperation in having twenty-three million dollars transferred out of their banks and into my account. No thank you. As impossible as that Nigerian thing seems, the IFCC states that it generates over fifteen percent of the complaints that come in. A foreign news correspondent I know tells me that every week the British police find people sitting in London's Heathrow Airport waiting to meet some non-existent Nigerian official who they've wired money to for one phony reason or another, to get the money released so it could be brought to them in London.

The greedy suckers fly in from all over the world expecting to meet the Nigerian con men.

The phone is ringing. It's Myra calling.
"Hello sweetheart. Yes, I am available for my free dinner. Is tonight too soon?
"You've got a lot of nerve pulling that stunt with Snell. If you knew your guy was a fed you should've told me at the beginning. I could have avoided making a fool out myself by getting that indictment."
"Okay, I'll pay for dinner."
"I'm not having dinner with you tonight, or maybe any other night ever. Every time I get involved with you I wind up losing. I'm getting tired of it, Peter."
"I apologize for any inconvenience that the FBI has caused you, but you surely must realize that I'm not smart enough to have purposely caused you such aggravation. I'll tell you what I'm going to do. I'm working on a case right now that might possibly lead to a really nice bust for some police agency. If you're nice to me, I'll see to it that you're first in line to nab this white-collar fraud gang. You'll have a chance to rub Snell's nose in it too, because I think he'd also like to get these guys. Whatta ya think? Can we play nice now.?"

Silence on the other end of the line. She hasn't hung up yet, so I think she's weakening. I'm succeeding in wearing her down. Now I go in for the kill.
"Hey, why don't we get together for dinner tonight? I'll pick up the tab and fill you in a little."
It doesn't work. She snaps out of the ether.

"Sorry Peter, but your days of filling me in are over. I'll wait and see what you come up with on that white-collar gang. If it pans out, I'll take you and your crew out to dinner, just like our bet on that aborted John Doe case."

I agree to the deal. As a result of her late grandfather's will, Myra is worth more than Stuart is, but she still holds on to every buck like it's her last one. My timing is really terrible. I was asked to depart from our marital residence about six months before the rich old guy bowed out.

The greatest feat of strength any human being can exhibit is the picking up of a dinner check. I'm constantly amazed at how people of all income levels try to avoid that strenuous activity, and Myra is no exception. It's always the people who can afford it the least who usually get stuck with the check. That's no doubt why they're poor. It's a combination of their inability to avoid getting snookered into paying, along with some need to boost their own ego by showing they can afford to pay the tab.

The paws are approaching. Another incoming dog-mail telling me that I should have kept my mouth shut with Myra. According to the little genius' plan, we don't want to see that fraud ring busted until we have a chance to recover punitive damages from them for defrauding Stuart. She's absolutely correct. Once we turn that gang over to the authorities all of their assets will immediately be seized. The proper procedure would be to act on Stuart's behalf and not let them know we're onto the whole operation. All we want is to make our client whole.

Maybe if they think Stuart got lucky and by a fluke happened to find them, they might pay off, hoping that they're still in business. We'll get Stuart's money back and then turn them in. I love it when a good plan emerges. Now all we have to do is find out who and where they are.

My timing must be improving. The kid is now standing in front of me. She and the dog just stand there and look at me. I'll never figure her out. I might as well break this deafening silence.

"What?"

"We got a hit on the van driver's face."

"The facial recognition software we bought?"

She nods in the affirmative.

"So if you've got a hit, that means you know who he really is, right?"

Another positive nod.

"Okay, it's your turn to speak now. The guessing game stops working when I have to start calling names out of the telephone directory."

She hands me a piece of paper and then they both walk away. The small sheet has 'Marvin Shackler' written on it. This is nice to know, but it means absolutely nothing to me. I call out to her, hoping to get some answer before she retreats to her stateroom for the night.

"Hey, do we know anything else about this guy Shackler?"

As her stateroom door is closing, I get an answer.

"He's Neil Kaplan's uncle."

16

I hate coincidences because they always lead to a lot of work. I call Jack Bibberman and give him his new instructions. If the kid knows about all this and hasn't told me, she's in big trouble. If what I'm thinking now is actually true, that means Neil Kaplan is part of the internet credit card and auction fraud ring.

But how does this young college student get connected to an internet fraud ring? Come to think of it, why not? Guys like Bill Gates, Steve Wozniak and Michael Wang were just young college students fooling around with computers in their parents' garages when they started businesses that we now know as Microsoft, Apple Computers and Yahoo. It's not the large corporations that are driving the new innovative hi-tech industry, it's college kids like Neil Kaplan.

I met him. I took his deposition and he doesn't impress me as the type who is smart enough to create a successful business of any kind, whether it's legal or not. On the other hand, he is kind of a nerdy guy. I guess he fits the geek profile, but being a defense lawyer, I still want to give him the benefit of the doubt. Granted it's a big coincidence that his uncle may be the pick-up van driver, but it's not conclusive evidence that Kaplan is involved too. We've got more work to do if we're going to connect them together in this fraud ring.

Just to make sure of Suzi's investigative results, I call Jack Bibberman and add another task to his assignment. He is to park outside of Shackler's house tomorrow morning and get a good look at him. Jack saw the van driver and I want a positive identification from him. He'll probably use his telephoto lens to get a picture of Shackler coming out of his house in the morning and another one of him returning the van to the large mailbox place. I'll wait to see both of those pictures side-by-side before jumping to any conclusions.

I've just jumped to the conclusion. Today Jack did exactly what I asked him to do. Using his new digital camera, he took those photos of Shackler. Then he loaded them into his laptop computer, drove by a known wireless hotspot and emailed them to us here at the boat. Shackler is the van driver. Another piece of the puzzle just fell into place.

Because our case against Kaplan is already filed with the court, all we have to do is add another few causes of action and name his uncle as one of the 'John Doe's' discovered subsequent to our filing of the case.

The strategy will be to not divulge too much in the pleadings, because not only the defendants will see them, but they're public record too. We don't want to say that they're part of a fraud ring... only that for some unknown reason, the credit card company did not honor the credit cards they used. The complaint should only seek to recover the actual cost of the merchandise they purchased, plus court costs, a minimal amount of punitive damages and attorney's fees.

We want to give them the idea that this is an isolated case they can easily buy their way out of for less than a grand.

In the meantime, we've still got the names and addresses of everyone who sent them merchandise, and Jack succeeded in getting a copy of the large mailbox place's UPS manifest, so we also know who their customers were. They do everything by computers now, so we have a printout of every person who the gang bought from and sold stuff to.

One of the things I also instructed Jack to do was start contacting the people who bought things from the gang. If we're going to follow the money, we'll have to start right where it comes from. Those buyers had to find this gang somewhere on an internet site. Once we discover the site we can do a lot of tracing. We can follow the money and also go to their internet server to see if they are paying for other domain names to be hosted. We can also discover the methods of payment they accept and then subpoena information from the companies that have processed all of the transactions, finding another money trail to follow and see where it all winds up.

This is the part I don't like. Sitting back and waiting for something to happen that will give us a new direction. We need a new lead. We need to get lucky. The phone is ringing. It's a number I don't recognize. I'll let the answering machine pick this one up while I sit here and screen the call. After the fourth ring the machine picks up and I hear my outgoing announcement.

"This is the law firm of Peter Sharp and associates. Please leave your number and we'll call you back." Beep.

"Hello Mister Sharp, My name is Todd. I'm a friend of Neil Kaplan, and that was my laptop the guy took out of his back seat. He gave me a ride part way downtown and when I got out of the car I ran to catch a bus and forgot to grab my laptop. I know that you're the attorney who was representing that John Doe guy. Now that he's disappeared, I wonder if I could get my computer back. You can call me at 818,…"

This is too good to miss out on. I grab the phone. "Yes, hello. This is Peter Sharp. I just walked in and heard the last couple of words of your message. What can I do for you?"

I can't believe the guy just dropped into our lap like this. He tells me his story over again and I make sure to get down his name, address, telephone number and whatever else I can find out about him. While I've got him on the phone I try to pump him just a little bit more.

"Todd, because that computer is still locked up in an evidence locker, no one has really had a chance to look at it very closely. Is there any particular reason you need that exact one, because if the county prosecutor won't release it to you, I can probably get them to lend you a substitute computer until that one is ready to be returned."

This is a very nice offer I've just made to him, but as I hoped, it freaks him out a little. He tries to maintain his composure, but he's definitely on edge. He tells me that there's a lot of personal family information on it, so no loaner will do. I can tell he's lying. It almost sounds as if there's someone there with him, prodding him to get that computer back. Not a loaner, not another, better computer, but that exact computer. I tell him that I'll see what I can do for him and get back to him in a while. I get his e-mail address and our conversation ends.

Looking up after hanging up the phone I see that the dynamic duo is standing in front of me. No conversation. They're just looking at me. I don't know why they do this, but it's starting to spook me. If I don't say something, I have no idea how long they'll stay there, so I speak.

"Now what? I don't remember calling for a staff meeting."

"We need him. He thinks he needs us to help him get that computer back, but we need him."

She doesn't say very much. I liken her expectations of me to the conversation of two old time comedians who have been working together for many years. Between the two of them they know every joke ever written or performed. They know the jokes so well, that all one of them has to do is say a punch line and the other will automatically know what his partner meant. That's what I think is going on here. Suzi will ponder a situation for a while. After she's got the whole thing figured out in her own brilliant little mind, she walks out into my area of the boat and looks at me, expecting me to know exactly what she's been thinking about, so that I can say the punch line. I disappoint her every time.

"Why do we need him so badly?"

"Because he's our link to the whole gang. He didn't make that call on the spur of the moment. They must have thought it over for a while and waited to see if they were being followed or in danger of being arrested. When they thought the coast was clear, they must have believed that their secrets are safe in that laptop's hard drive, so they put that man up to calling you."

"I'm sorry. I can't work in the dark any more. I know you went through that hard drive with a fine-tooth comb and probably got a lot of information out of it. You haven't told me one thing that you found, and now Snell's got it and we're out in the cold again. So if you want to really be a part of a team, then you'll have to trust me."

She's obviously only capable of a limited amount of conversation with me, so now they're heading back to her stateroom. I patiently wait, because her usual routine is to throw me a one-liner before closing the door. Here it comes.

"Snell doesn't have what he thinks he has."

I don't believe it. First she fools Myra by giving the computer back with a substitute hard drive in it. Now she's tricked the FBI into dismissing charges against our client in exchange for another switched hard drive. The feds are going to have their experts going through that thing. The difference between them and Myra's people is that the feds have some idea of what they're looking for. Oh boy, are we in trouble. I know I'm going to be getting a call from Snell. I wonder how many federal crimes he'll threaten to prosecute me for. Wait a minute. I didn't do anything. He dealt with the kid. He can't threaten her with prosecution because then he'd be forced to admit that he was tricked by a kid, and that would be too much for his FBI ego to tolerate. I think we've got him. In fact, I think we've got everyone.

It's too bad that our John Doe disappeared on us. It would have been nice if that dismissal came during the trial. We've done pretty good wrapping things up in courtrooms before.

In the old black-and-white detective movies, there was always a grand finale scene that was called the 'showdown.' It usually took place when the sleuth solved the case and arranged for all the suspects and the police to be in the same location, at which time the detective would espouse his theory and brilliant crime-solving methods, eliminating each suspect until only one remained. The guilty person. The one who no one ever suspected. Then the befuddled police would suddenly try to make it look like they knew who the real culprit was all along.

The thing that Suzi really seems to enjoy is performing in her own dramatic showdown. Unfortunately that only works well in a court-room where a judge, all the suspects and the authorities can be together in one place while she does her super-sleuth routine.

The first time I saw it happen I was shocked. Next time the shock was a little less. Now I'm kind of looking forward to it, mainly because I'm in awe of the way she arranges it. But with our client having disappeared forever as far as the public is concerned, and with the case really having been dismissed, I think this time she's just going to have to learn a lesson about how it feels to be disappointed.

I know that the kid is in her stateroom plotting full time. I hope the failure she's going to experience won't hurt her too much. I might as well relax and let nature take its course. She may be bright for her chronological age, but she's still just a kid and there's a learning process she has to go through on her way to adulthood.

The ultimate waste of time is watching local news. I usually wait at least five minutes before turning it on, because of their 'if it bleeds, it leads' policy. After the carnage portion is over I then watch to see if Myra is making a statement. If she doesn't, then the sports will be forth-coming. The most ridiculous thing they ever put on the air is one of those self-appointed UFO experts. They usually pop up during the 'sweeps' months that TV ratings are compiled. In a court of law, in order to testify as a witness, the attorney calling an expert must first show the court that the witness is qualified to testify as an expert. The court demands this because according to rules of evidence, expert witnesses are the only ones allowed to offer their opinions. My dream as a trial lawyer is to have the other side attempt to call a witness to the stand and qualify him or her as a UFO expert. I just want three minutes of cross-examination of this alleged expert and then my life will be complete.

Tonight I'm a little surprised. There's no UFO expert, but the blow-dried anchorperson is not only reading the news, she is holding up a brand new issue of a tabloid newspaper and showing the headline. It's in big bold type and screams out the one thing I was never expecting to see. **JOHN DOE HAS BEEN FOUND AND IS BACK IN CUSTODY.**

17

It's a good thing I'm sitting down in this deep plush couch, because I surely would have fallen off of a chair. Not only does the anchorperson say that our client is back in custody, it credits the story's source as being a high-ranking member of John Doe's defense team. Gee, I wonder who that could be. I know it's not me, so that only leaves two other living creatures, and I have a suspicion which one it is.

This is crazy. John Doe isn't in custody. There is no more John Doe. Why has she done this? I'm now considering turning off the ringer on my phone. Too late. It's Myra calling. I don't waste any time.

"Myra, I swear to God I didn't do it. You and I both know who that story was leaked from, and I haven't the slightest idea of what she's up to. If you want, maybe you should call her. She's already spoken to me twice this week, so I've received my quota of words from her."

"Peter, why is she doing this to us? You know Snell will really be pissed, and that's nothing compared to how the judge will feel. If she plans on doing her super-sleuth routine again, she's on her own. I want no part of it."

I barely hang up the phone when it starts ringing again. I recognize this number, so I start the same routine over again. Snell definitely is not a happy camper. He wants Suzi in his office tomorrow at ten A.M. I've got a good mind to have Jack take her over there so she can see what it's like to be surrounded by the big bad federal agents all by herself. Nah. I better tag along. Maybe they'll shout at me and it'll take some of the heat off of her.

I rattle the dog biscuit box. The foreward stateroom door opens and she sticks her head out, saving me the trouble of sending a dog-mail. She informs me that she'll be ready at nine-fifteen tomorrow morning. If this wasn't such a miserable situation for us to be in, I might even enjoy watching the upcoming confrontation between Suzi and the FBI.

The seventeenth floor of this building gives its visitors a beautiful view. You can see all the way to the Pacific Ocean and on a clear day Catalina Island is visible. It's too bad that the tenants of the floor don't have the vision to enjoy it.

Against my advice, the kid has not only brought the dog, she is prominently wearing her Detective Sergeant's badge on a gold chain around her neck. When one of Snell's rookies comes to the waiting room to act as our escort he sees that Suzi is bringing the huge dog with her.

"I'm sorry young lady, but I don't think you can bring the dog with you to Special Agent in Charge Snell's office."

True to form, she completely ignores this guy and continues walking down the hall. He looks at me with one of those 'is she deaf, or what?' looks on his face. I merely give him one of those 'I have no idea' shrugs. When we get to Snell's office the rookie raps quietly once and then opens the door for us. The kid marches in like she owns the place and with a hop, jumps up and sits down in the chair directly in front of Snell, who is slightly surprised at this little girl with the badge and big dog who have invaded his office. I am intelligent enough to keep my mouth shut. As I look around I see that Snell has arranged his own little 'showdown,' because others in the room for today's meeting include the judge, Myra and Special Agent Karl Shaeffer.

Snell starts out with a small display to show that he's in charge here. The alpha male in some animal groups may do this by marking the perimeter of his domain with urine. Snell is slightly more sophisticated with his opening salvo.

"Young lady, I would have preferred that you hadn't brought that animal in here with you. These are new carpets. And I notice that you are wearing a peace officer's badge, in violation of the law."

Oh, oh. I wouldn't have done that if I were him. He obviously doesn't know her very well. Even Myra is now directing her own gaze to the floor in anticipation of what the kid's response might be. The judge has seen her in action too, so with the exception of Snell and Shaeffer, the rest of us wish we could get out of the way, in fear of what the kid may come up with. She looks him directly in the eye.

"Mister Agent Snell, to begin with, if there is any regulation against me wearing this badge, it's definitely not a federal offense, so please stop trying to intimidate me. Secondly, the reason I leaked that story to the press is because you've got to bring John Doe back to life for a trial."

Snell doesn't blink an eye.

"I'm sorry young lady, but we've made our final decision and the Federal Bureau of Investigation is not going to change its plans because of an uppity little girl's wishes."

There's a brief silence. Myra and I exchange glances. It looks like we'd both like to sneak out of the room for a minute. We don't have time. The kid's ready with her final salvo. The first time, she called him 'mister agent Snell.' He was lucky. Let's see what he is this time.

"Mister Snell, I'm sorry, but you really don't know what you've got here. The hard drive I gave you is the original one that was in that computer, but it had something on it that was so terrible, I erased it. As soon as that computer was delivered to us the first thing I did was copy the entire drive's data onto my own computer, so the erased portion still exists.

"The reason I found it so nasty was because I believe there is a plot to blow up this very building on the anniversary of the horrible thing that happened to the Federal Building in Oklahoma. I wasn't born yet when that happened, but I researched it on the Internet and I don't want to ever see anything like that happen again."

Snell doesn't know whether to believe her or not. He opts for 'not.'

"Oh my, that sounds serious. Did they happen to mention how they intend to accomplish such a nasty feat?"

Big mistake. Not only does he not believe her, but he's talking down to her like she's some kid. Of course that's all she is, but she doesn't know that.

"Your agency originally grabbed Kaplan's laptop computer because of his suspected complicity in a credit card fraud ring, but what you didn't realize was that he and his gang didn't even know that the information I found on that laptop was there.

"If it will help convince you that I have some idea of what I'm talking about, perhaps names like William L. Pierce and the Turner Diaries will ring a bell somewhere.

"Its previous owner had deleted it before Kaplan got the computer, but I was able to retrieve it. If you will allow my partner to conduct his John Doe trial in a courtroom and win it there, I will deliver the real bad guys to you. You can now do either one of two things. Let attorney Peter Sharp finish his case in court, or send me to Guantanamo Bay in Cuba under some trumped up imaginary violation of your Homeland Security Patriot Act and let the press see what you've done to a poor little defenseless girl."

Having finished her monologue and caused every jaw in the room to drop, she hops out of the chair and walks out of Snell's office with the dog following closely. In her usual style, she tosses me one last line before going through the door.

"I'll be waiting for you at the car."

I knew she would be able to hold her own with Snell, but she's outdone herself this time. Snell's only remaining target is me.

"What's she talking about, Sharp?"

"I have no idea. I never even knew she switched hard drives on Myra."

Myra's eyes open wide in astonishment.

"What do you mean switched hard drives? You mean she removed the hard drive from that computer without breaking the seal on that evidence bag?"

"Not exactly. She never touched that evidence bag. The hard drive was switched before, when it was sent to us as a return of our client's property. That was before you filed charges and before it was evidence. After the indictment she wouldn't touch it because she remembers how you subpoenaed her as a witness the last time you found her fingerprints somewhere."

Now to try and convince Snell that I'm dumber than I look.

"And as for what she's said here today, I know nothing about it, but I am sure about one thing. If she says there's a danger, then you'd better believe her because she's rarely wrong about things like that. And if she promises to deliver some bad guys to you, I would take her up on it.

"Now if you'll excuse me, I've got a kid all by herself in a big public parking lot and there are a lot of bad people who might try to bother her, so I better get out there to protect anyone who tries."

This meeting is over and I'm on my way back downstairs in the elevator. Myra stayed behind with Snell and the judge, no doubt to figure out some way to get the John Doe trial back on track.

The ride back to our boat should be an interesting one. It seems like the only time I can ever get her to talk to me is when she doesn't have a foreward stateroom to head for. I was successful during our ride back from court last time, so I might as well give it another shot.

"That was nice the way you were able to hold an adult conversation with Mister Snell, but I think he would prefer being addressed as Special Agent In Charge Snell."

"Please don't patronize me. I know exactly what his title is."

"I thought you did. What about that plot to blow up his building? That was a little much just to try and get your way. I appreciate the fact that you enjoy sitting as second chair during a trial, but don't you think you've gone a little too far in trying to get that trial started again? I mean, if that's all you're interested in, I could bring you into court with me on other trials. You don't have to make bomb scares just to get back into court."

"I wasn't making an idle threat. When you delete something on a computer, it's really still there. All you've done is make space on the drive where the deleted data is available to be written over, like you record over an audio or videotape. If you never get around to actually writing over the data, then it may have been deleted from the file directories, but it can still be found hidden in some areas of the hard drive.

"When I first started going through that laptop I didn't find it, but when I found out that Snell was involved, I went back and searched a little deeper."

"And exactly when did you decide that Snell was involved?"

"Right at the beginning. When you went to the hospital the first time and Victor took that DNA swab from John Doe. At that time, his memory really hadn't returned. If it had, he would've known he was an FBI person and he never would have let Victor take his prints and DNA.

"When running through the DNA database I found him in there, but the information was blocked.

That meant he was either federal law enforcement or a protected witness. Either way, the FBI was involved so I called Snell to find out. He denied knowing anything, but the mere fact that an organized group of people were able to get him out of that hospital means that Snell was involved.

"The first time that John Doe called wanting you to believe he was still in custody at the county jail, I told him that I knew what was going on, so Snell was sort of forced into making that deal with us to have the charges dismissed.

"It wasn't until then that I started to dig deeper onto the hard drive information that was still on my computer. Snell was happy because he found the credit card info on the drive we returned to him, but he never realized there was more on it, because his experts stopped looking when they found what was important to the case they were working on."

"What do you suggest we do now?"

"I'm working on a plan. Kaplan didn't know what he had there, so it must be the person he got that used computer from. That's who we're after. Uncle Jack is now running down some leads I gave him. Maybe we'll get a report from him soon."

The rest of the ride is in silence, but that's okay with me. I'm already overloaded with more information than I wanted to know. I heard her do a little name-dropping to Snell, so it looks like I've got some research to do when we get back to the boat.

18

An abbreviated bio of William L. Pierce shows that he is a former Oregon State University college instructor who holds a Ph.D. in physics and has quite a background. In the 1960's he was an assistant to George Lincoln Rockwell, the founder and head of the American Nazi Party.

In 1978 Pierce used the fictitious name of Andrew Macdonald and published a book about the future entitled *The Turner Diaries*. This was a fictional account of the activities of a racist, anti-Semitic underground that gains power over the United States and eventually the world. Like another deranged leader of the 40's, Pierce's futuristic scenario also included the systematic killing of all Jews and non-whites in order to establish an 'Aryan' world.

The events he wrote about were supposed to take place during the 1990's and included certain white-supremist militias carrying out a mortar attack on the White House, the destruction of public utilities and communications systems and the 'liberation' of this country after nuclear bombs had been dropped on several East Coast cities. In the 1970's Pierce took over as leader of a neo-nazi organization called the National Alliance.

Pierce's book has become very popular with the far-right extremists who can read, and it is known that Oklahoma City bomber Timothy McVeigh was an avid fan and enthusiastic promoter of The Turner Diaries. There appear to be incredible similarities between McVeigh's bombing of the Murrah Federal Building in Oklahoma City and a scene in *The Turner Diaries* that graphically describes the preparation and use of a bomb used to destroy the FBI's national headquarters.

The *Turner Diaries* is also thought to be the inspiration for a violent extremist group called 'The Order,' which was founded by Robert Matthews, a man who Pierce mentored. This group committed a string of murders, robberies, counterfeiting and the bombing of a synagogue in the 1990's.

It's no wonder that Snell turned ash-gray when Suzi mentioned Pierce's name, which I'm sure can push as many buttons in an FBI office as the word 'bomb' can push in an airport. I'm surprised that she even knew about Pierce.

Now that it looks like she's talking to me a little, maybe I can get some more information out of her. I rattle the dog-biscuit box and send her a message asking what plan she has for finding out about the alleged bombers from that computer hard drive. A message comes back with only one word. "Cookies."

This is getting rather fatiguing. Working with her is like going back to college. Every time she says something, I'm forced 'back to the books' in an effort to keep up with her. Instead of wasting all those nights on Laverne's boat, perhaps I would have been better served researching things on the internet. On second thought, doing research on-demand works too.

I've heard the word Cookies before with respect to computers, but never really understood what they did. From what my research now tells me, Cookies are small data structures used by a commercial web server. Once a user reaches certain websites, the site will send information back to the user. This information is stored in the user's computer and only comes into play when that user returns to the same web site once again.

In this way the operator of a website can tell where each of the different unique visitors are going on the commercial web site and which pages of the site are visited most. Cookies are stored in the user's computer. If I understand what I've learned about them and what our dock computer guru explained to me about them, if you really know what you're doing you can get into a hard drive and find the Cookies that are stored there. Very few people waste the time to periodically delete the stored Cookies in their computer because they take up so little storage space. And even it they did try to delete them, a proficient 'recovery' expert could probably retrieve them.

By a close inspection of a computer's Cookies, an expert can re-construct a complete trail of every website the user visited. My research also reveals that emails are also stored in the computer's memory. It sounds a lot like human memory. Everything's in there... it's just a matter of how to access it. Some people use mnemonic devices, others use word association, and others have devised different methods.

A computer with all its information deleted resembles a human being with amnesia. The information is still there... all you have to do is know how to get in there to retrieve it. I don't know how good she can be with a human brain, but I have a feeling that given enough time, Suzi will be able to put together a pretty good picture of what the previous owner of Kaplan's computer was up to, what sites he visited, the people he communicated with and exactly what they're up to.

When the FBI got their hands on the computer they were only looking for information that led to one thing... putting an end to the credit card fraud gang and convicting the perpetrators. That's all they were looking for. Seek and ye shall find. Don't seek and ye shant find. They weren't looking for Cookies; they were looking for credit card crooks.

The phone is ringing. It's Myra calling.

"Don't shout at me Myra, I'm just along for the ride. The kid's driving this train."

"I know that. I also know that the rest of us are all on the same train. Do you know what her plan is?"

"Not really, but I think she'll follow a suggestion from me that might be a win-win for most of the people involved."

"And what would that be?"

"I don't know yet, but as soon as she tells me what to think of, you'll be the first to know."

Jack B. has just come aboard the boat. He nods hello to me and then walks into the foreward stateroom. I'm beginning to feel left out of the loop.

I turn on the evening's local news show. Just after the car chase du jour, the on-screen person talks about an interview earlier today with our district attorney. Myra's face appears. They caught her walking into her office building. They must have staked out her private parking space in the underground garage. It doesn't look like she had any prepared statement to make, but she's a pro and made it look good anyway, just winging it.

The only question that had any merit was from a reporter who asked her where they were keeping Karl Shaeffer alias John Doe this time. Of course Myra knew that he isn't in custody, so she gracefully danced around that question by simply stating that this time they're not revealing the very secure place he's being kept at, and that her office is now making preparations for the upcoming trial, which will be resumed without a jury, per stipulation of both prosecution and defense counsel.

That's nice. I don't remember making any stipulation like that but it's a moot point anyway because there really is no case. When the trial resumes it will just be an act to try and round up two gangs of criminals. One semi-harmless group that steals money by defrauding people on the internet, and one dangerous group that may be planning mass murder. I hope the courthouse metal detectors are working the day we go back to our mock trial.

Jack comes out of the foreward stateroom.

"What's up, Jack? You look like you're carrying the weight of the world on your face."

"I've got a lot to do. Suzi's got me going to meetings at the FBI building. It looks like they're devoting their entire resources to her investigation. I'm just doing the leg work, but that'll keep me busy full time for several days."

Interesting. She must have really said the right thing to Snell if he's going that far to cooperate with her. The FBI isn't necessarily the intelligentsia of this country, but they are in a much better position to backtrack Internet service providers and email carriers than we are.

The combined efforts of Jack B., Suzi B., and the 'B' of FBI must be working out because just a day or two into their investigation I receive a dog-mail giving me a heads-up that a special letter is going out to certain selected people.

To whom it may concern:
It has come to the attention of this office that you have recently sold an electronic or computing device to someone by availing yourself of an online auction service.

There is a group of individuals who have been making unauthorized online purchases using other people's credit cards and victimizing online sellers.

If you have been victimized in this manner, you may appear at a time yet to be determined to reclaim your property.

Please contact this office at your earliest convenience with the description of your property, along with any identification information such as make, model and serial number. It would also be convenient if you would provide copies of any e-mail correspondence you may have concerning the sale and shipping of the item of personal property, including UPS receipt and tracking number.

Unclaimed merchandise may be auctioned off on the spot to persons present, so it might be advisable to bring some friends with to help you carry items.

This is clever. I like the type of plan where the bad guys are tricked into coming to a controlled place. Several times in the past, television shows like *Cops* featured programs where people with outstanding warrants were tricked into coming to some location under the guise of having won a large screen television set. The main requirement for each person before claiming his or her prize was the showing of proper photo identification. One by one the crooks would arrive, show their identification, admit that they are indeed the person requested to appear, and are then be led into the 'prize' area, where they were rewarded with an all expenses paid trip to the local jail.

Anyone with a brain wouldn't believe that last sentence of the letter that offers the auctioning off of other merchandise. Fortunately we're not dealing with very bright people, who will probably be skinheads. In any event, if there is some way we could fill the courtroom only with black people, the really bad guys should stick out nicely. That's not going to happen, but my suggestion would be to have the court set aside a special 'prize' area, complete with items on a table where they can go in and pick out their property. The jury room would probably be the best place, now that there won't be a jury there that day.

The news reports say that our John Doe trial resumes in two weeks. No one felt it necessary to clear it with my calendar, but not to worry... I'll be there.

Jack B. has been a busy guy. With UPS's cooperation we've managed to hold up all the outgoing shipments from the large mailbox place. This means that everyone who bought something will be disappointed, but they will be notified to contact their respective credit card companies and inform them that the merchandise was not received. The credit card companies will charge back the paid monies from the credit-card gang's bank account. We purposely delayed contacting the purchasers for fear of alerting the gang too soon.

We've also started a 'switch' routine of incoming packages. Each of the people who have sold items to the gang will receive their merchandise back. Jack and his crew are going to each of the mailbox places daily and picking up the newly arrived items. They then get replaced by dummy packages of the same approximate size, weight and return address.

Once the incoming packages have been replaced, the original items are shipped back to their owners with instructions to be careful in the future and to refrain from contacting the buyers, for fear of being caught up in the dragnet that the authorities are spreading.

The outgoing letters intended to snare the bombers contain our post office box as a return address and the clerk there has been instructed to not handle any envelopes delivered there for us. The mail carrier and sorters at the post office were also cautioned to be on the lookout for anything addressed to our P.O. box. Hopefully, we can intercept a letter before too many fingerprints have been placed on it.

Victor is standing by to perform DNA tests on the mucilage of the envelopes and postage stamps.

Our email address has been included with the letter, but anyone responding to it will be notified that they must respond in writing also, so that we can make room for all the people who are expected to show up that day to reclaim merchandise.

Snell has an entire cadre of men and women who will shill as other people there to pick up their merchandise. They'll all be FBI agents, who will accompany the bombers into the 'prize' area.

We've also notified Kaplan and his alleged friend Todd to show up to retrieve the laptop, which will no longer be needed in evidence. This will be interesting, with two criminal gangs showing up to pick up the same laptop. Hopefully they'll be properly separated. They've never seen each other before, so we shouldn't have any accidental recognition problems

So far the plan has been moving right along. Suzi has made separate gift packages for the authorities. I originally led Myra to believe that she'd have first crack at the credit card fraud guys. Snell spent a lot of time and money trying to get Kaplan and his gang and doesn't want to let them slip away, but we convinced him that he'd be a bigger hero by saying he used the credit card fraud ring as a way to reach the white supremist bombers. That way we talked him into letting Myra have first crack at Kaplan's gang.

Stuart will lose out on his lawsuit against Kaplan for the loss of his computer, but Suzi has promised him that she has a plan that will allow him to recover from his losses. He's curious about what she has in mind, so at his request we get him a reserved seat at the so-called trial.

The arrangements have all been made. I've been fronting for the FBI, who have been sending out some of those enticing 'reclaim your property' letters with my name on the stationery. They decided it would be best to make it look like John Doe's lawyer sent each letter. I don't know exactly who the letters were sent to, but that's okay. Anyone who shows up won't be dealing with me anyway, and truth be told, I'm really not interesting in becoming acquainted with any skinhead terrorists. I do know that once Suzi put the feds onto the right track, their experts looked in the right portions of that computer hard drive and even Suzi had to admit that the resources of the FBI are slightly better than the ones in our foreward stateroom.

From the bits and pieces of information I've been getting, Snell's team was able to get the complete cooperation of eBay and their money distribution network PayPal, UPS, the mailbox and vehicle rental places, DMV, the Post Office and various Internet Service Providers. With all that help available to them, I'm sure they'll succeed in inviting the bombers to our phony trial.

THE PHONY TRIAL

The press mob is outside the courthouse. Too bad they're going to be disappointed when they find out that our trial was really over some time ago and is now just being used as bait.

Myra arranged for us to be allowed use of the judge's entrance and elevator so we can avoid the reporters. Once inside the courtroom Stuart immediately picks a good seat in the front row. The judge has absolutely denied us the ability to pretend like the trial is going on, claiming that he refuses to preside over 'entertainment' in his courtroom, even if it serves a useful purpose. Instead he has gotten the federal and state authorities to agree to let him publicly conclude the John Doe criminal trial in a quick efficient manner as the court's first order of business.

This actually isn't a bad idea, because that will probably clear the area of most of the press and thereby give the good guys a better chance of spotting and dealing with the bad guys.

It takes a while for the courtroom to fill up. Snell and his men are nowhere to be seen but I'm sure they're around, watching. Looking around the courtroom walls I notice some additional cameras have been added. Court TV doesn't usually have the luxury of five-camera trial coverage so I assume that today we'll also be on FBI-TV.

Mister Uniman and Neil Kaplan returned to watch the trial and so have Michelle Chang and her daughter Lotus. Suzi has had several meetings with Myra and the judge. In a normal criminal case there is no such thing as a meeting of only one side with the judge unless the other side is present also. In this case it doesn't matter, because it's really been over for a while now. These meetings are to plan the statement that the judge will agree to make when he takes the bench.

The bailiff steps to center front of the courtroom, gets everyone's attention and calls the court to order. The proper buzzes are exchanged and the judge comes out to take the bench. From what I've been told, he will make an opening statement that closes all the loose ends. I don't expect to hear anything surprising in it. He bangs his gavel down lightly once, as his own sort of 'drum-roll' before starting his monologue. Here it comes.

"Ladies and gentlemen, the court will now describe some events for the record. These events have led to the court making certain rulings. First of all, notwithstanding the fact that it may disappoint the press, the criminal case against John Doe has been dismissed in its entirety."

This gets a round of gasps from the press, and a look of angry indignation from the deceased woman's attorney. The judge goes on.

"It has been brought to the court's attention that notwithstanding the fact that evidence supports the physical removal of certain property from a vehicle and that a chain of events followed causing the death of a female driver, there have been some technical and legal details that present insurmountable difficulties for maintenance of the indictment against John Doe.

"Firstly is the matter of the underlying theft charge. Due to a failure of communications and lack of willingness, the prosecution has been unable to obtain the requisite cooperation of a victim to testify under oath that removal of said personal property was not consented to.

"Without this supporting evidence, all that remains as a valid charge against the defendant are those of attempted burglary of a vehicle and or malicious mischief. That brings us to the vehicular collision causing the death of a female driver as she ran into the rear of a police squad car that stopped to prevent what they perceived to be a crime, and to avoid running over the defendant who had lost his balance and fallen into the squad car's path. As you are all aware he was struck and suffered a broken leg and concussion, which then caused a memory loss that gained international attention. That matter is now irrelevant to this court's rulings.

"Secondly, additional evidence has been provided to this court by defendant's legal team that bears on the causation of the collision causing decedent's loss."

What is this? We don't have any evidence about her death. This must be the kid's doing. That's probably what those meeting were partly about. Okay, I'm listening. Let's see what she's done this time. I glance down at my second-chair assistant and notice that she's got her attention focused on the judge, with that academy-award look of innocence on her face. The judge continues.

"Outside security camera tape previously admitted into evidence to support alleged criminal acts of the defendant have been more fully analyzed, said analysis expanded to include what happened up to thirty seconds prior to the fatal vehicle collision. That analysis showed what appeared to be certain action of the deceased driver more precisely described as holding a cell phone up in front of her face and attempting to make an outgoing call. Records subpoenaed from her cell phone service provider have confirmed this purported action of hers.

"The City of Los Angeles' insurance carriers demand that an extensive report and investigation must be done whenever there is any damage to a city owned vehicle. The report of this event shows a complete absence of skid marks under the decedent's Plymouth vehicle. Furthermore, judicial notice of certain times of the day have been taken of evidence presented to the court regarding the exact hour, minute and second of a telephone call attempted from the decedent's assigned cell phone number. That timing has been compared with time-code indications on footage from the several exterior security cameras and the court therefore finds that decedent's injuries were caused by her violation of two statutes. Following a vehicle too closely and inattentiveness due to unauthorized use of a cell phone while driving.

"Accordingly, this court hereby rules that all aforementioned criminal charges against the defendant are dismissed and that liability for the fatal collision lie with the decedent."

He bangs his gavel down and leaves the bench. The reporters go ballistic. Not only do they not find out the real truth that they rightfully suspect has been withheld, but they also miss out on a chance to get at our John Doe, who was revealed as Karl

Shaeffer during our previous court date. No doubt they tried to find out who Karl was, but the FBI does a pretty good job of protecting their special agents from that kind of scrutiny. The bailiff takes center stage again with another announcement.

"All members of the press are now asked to exit the courtroom so another related matter can be addressed."

This gets their attention again as they wonder what kind of other related matter could the bailiff be referring to. They get their answer as the bailiff finishes.

"Certain issues regarding disposal of personal property involved in the instant case will now be resolved."

This sounds completely void of any facts that will sell newspapers or get television ratings, so the press leaves the courtroom. There are very few people remaining and I recognize them all. My second chair assistant is now talking to one of them. It is Mister Uniman, who is handing an envelope to Suzi. He smiles and gives me a 'thumbs-up' sign as he pats Suzi on the head and leaves the courtroom. If that envelope contains what I think it is, our law firm is one hundred grand richer now because the judge got Uniman off the hook for that double indemnity portion of the deceased's policy. She caused that accident and the terms of the policy won't allow someone to benefit from his or her own acts of wrongdoing.

The other recognizable ones remaining are Stuart, Michelle, Lotus and Neil Kaplan. The clerk tells everyone that it will be a short while before the judge comes back out to handle the personal property issue. The clock on the wall indicates that it's now a little before ten in the morning. The letters that were sent out requested that interested people be in court by nine. It's almost an hour past that time and I still don't see any skinheads. Something must be wrong here. A guy sticks his head into the courtroom and calls out Stuart's name. Turning around, Stuart sees that the man is motioning for him to step out into the hallway. Stuart politely excuses himself to Michelle and Lotus as he walks out. He's got a bad habit of parking wherever he feels like it and this time it's probably some big shot's parking space. I hope they haven't towed his car, because there isn't room for Stuart and the Changs to fit in the Hummer with my other passengers.

A few minutes later Snell comes into the courtroom and tells us we can all go home now because they've made their arrest. They've got the bomber. We're all relieved to hear this information. I had my doubts about the FBI's methods before, but I've got to give credit where it's due. They did their job and I feel good about it. Suzi looks a little disappointed because she probably wanted to watch the whole thing go down. We all get ready to leave. Neil Kaplan looks around as if he's been forgotten. He goes over to the court clerk and inquires about the personal property issue. She looks over to me. I look back at her with a shrug indicating that she's on her own and hear her as she tells Kaplan to leave his number and the court will call him with their decision as to the computer's disposition. He does so and leaves.

Myra's not too happy now. She was promised the delivery of a credit card fraud ring and feels left out. The feds got their bomber, but she wound up with nothing. I try to make her feel a little better by promising her that she'll still get her gang. Suzi backs me up. She believes it when Suzi promises it.

Michelle Chang and Lotus are still here, but Stuart hasn't returned. We all walk out into the hallway together. The press is gone and only one person remains. Special Agent Snell. I'm no fan of his, but he still deserves my congratulations, and Michelle asks me to inquire about Stuart's whereabouts.

"Well, well, you guys certainly did your job today. I feel safer already."

"I hate to admit it Sharp, but we couldn't have done it without you."

This acknowledgement from the FBI gets everyone's attention. Now Michelle, Lotus, Myra and Suzi have walked over to us to see if more thanks might be forthcoming. They're not disappointed. Snell continues.

"That's right Mister Sharp, with the cooperation of your office, we now have succeeded in striking a blow to a very dangerous gang."

My curiosity is getting the best of me now. I have to ask him.

"That's great Snell. By the way, I was wondering. Were they skinheads like I thought they might be?"

"On the contrary. We arrested only one person, and we believe him to be the leader of the gang."

"Gee, only one person? And he wasn't a skinhead?"

"Not at all Mister Sharp. We were as surprised as you probably will be. Our prisoner, the leader of the terrorist gang, is none other than your close friend and new criminal client Stuart Schwarzman."

19

We're all in a state of shock. I ask Snell if it's okay to see Stuart now. He tells me that I can see him tomorrow afternoon because they'll be holding him in a safe house tonight while they ask him some questions.

"I'm his attorney. I have a right to be present during any interrogation."

"Sorry to disappoint you Sharp, but you better check the details of the Patriot Act. At this point we don't actually know who this Stuart Schwarzman fellow really is, so until we get some fingerprint and passport history on him, he's not being visited by anyone."

"Snell, I tell you this on my word as a natural-born American citizen and sworn officer of the court for over twenty years now. I personally have been acquainted with Stuart Schwarzman for over fifteen years. He has been a neighbor, a client and a good friend for all that time." That doesn't stop Snell. He has another question for me.

"To the best of your knowledge, has he been out of the country recently?"

"If you check his passport you'll see that he travels to Thailand occasionally. His uncle owned a condominium there and Stuart stays in it once or twice a year. Look Snell, I know in my heart that Stuart isn't the guy you're looking for, so please – do yourself a favor: don't dig a hole so deep that you can't get out of it.

"I know that it's your job to follow through on leads and if you feel it's necessary to keep him in custody, I understand, but before you put him in the system as a terrorist, please give us a day or so to try and find out what's going on here."

He looks me straight in the eye for what seems like minutes.

"Okay Sharp. You've done a couple of favors for us in the past, so maybe I owe you one. You've got forty-eight hours to convince me that we've got the wrong man and we won't interrogate him during that period of time. If you do prove us wrong, then I'll expect you to have him sign a form that releases us from any liability for his detention. But if you're wrong, we're going all the way with him. No holds barred."

I feel a tugging at my sleeve. It's the kid, with an expression of urgency on her face.

"C'mon Peter, let's get back to the boat. I've got a lot of work to do."

After we drop Michelle and Lotus off I see that Suzi is busy on her cell phone talking to Jack Bibberman. Her next call is to Victor Gutierrez. She gives them both assignments concerning further investigation into matters I didn't even know they were working on.

Once back at the boat she disappears into her stateroom, probably to turn on her computer and work on it until the next day. There's no mention of food, so I make my own plans for dinner. Hopefully, my pasta du jour's bouquet will attract their attention.

I thought I had this whole case figured out but Stuart's arrest has thrown a monkey wrench into everything. For the life of me I can't imagine why anyone would think that Stuart has any connection to some crazy gang that wants to bomb a federal building.

I haven't got the mental energy to create a new pasta dish this evening, so I'm taking the easy way out. Trader Joe's Roasted Vegetable Ravioli. I'll prepare three of their ten-ounce packages. That'll be almost two pounds, but because the dog will be joining us for dinner, I want to make sure I've got enough to go around. He doesn't like to leave the table hungry. Come to think of it, he just hates to leave the table. I try some sprinkled-on garlic salt and grated Parmesan cheese in an attempt to create a 'come-and-get-it' invitation aroma.

Aside from the fact that I want her to get some food digested for energy, having the kid present at the table may give me an opportunity to get a couple of questions answered. She hasn't spoken to me much today, so perhaps I'll be graced with some of her precious dialogue.

The recipe worked. After almost three minutes of my slaving away and working my fingers to the bone over a hot microwave oven, I turn around and see that our table is already set and she's sitting there with a fork in her hand. Bernie's empty bowl has conveniently been placed on the floor atop a placemat.

When the food is brought to the table and set down on its trivet, the dog gives us a short, soft whine. We interpret that as his saying Grace, and accept it s a signal for us to dig in. Once the eating has commenced I start to think out loud. Hopefully she'll find some errors in my thoughts and make some verbal attempt to correct them. I'd rather her comments be made voluntarily like that instead of as answers to my direct questions. In between mouthfuls I start.

"Let's see. They've got Stuart. That must mean something gave them the idea he's involved with the bombers. We all know in our hearts that he's not, so what could have given them that idea?

"It couldn't have been anything we've said or done, because we haven't said or done anything. That leaves physical evidence, and the only thing they have that we know about is that computer and the hard drive you sent over to them.

"If my memory serves me correctly, you said that the only thing you did when Myra sent that computer over here the first time was to copy the entire hard drive onto your computer. That was before you switched hard drives and sent it back to Myra. I can't think of anything else they might have, so it has to be that computer… and you've got the same information that they have.

"Wait a minute. You've got more than they have. I remember you saying that some of the stuff was so terrible that you erased it. When we were in Snell's office that day you also alluded to the fact that the previous owner before Kaplan may have visited some websites and had communications with the bomb gang. We never found out exactly who that previous owner was, did we?"

That last question must have hit a special note because she's staring at me with an astonished look. She now jumps up and runs to her stateroom. The dog looks up for a second to make sure she's okay and then probably figures that she can get along without him for another minute or two, so before leaving he's going to finish everything that was in his bowl... and on her plate.

Now that our family dinner is apparently over, I might as well sit back and watch the local news. It's already in progress, but I'm in time to see a special late-breaking story, in which they're showing file footage of Snell at one of his previous press appearances. The anchorperson's voice-over tells the story.

"We have been informed that Special Agent in Charge Robert Snell of the West Los Angeles office of the FBI has made an arrest. Details haven't been released yet but we have been led to believe by an inside source that the person detained is an American citizen and the mastermind of a group of persons with terrorist intentions.

Special Agent Snell wasn't available for comment, but we understand that the FBI feels they have discovered and put an end to a plot to bomb a federal building. Further details will be brought to you on this station as soon as they come in."

Hah! An inside source. Who do they think they're kidding? This local news show doesn't have any inside source at the FBI… this is one of Snell's contrived leaks. If he really had anything on Stuart he'd be front and center on camera bragging about it. The mere fact that he's made this leak begs the question of why. Why would he want to let the real bombers know that he thinks he's got their ringleader?

Suzi also heard the newscast and she's returned to the boat's main saloon to watch it with me. I continue my thoughts aloud.

"I don't think we gave Snell enough credit. He may be leaking that information to put the real gang at ease. He wants them to relax and think that they're safe because the stupid FBI arrested the wrong guy."

I look down at her. "Any comments?"

Her answer isn't what I expected.

"They found out about Stuart from me."

"What are you talking about? Did you call them with some information?"

"No. I gave them the real hard drive and I now know who the previous owner was."

"So? That means the previous owner is the bomber. Let's call Snell and let him know he's got the wrong guy. We'll give him the name of the real bad guy and let the FBI go out and earn their money."

She stands there silently, looking down at the floor. The suspense is starting to get to me.

"Okay, out with it. Who was the previous owner of that computer?"

After another hesitation, she gives me her answer.

"Stuart was. I've been checking its history. The factory that made the computer originally sent it to their leasing division. From there is was part of a fifty-computer package sent out on a one-year lease to some big corporation. After the year's lease was up, the computers were returned to the leasing division in exchange for fifty new models.

"The leasing division then put those fifty, along with many more returned from other leases, onto an online auction site that specializes in liquidating excess and surplus inventory. Stuart has an account on that auction site and he was the winning bidder for a group of twenty of those computers, all having consecutive serial numbers. One of those ultimately wound up in Kaplan's car, where John Doe got it.

"Are you sure about that? How do you know that it was one of Stuart's computers?"

"When I switched hard drives before sending it back to Myra the first time I didn't bother writing down the drive's serial number. That sealed evidence bag sent over to us it had the serial numbers of both the computer and the hard drive prominently marked on that sheet of paper inside the bag, so I wrote them down.

"It wasn't until you were talking during dinner that the hunch about those serial numbers hit me, so I went back to my room to check the numbers I had recorded. The serial number of the original hard drive and the number of the one I got from one of Stuart's computers to use in the switch were only one number apart. They were consecutive. The odds against that coincidence are astronomical. That means that both hard drives were from computers in the same batch of computers, from the same manufacturer's leasing division.

"I had given uncle Jack an assignment several weeks ago to get the serial numbers off of Stuart's computers. I don't know why I did that, but I thought it couldn't hurt. I never even looked at the list until just now. All twenty computers that Stuart bought contained consecutive serial numbers. Kaplan's computer was one of those twenty.

"That means the computer went from the leasing division, to Stuart, to the bomber, and then to Kaplan."

"Great, Suzi. Now all you have to do is find out who Stuart sold that computer to."

"That's not enough. I think the computer was bought by an unauthorized credit card charge. All we'd find out is who the real credit card holder is, and not who actually received the computer."

She's right on track. I agree with everything she's said and for once I think I'm actually understanding and keeping up with her. I give her my idea of what should be done next.

"Suzi, Stuart's obviously in no position to help us now, so we'll have to get hold of Vinnie and Olive. They help with the shipping at Stuart's warehouse. We need Stuart's UPS records to see where he shipped every one of those computers. Kaplan's too reluctant a witness for us to expect cooperation from him. Without information from him as to how he got that computer, we're on our own"

I kept up with her thoughts, but not with her actions, because now she informs me that Jack B. has already been given that assignment, and he's probably going over Stuart's UPS shipping records as we speak. I hope we're in time because there's definitely a clock ticking now. If the bombing gang watches the news they know that Snell has the wrong guy. Even with vigorous interrogation the wrong guy can't give them any real information. It'll only be a matter of time before the feds figure that out, so if the gang is going to make a move it'll have to be soon.

The phone rings. It's Jack B. calling. He's got the list and is bringing it over to us tomorrow morning. It's Saturday, so we'll have all day to make some plans.

Jack just called to say that he's on his way. We may need Snell's help on this because UPS won't give up the information we need without a warrant or someone really important insisting on it. It isn't necessarily privileged information, but companies are very protective of their customers' business details. Just having Stuart's shipping list isn't enough. We want to know exactly where each computer was delivered, when it was delivered, and who signed for it.

I call Snell to give him a heads-up and to support our contention that Stuart's not the real bad guy. He' out of the office today but when I tell the service that it's information about his bombing suspect they patch me through to him.

"Snell here. To whom am I speaking to?"

"This is Peter Sharp. I've got some information being delivered here to my boat. I think you might be interested in it."

"I'm listening, Sharp."

I tell him everything that was discussed on the boat last night and let him know about Jack bringing the shipping list to the boat later today. For once he seems interested. I think that his main concern is my theory that the real bad guys are running out of time and may be pushing their schedule up. He surprises me with his enthusiasm.

"I'm in my car now and can be at your boat in less than an hour. Hold on to that list and don't do anything stupid. I'm on my way there."

This is getting interesting. Not only am I keeping up with the kid's mental process, I think I'm pretty close to actually convincing Snell that he's got the wrong guy. In all fairness, I should let Myra know what's happening too. I dial her home number. No need to ever look it up because it used to be mine too.

"What is it Peter?"

"I'm fine thanks, how about yourself."

"Please. You know what I do on Saturday, and I'm in the middle of another load right now."

"The laundry can wait a little while. You know that Stuart's not part of any bombing gang, and I think Snell may be convinced of it too."

I tell Myra about our recent discoveries, and when she hears that Snell is coming to the boat, she can't resist joining in the fun.

"I hate to drive to the Marina on the weekends. Besides, my assigned driver only is available during the week. Can't we all meet here at my house?"

"You poor thing. I don't want to see you exert yourself by driving. I'll have Jack pick you up. Your house is on his way, so get out of those ratty old laundry jeans. He'll be there in about twenty minutes."

I call Jack to give him Myra's address and tell him to call me when he gets to her house. While waiting, I summon the dog and send him to the foreward stateroom with my message requesting a status report. I haven't heard a peep from Suzi's computer room since last night. If she's been working like I think she has, there must be something to report. It worked. She's coming out now.

"I know that Snell, Myra, and uncle Jack are on their way here. I think I may have found something useful on my copy of the hard drive. Checking the Cookies that were planted there by various websites I found that there is a record of many of the sites that were visited. I made a list of the URL's… that means Universal Resource Locations, or web addresses."

I appreciate her translating things into English for me.

"Every one of those websites has been put down on a list I compiled, and the places he went to are really bad."

"You said 'he' went to. Do you have anyone particular in mind?"

"Yes. Neil Kaplan."

"What makes you think that Neil Kaplan went to those websites? I thought we were looking for the guy who had that computer before he did."

"No. There was no time. I checked the dates of the Cookies and can definitely prove that it was after the computer left Stuart's warehouse, so we can now get him released. Also, there is no indication of any other user identification, email address, or anything else that would indicate someone other than Kaplan is the person who visited all those sites."

"Suzi, are telling me that scrawny, young, Jewish computer nerd is our mad bomber?"

"I'm not saying he's anything. All I can tell you is what that computer was used for and where its user went on the internet."

"Then there's a possibility he's covering for someone else. Maybe his friend Todd, the one who called you and said that he's the one who left it behind in Neil's car."

"I don't think so Peter. I heard his voice and it sounded like he was scared stiff, like someone else was forcing him to make that call and telling him what to say. In my opinion, there's got to be some grown up behind all this."

It's nice to see she holds us adults in such high esteem, but I have to agree with her. I've talked to both Kaplan and Todd. Whoever's behind this plot is definitely above their pay scale.

Jack calls in from outside Myra's house and she should be ready in another minute or two. I guess that becoming the elected district attorney of our county didn't do much to improve her ability to get dressed on time.

A few minutes Jack calls again. Myra's in his car and they're on their way here to the boat.

Just then the phone rings again. It's Snell calling.

"I don't believe it. My car just broke down. I have no idea what it is, but the car is completely dead and I'm waiting for a tow truck."

"You must be driving an American car."

"Yeah, it's one of the Bureau's Fords. They don't want us to drive foreign cars."

"Tell me where you are. I've got someone driving here to the boat and I can have him pick you up on his way."

I call Jack and tell him to pick up Mister FBI. It'll be just a little out of his way but they should be here within the hour if Jack's old clunker doesn't fall apart on the way.

So far everything has worked. Jack and Myra picked up Snell and the gang's all here. Our boat is starting to look like the Pentagon's War Room. Jack brought Stuart's shipping list for the past six months and we've got papers spread out all over the floor. I hope the dog doesn't mistake the paper-covered floor for some attempt of ours to housebreak him into dropping something inside the boat.

We know what the computer weighed when packed, so while Myra and Suzi are looking for outgoing packages weighing that exact amount, Jack and I are going over the alphabetical list of customers. Snell is on the phone shouting to some poor soul at the UPS tracking center, trying to explain how important he is and that UPS' cooperation is necessary for homeland security. What a pompous ass. All he needed to do was ask for a supervisor, give his name and ID number and let her call his office to verify it. But does he do that? Noooo. He has to try and beat some cooperation out of the girl whose only job is to answer the phone on Saturdays.

While we're in the midst of sorting through all of our 'intelligence' paperwork, Jack's cell phone rings. He steps up into the boat's wheelhouse to take the call. I see him up there feverishly writing something down and then making another call. For some strange reason everyone on the boat seems to sense that Jack's onto something really important. Jack comes back into the saloon with a report on his new information.

"That phone call I just got was from a clerk I know at the car rental place. The place where the van driver rents his auto every Thursday... the auto he drives to get the van he uses to pick up incoming packages at the various mailbox places where the stuff they purchased with stolen credit card numbers comes into."

These are more details than would ordinarily be necessary, but Jack knows that Snell and Myra were never brought up to speed on all of our investigations, so he's expanding his explanation to bring them up to speed. It's working. Myra's mouth is open almost as far as Snell's as they sit here silently gaping and waiting for Jack to continue. Without losing a beat, he goes on.

"This isn't Thursday, it's Saturday, and UPS doesn't make regular deliveries today, so he's not going on his regular pick-up route. And the clerk tells me that he didn't rent a van today, he rented a high cube. That's one of those big box vans with a square payload area of about eight-by-eight-by-eight, so it means he's got a much bigger load to pick up.

"And the clerk noticed that he was carrying several sets of those heavy rubber industrial gloves, like the kind you'd use with chemicals. I got the license number of the truck, but the clerk doesn't know where he's going with it.

"Next I called Victor at his lab, the 1800AUTOPSY place. You know, he's the one who does all our CSI work like fingerprints and DNA."

Once again Jack is overstating things for Snell's benefits and he is impressed to know that we have an asset like Victor, but that's okay because this afternoon we're really all on the same side for once. Jack continues.

"Victor says that we should check the UPS shipments for anything sent to a Gus Koeppler. That's the closest match he could get on those prints I brought in on Kaplan's uncle. The ones he left on the glass counter-top at the rental place last week."

We all drop to the floor and start checking the UPS lists. Sure enough, there's a Gus Koeppler on the list. He bought something from Stuart using his own credit card. Suzi now runs out of the room toward her stateroom. She's got a new name to research.

A few minutes later we get her report.

"There's a GK that signed in on numerous occasions at online chat rooms discussing feature articles from *Ragnar's Big Book of Explosives* and the *Anarchist's Cookbook*.

This gets an immediate reaction from Snell.

"Those are the two books of choice if you're planning an explosion. This guy plans to do some serious damage and we have no idea where he is now."

Jack comes up with a brilliant idea.

"Mister Snell, now that you've got Gus Koeppler's name, talk to UPS and try to find out if he had any large packages delivered in the last few days. If he ordered chemicals from some company and had them shipped somewhere, maybe UPS will have a record."

Snell takes his cell phone and a legal pad onto the rear deck and starts his investigation. Myra comes up with another idea.

"Jack, you mentioned you knew some places where this Gus fellow picks up incoming packages. Why don't you get on the phone and start calling those places. Maybe one or two of them have received some large heavy objects... the kind he would want to pick up with that high-cube truck."

Jack immediately realizes that Myra's right, so he goes back to his improvised office in the wheelhouse. Jack gave Myra the license number of the truck that Gus rented, but after a quick meeting we decide not to bring the local police in just yet.

We now know that Kaplan's uncle Marvin Shackler is really Gus Koeppler. This could also mean that Kaplan probably isn't really Kaplan. I've never heard of any Jewish militia locally, so it's probably a fair guess he's using that name as a cover. Jack and Snell come back into the room at about the same time, both with results of their separate efforts. Snell says that UPS reports having made a shipment to Koeppler that was delivered to one of the mailbox places. Jack also has some information from a different source, about the same shipment. He spoke to the clerk at the mailbox place where the UPS shipment to Koeppler was delivered and learned that some other large items came in for Koeppler too, but they weren't delivered by UPS... they came from a freight forwarder. Jack says the clerk told him that he called Koeppler early this morning to come and pick up the large packages and Koeppler said he'd be there with a truck to get them some time later today.

Snell asks Jack for the telephone number of the rental place where Koeppler rented the truck and calls the clerk there to ask him whether or not Koeppler took out any insurance on the truck. The answer was no. Snell then tells the clerk to do himself a favor and add it on, charging it to Koeppler's credit card. Snell tells us that a person who normally gets insurance on his rental vehicles and then suddenly decides to skip it one time is an indication that he isn't planning on returning the truck. He may not even be planning on personally returning. It's the same type of thing that airline personnel are suspicious of when someone pays cash for a one-way plane ticket.

Snell then gets the clerk's number at the place where Koeppler will be picking up the large parcels. He calls there, identifies himself, and tells the clerk to stall Koeppler with paperwork as long as he can. He then looks up at me with a quick order.

"Give me your car keys. I have to go."

"Go? Go where? Not with my car. If my car has to go somewhere, it'll be with me driving it, not you."

Wow… it just dawned on me. Snell doesn't have his car here and he doesn't trust Jack's jalopy to get him very far, so on behalf of the federal government, he's trying to commandeer my Hummer.

That might work with a federally documented vessel and was quite common during many past wars, giving rise to a nautical description of 'privateer.' But my car isn't documented with the Coast Guard, it's registered with California's Department of Motor Vehicles, and our state DMV doesn't recognize commandeering.

"Sorry, Special Agent Man. If you want to go somewhere I'll either call your a cab or give you a lift, but you're not taking my Hummer. That car's my pride and joy and I've been watching television. You G-men are terrible drivers."

Snell isn't used to being around people who don't work for him and ready to follow his every order. He's frustrated by my refusal, but because of what he perceives to be the urgency of the situation, he gives in.

"Okay Sharp. You're driving, but let's make it quick. We may have a serious problem on our hands. I'll make some calls for back-up once we're on the road."

Snell leaves the boat and we all follow. He doesn't even notice how many people are behind him until he gets to the car. When I open the front door the dog immediately jumps in and assumes his position. Snell looks surprised, like he was intending to sit there. I clue him in on the facts of life.

"Sorry pal, but that front seat is his and I've yet to see the human who can discourage him from sitting there. I suggest that you, Jack and Myra hop into the back seat. Suzi will sit up front with me because she has to put Bernie's Doggles on for him."

Snell doesn't look too happy about losing his front seat or that so many people are going along for the ride, but he has no choice. He follows my instructions and from the rear seat watches in wonder as we pull out of the underground parking area while Suzi fastens Bernie's Doggles and he sticks his head up out of the sunroof. I turn around to Snell, and in my best Rochester voice ask him the question.

"Where to, boss?"

Snell shouts out an address. Jack tells me that Snell is directing us to the place where Gus' large packages are waiting for him. Snell gives me another piece of advice.

"Listen here Sharp, we've got to get to that mailbox place in time, so don't worry about speeding tickets. I've got my ID with me and you won't get a ticket as long as I'm in the car with you."

Myra isn't satisfied sitting second-chair to Snell, so she puts her two cents in.

"Forget that FBI identification card. The cops don't know who Snell is. I've got my own badge, and it carries more weight with the local cops than his flimsy ID does."

I see that we're playing 'Can You Top This,' because Suzi's got something to say too. She opens up her jacket to reveal the police sergeant's badge hanging around her neck.

"Forget about all their chest-pounding. This is the only thing you need today, so step on it." That's good enough for me, so I follow her advice and in no time at all we're on the Marina Freeway heading east to the 405 San Diego Freeway. Traffic is pretty light this weekend, so it's smooth sailing all the way north to Wilshire as we past by Snell's Westwood office. There are more cars here than we saw earlier, so I finally get a chance to legally use the car-pool lane. I think that four-and-a-half people plus one dog gives me the right to drive in it.

In less than ten minutes we're cruising uphill towards the Mulholland Drive exit and once at the top it's a downhill drive, during which time you can see most of the San Fernando Valley ahead of you. Jack and Snell are both on their cell phones with the speakerphone attachments on, freeing up their hands to make notes while they're talking.

Snell gets through to the clerk at the mailbox place and just as he starts to talk to him the clerk tells him to hold on because another call is coming in. Snell sees the mailbox place's number on Jack's phone. They both called the same place at the same time.

Snell reaches over and slams Jack's phone shut. The clerk tells Snell "never mind, the other caller must've hung up." Snell wants to know if Gus is there with the truck yet. The answer he gets is 'yes. Gus just pulled up.' The clerk says he'll try and stall him as long as possible. We're still about ten or fifteen minutes away from the mailbox place.

It's Myra's turn to make a call. She calls the CHP and puts them on alert to watch for the truck. She then calls Valley Services Division, the Van Nuys L.A.P.D. station, and tells them to have an unmarked vehicle go to the mailbox place and follow the truck at a distance, reporting to both her and the CHP if and when the truck starts moving. I remind her to tell everyone to not interfere with the Yellow Hummer. Myra asks me what the license plate is so she can make sure the cops know we're the good guys. My answer is simple.

"Honey, just tell them we're in the yellow Hummer with a goggled Saint Bernard sticking up out of the sunroof and a district attorney and supervising special FBI agent in the back seat. I don't think there are too many vehicles exactly like this in the Valley today."

Jack's cell phone rings. It's the clerk calling to let us know that Gus has loaded the truck and is pulling out of the driveway, heading south on Sepulveda Boulevard. I'm now at the Ventura Boulevard off-ramp, so I leave the freeway and turn north on Sepulveda. Just after we cross Ventura Boulevard we see Gus coming the other way. He's still going south on Sepulveda and probably intends to take it all the way through the pass towards West Los Angeles. This will allow him to avoid being caught up in any southbound San Diego Freeway traffic and also minimize his chances of getting stopped. We see an unmarked vehicle not too far behind with two mustached cop-types in plain clothes. They nod at us in passing, letting us know that they've got everything in control and that they recognize our vehicle.

We cross over Ventura Boulevard and Snell tells me to make a U-turn to follow Gus' truck. I see a black-and-white CHP cruiser approaching us from the north. Ordinarily I would never have the nerve to make a U-turn here, especially in front of an oncoming cop car. To my surprise, as soon as I start my turn the CHP squad car slows to a stop and the driver signals for us to go ahead. He obviously recognizes us too and wants to signal that he's also part of the team.

The light at Ventura is green, so there's no need for any special stunt driving getting across the Boulevard. We've got another mile or so to go before the road starts to turn into a winding uphill motor course through the pass. This Hummer is definitely not a performance vehicle but its large eight-cylinder engine does pack a punch. Without too much effort we catch up to the unmarked police vehicle and pass them up. They know we'll be the primary on this medium-speed chase, so they back off and give us some room to get in behind the truck, which has now slowed down due to the steepening uphill grade and the heavy load it's carrying.

We're not too worried about being noticed, because trucks like the one Gus is driving have very limited visibility. As long as you're directly behind one, you're almost completely invisible to its driver. I look into my rear-view mirror at Snell.

"Any suggestions?"

"You're going to have to run him off the road."

"Me? What do you think I am, some studio stunt driver?

Our local Los Angeles television newscasts usually show at least one or two idiots each week who think they can get away from the cops by out driving them. Big mistake. Maybe you can outrun a cop, but you can't outrun a Motorola. Many times if the police think that the escaping drive is a danger to the public, they'll try what's been nicknamed the PIT maneuver, which really only an acronym for **P**ursuit **I**ntervention **T**echnique.

If it's done properly, the cop car speeds up and aims to ram into a side portion of the subject vehicle's rear end, in an effort to make the fleeing car spin out of control. Sometimes it even tips the bad guys over, too.

"Wait a minute, Snell. Are you suggesting I try a PIT maneuver on this truck? That's crazy. All you have to do is tell that CHP patrol car to hit the siren and pull the guy over. End of story. He'll get out of the truck, it'll all be over, and we can all go for some pizza."

"Nice try Sharp, but that won't work here. If he's got something in there that can be detonated to make a big bang, then we can't use a siren because that'll only tell him it's time to arm the detonator and use it as a negotiating device. And if he's a real nut, he might just set it off and take us all with him. No, it's gotta be the PIT maneuver, and I'm afraid you're in the barrel on this one."

"What about that CHP cruiser back there? He's been trained to do that sort of thing. He's even got those big black bumper extensions sticking up in front of his car."

"You're right Peter, but his vehicle isn't high enough or heavy enough to get this job done. It's got to be you, and it has to be done while we're still winding through the pass. You'll have to catch him on a curve. It'll be a lot easier then. His truck will spin out and probably tip over. He won't have any advance warning and no chance to arm the detonator. That's the way it's got to go down."

For some strange reason Mister Uniman comes to my mind. His company carries the insurance on this yellow tank of mine and he's not going to be happy with me rear-ending another vehicle. I realize that I'm just stalling, but that's natural. I really don't care much about the Hummer, but I've got some valuable passengers. I tell Suzi to get Bernie down and to close the sunroof. The back seat passengers see that we're getting ready for action so they tighten their seat belts as I speed up a little and try to get closer to the truck. Snell tries to give me some assurance.

"Peter, I've seen this maneuver done hundreds of times. I've even gone through the training myself. In all those times there was never any damage to the vehicle instituting the maneuver."

Thank you very much, Snell. What he's just told me is that with the proper training and an extensive driving course taught by professionals, there's a slim chance of anything going wrong. I'm one of the admittedly poorest drivers I know, with an almost complete lack of depth vision. This is going to be hairy.

I've seen several of those disaster movies over the years in which some disability befalls the flight crew of an airliner and a passenger with no flying experience is forced to take over and land the airplane, with some assistance from a nervous ground crew desperately trying to explain what all those little gauges and levers mean to the new pilot. I always imagined that if a situation like that ever came up in a commercial airliner that I was a passenger in, I'd be the first volunteer to go up there and take over the controls.

This may sound strange coming from person who perspires when the engines on our boat start up, but I always thought that I could really come through when the pressure was on and it was a life-and-death situation.

That was then. This is now. This may not be a 747 in trouble, but I'm at the controls of a heavy vehicle speeding downhill after a terrorist bomber who must be rammed and forced off the road. And to make things worse, the people I care most about have been forced to be along for the wild ride. If I survive this day, I may re-think my previous desire to volunteer in an unfavorable airliner situation.

We've already gone through the tunnel and are still going downhill. The bottom is only a mile or so ahead. Suzi is hugging the dog very tightly and they're both strapped in as securely possible, in the same seatbelt. We're now rapidly approaching the bottom of the incline and I know for a fact that there's a sharp left turn ahead just before southbound Sepulveda goes under the San Diego Freeway overpass. The truck is slowing down for this upcoming curve. He's obviously familiar with this route too.

I'm trying to get a mental image of how to pull this thing off. If I'm going to ram the left rear portion of his truck, I should come at him from as far to the side as possible so as to give me the best chance of forcing him to spin out. The only problem with that part of the plan is that it in order to approach him from the left I'm going to have to first swing out into the oncoming traffic lane, and trying a stunt like that on a curve can have a disastrous result. I try to visualize how many seconds the out-swing will be and feel confident I can get back in time to ram his rear end before getting hit by opposing traffic.

I know this is wishful thinking, but that's all I've got now and I also know that it's now or never. One noticeable thing about this whole event is the silence in the car. Everyone is probably as scared as I am, if that's possible.

It's time. The left turn under the freeway overpass at the bottom of the hill has just come into sight so I slowly start to pick up speed to close the distance between us and the truck, and try to calculate where to start my swing into the other lane. Now's the time. He's slowing down a bit in anticipation of the tight left turn ahead. If I can clip him hard enough on his left rear as he's attempting that tight left turn, I think there's a good chance I can either spin him out or tip him over, or both. The real trick is to do it in such a way as to allow our vehicle to remain upright, while not getting hit by oncoming traffic.

My moist fists are clenched around the steering wheel. The silence in the Hummer is deafening. We all know what's going to happen in a few seconds. He's making his turn. Now's my chance. Just as I speed up to swing out into the other lane and prepare to swing back and ram him, a cell phone rings in the back seat. All three people back there have cell phones, but no one seems interested in answering the one that's ringing.

This is it. I swing out to the left and then back to the right, speeding up and catching him during his turn. We all feel the jolt as the vehicles collide, but fortunately our air bags don't deploy, so there's no impairment of my vision. The truck is heavy and doesn't spin out, but due to our momentum, we keep moving and because our bumpers are still touching, his rear end swings around as he starts to spin out.

With his forward momentum stopped, I slam on my brakes to avoid hitting the truck as it ends its spin perpendicular to the road. My brakes can't do the job for us, so my only alternative is a desperate turn to the right, hoping to avoid slamming into the truck. As we screech by, I see the truck's spin has ended and it's now starting to roll.

The Hummer comes to a stop up on the road's shoulder and we all look to our left to see the truck rolling over several times before finally coming to a stop. At that instant, it seems like every squad car in town has reached the truck. Our rear door pops open as Snell makes his quick exit. Before he's completely out of the Hummer he shouts at me to get the Hummer out of here fast. That's an order I intend to obey immediately. Our engine died, but it turns starts right up and to my pleasant surprise we're still mobile. I make a U-turn by going to my right. This is completely in violation of every rule of driving I've ever learned, but I don't care.

From our safe position a hundred feet away, we watch as Snell joins the uniformed officers, all guns drawn. They jump up on the overturned truck and pull the driver out.

The next vehicle to pull up is a police bomb squad truck. Several men dressed in armored gear are opening the truck's rear doors, obviously trying to get inside to de-fuse whatever might be in there.

I haven't seen any traffic coming from either direction for the past few minutes and am glad to see that it's a slow day. When the bomb squad guys give the 'thumbs-up' signal, I learn why the traffic seemed so light. Snell alerted the CHP car that we'd be using the PIT maneuver, so they radioed other squad cars to stop oncoming traffic from both directions.

This now looks like the final scene of a big-budge motion picture. I never realized how large this operation became while we were going up and down the hill for that ten minutes or so, but the police, FBI and CHP must have been in constant contact with each other in a desperate effort to coordinate their respective movements. Looking up to the freeway, I see that they had stopped traffic up there too. All these plans were probably contingencies, just in case my actions would fail. Oh, ye of little faith.

The coast is now clear. CHP cruisers now allow the freeway traffic to resume. A large police tow truck has arrived and is getting the truck back upright so that it can be towed away.

Snell walks up the hill to the Hummer. I realize that we've all been sitting here in complete silence for the past five or ten minutes, or however long it's been. I don't really know.

"You've done a good job, Peter. I owe you one."

Suzi finally speaks up. "What about Stuart?"

Snell hands us a piece of paper with an address and room number written on it.

"Here's where your friend is waiting for you. I see that there's hardly a scratch on the front of your vehicle, which means you hit him just right. I guess those big bold bumper guards did the trick for you because they really protected your front end. Here, give my card to your insurance man. The Bureau will cover any repairs your might find later. And Peter…"

"I'm sorry Snell. No more stunts today, please."

"Dinner's on us tonight. The word's already been passed on."

I hand the address to Suzi. She recognizes it and gives me directions.

Before too long I'm pulling up in front of the Marina's Ritz Carlton Hotel on Admiralty Way. The valet takes my car and none other than our own John Doe, Special Agent Karl Shaeffer, escorts us into the hotel and surprises me with the plans that the FBI has made.

"Your friends are waiting in a suite upstairs. From what I've heard, you've probably worked up an appetite. Dinner will be served in about twenty minutes."

We are all pleasantly surprised to find Stuart, Michelle and Lotus waiting for us in the luxuriously appointed hotel suite. A beautiful dining table has been set for seven and a large dog bowl is in place on the floor. This is the longest period of time that I've ever seen Myra go without speaking. It's wonderful. Why couldn't she have learned this trick while we were married?

John Doe has a message for Myra. He whispers it in her ear and she looks over to me with a kind look on her face. Another trick she learned too late. As John walks out of the room he stops to let me know what the message was.

"I just informed the district attorney that Special Agent in Charge Snell has had the rest of Gus' gang arrested. They were all sitting with Kaplan in the trailer. We're going to hold off on filing federal conspiracy charges against them to give Ms. Scot's office a chance to indict them for their credit card operation. Snell says he owes you both that.."

Special Agent Shaeffer shakes my hand and thanks me for all my efforts from the time he was arrested up to now, and leaves the suite. He's a pretty nice guy but I wish he would have confided in me before Suzi dragged him out of the FBI's closet by out-investigating Snell's guys.

20

We're all now seated at the table watching some waiters bringing in what looks like a large gourmet meal - and it's not a minute too soon. Crime busting gives one a real appetite. I turn to Stuart.

"You look happy Stuart. I thought that being arrested by the FBI would have a sobering affect on you."

"Peter to be quite honest, I wasn't worried at all. I knew from the beginning that I didn't do anything wrong, so I didn't have anything to worry about. I also knew that Suzi here was still working on the computer's hard drive and it would only be a matter of time before she would be able to prove that I was innocent."

"That's reassuring to hear, but how did you ever wind up in this hotel suite?"

"As soon as they took me out of the courthouse Snell had them remove the handcuffs. Back at his office he confided in me that he really didn't think I was guilty. He asked for my cooperation and told me about his plan to have it leaked that they had a suspect in custody on the bombing gang. The problem was that he couldn't make that leak if he didn't actually have someone in custody and he wanted me to play that part for him.

"He promised that I'd only be out of circulation for less than a week and that the Bureau would compensate me for my time. I agreed to go along with the program as long as I didn't have to sit in a cell, be identified to the press, or have an arrest or anything else go on my record. He agreed to my requests.

As for this suite, it's one that the government maintains for visiting foreign dignitaries. It isn't being used this week so they let me stay here. And the food's been great, as you can now see for yourself."

While we're getting ready for the dessert course, Lotus clicks on the large television's remote so that we can watch the news. As expected, the blow-dried anchorperson leads off with this evening's feature story about the heroic capture of a terrorist ringleader who was arrested with a large amount of explosives and a detonator. The FBI suspects that the Westwood Federal Building was his target, and from the amount of explosives in the truck, there would have been as much damage to our Federal Building as there was in the Oklahoma City tragedy. Everyone is happy that the attempt was made on a Saturday when there was hardly anyone in the building. The newscaster doesn't know why the attempt was made on a Saturday when the building would be almost empty, but all of us at the table now realize that Snell's leak to the press probably made them move their plans up.

All of those cell phone calls Snell and Myra made to local authorities were broadcast over police bands to many squad cars. Newspeople routinely use scanners to listen in on the police frequencies, so in no time at all there were several traffic helicopters following us.

They picked up the trail as soon as Gus turned southbound on Sepulveda and we're now sitting here in the safety and comfort of the Ritz Carlton, as we get a chance to re-live the afternoon.

There is a dramatic narrative as we watch the Hummer make its U-turn on Sepulveda Boulevard to go after the truck. The newscaster comments about some large police dog that was brought along in case a foot pursuit ensued. Suzi is especially proud that they got that shot of Bernie. They did a nice job of covering the whole chase, and I'm amazed at the way I pulled off that PIT maneuver. It really looked professional, but even sitting here in the hotel, I get a slight chill watching us swing out to the left and then ram that truck. In my younger years I spent quite a bit of time as a gentleman biker, riding my Harley Davidson through the canyons on the weekends. I've finally gotten all urges to play games with any kind of vehicle out of my system.

The news story's next shot is of FBI Special Agent in Charge Robert Snell, who naturally is taking credit for doing the driving, as if he was the only person in that Hummer. I never expected anything less than this and we all have a good laugh at his on-camera performance. It's nice to see a real hero once in a while.

Surprisingly, they also have helicopter footage of Kaplan's trailer. We now learn from the newscast that while we were doing our thing with the Hummer, the police had the trailer surrounded. The authorities were afraid that if the rest of the gang found out about Gus' capture they might try to all get away in different directions. Not only did the police have them all hemmed in, but their phone lines were cut and some special top-secret electronic interference device was used to stop any outgoing cell phone calls. They were afraid that members of the gang would see we were chasing Gus and they might try to call his cell phone to warn him. That would have been terrible, because knowing he was going to be intercepted might have pushed him over the edge and caused him to detonate his truckload, causing a lot of damage to us, the freeway, and nearby residential areas.

I've heard of interference devices like this before. One time I went to the federal prison facility on Terminal Island near Los Angeles Harbor. I remembered a phone call I was supposed to make, but discovered that my cell phone was out of order. Little did I know that I was too close to the prison and my phone signal was being blocked.

Snell is then seen announcing that the rest of the gang will be prosecuted by Myra Scot, the district attorney, who was instrumental in bringing both of those operations to a close.

Noticeably missing is any mention whatsoever of my name or the fact that with the help of my trusted staff, we broke this whole case open and made heroes out of everyone but us. Stuart doesn't even mind that we couldn't recover the couple of hundred dollars he lost to the unauthorized credit card charges. He says that the fun and excitement of being part of this whole adventure was well worth the loss.

I'm starting to worry about Myra. She still hasn't said anything since before we did the PIT maneuver. She did a fine job of finishing her dinner, but hasn't said a word. After dinner we all move to the living room portion of the suite and Suzi is sitting between Myra and I on a large couch. I guess the combination of today's activities, along with the fact that she probably worked most of last night on the computer have taken their toll. She's now sound asleep.

With dinner over and everyone seemingly satisfied, it would ordinarily be time for us to leave. Only one thing is keeping us back. Suzi is not only asleep between us, but she's also tightly holding on to us. One hand on Myra and the other on mine. She's off in some dream world now where she is very happy. I can't help but want to be there with her. I wish Myra would feel the same way.

EPILOGUE

In another couple of months it'll be Suzi's birthday and I've decided to throw her a surprise party at the Chinese restaurant. I would use the boat, but she's got so many fans that there wouldn't be enough room here. I'm sure it will be impossible to pull off a surprise that she hasn't learned about, but it'll be a party anyway and most of the cops in west Los Angeles will be there, including judges, prosecutors and everyone else she's managed to mesmerize in her short time on this earth so far.

I'm getting a lot of help with the party from Michelle Chang and her Daughter Lotus. I wasn't looking forward to being at the same party with two women I could be interested in because Myra will be there too. Fortunately Stuart has become friendly with Michelle, now that he's widowed. I'm sure it's just a matter of time before she finds out about the married-to-the-cat scam he pulled on her organization. I don't want to be around when that happens.

Unbeknownst to me, Suzi has been communicating with the major credit card companies who sustained losses from the credit card fraud ring. I don't know how she did it, but she managed to get us retained on a contingency agreement by which we would receive a percentage of whatever the companies recovered. Suzi's computer expertise led to her following the money to where the gang had it stashed. The agreement that merchants sign allows credit card processors to automatically recover charge-back amounts, so the providers were able to recover a substantial amount. Our fee was a handsome one and as soon as Suzi received the check she issued one to Stuart in the amount of his losses.

She also drew two more checks on that reward money. One was to her 'uncle' Jack Bibberman, who did all the legwork for us. The other one was to Michelle Chang. Another assignment Jack B. completed was to check out the Markle Janitorial Service that Kaplan and his uncle worked for in the evening. He found out that one of their accounts was a particular building in the Valley that housed several organizations, one of which was the IRS' audit branch where Michelle Chang was assigned as an investigator. The way it looks, Kaplan's uncle would get him into the IRS' offices as part of the night clean-up crew. While the uncle did the cleaning, Kaplan copied files from the IRS computers that contained records of people who were required to substantiate deductions, many of which were paid for by credit card bills.

In just a few hours a month Kaplan was able to get the name, address, credit card account numbers and social security number of each person audited. By later going over the files that were uploaded to his laptop, Kaplan was able to create a 'hit-list' of 'marks' living in the San Fernando Valley, whose credit card billing addresses could conveniently be changed to one of the chain of mailbox places the gang used.

Thanks to Michelle Chang's verification of the fact that every one of the partially stolen identities belonged to someone who had been audited by her particular office, the secret of how the gang got its information was discovered and new systems were put in place to avoid that leak from happening again. Michelle also got promoted.

I think she really knows about Stuart's married-to-the-cat scam, but she's keeping her mouth shut about it so that it doesn't do any damage to their social relationship.

I received a check from Bart Levin, along with his thanks for my lecturing at his review course... and he offered me the same teaching spot in his next seminar. I was also very pleased to learn that almost sixty percent of the students in my class on law exam writing were successful in passing the Baby Bar. That's almost twice the usual passing rate. He also informs me that Doctor Sheldon Eidoch was one of the students who passed the exam.

Included with the check is a DVD-18, which is a double-sided, double-layered disc capable of holding many hours of information. The enclosed brochure describes the material as being two lectures from Bart's review class that specifically covered my classroom performances, complete with Bar question analyses. Another attached envelope contains an advance on royalties for sales of the DVD's.

Bart also feels that many of the females in the class will look forward to meeting Myra when they get admitted to practice in a couple of years, and they'll probably be wanting to mention my name to her as a reference. I shoot a note back to him accepting his offer to teach in the next review course and tell him that if those students wait another couple of years to contact Myra, it may not be in the district attorney's office. By then they may have to reach her at the office of either the Mayor or the Governor.

I'm also now planning to add more than forty names to Suzi's birthday party list, to include the students of mine who passed the Baby Bar.

A check also came in from the Superior Court for my work on the John Doe case that I was appointed to handle. After Suzi took the firm's cut, there was still enough left for me to hop over to Maui for a week and hang out at the Lahaina Yacht Club, where I've been a member ever since Myra and I went there for a vacation. That's now history, as is our marriage, but because of the way Myra feels about boats and motion, it wasn't too hard for me to get custody of the club membership.

Myra did get her voice back and that golden evening of silence came to an end. She never cared much for anything involving motion, so skiing and sailing have always been out of the question. I guess that our fifteen minutes of extreme motion the Saturday afternoon of that PIT maneuver was a little too much for her. She probably was in a mild state of shock the rest of the day and that's what caused her to be naggingly challenged.

The Monday following our exciting week-end she was back on the local news shows being interviewed about how she worked with the FBI to break up that credit card fraud gang. She also announced that her office has retained an outside consultant to give advice and training to her new identity theft department. Hmmmn. I wonder who that 'consultant' could be.

Senators Diane Feinstein and Orrin Hatch successfully tacked an amendment onto an act that applied to violent and repeat offenders. Their extra-added provision was designed to prohibit teaching or demonstrating how to make explosives if the 'intent' is that the information will be used to commit a federal crime.

Of course the amendment was attacked by about as many organizations as there were supporting it. I don't know how a law like that would ever be enforced against people using the internet to disseminate their materials. As much as I'd like to see them stop printing and selling hateful things like the Turner Diaries, I wouldn't want to see that book or any other one be the subject of a public burning in the town square. I guess there is no middle-ground answer that most people can agree upon.

Olive and Vinnie have once again worked out their differences and are now planning to set another wedding date. I think it will really be more like an elopement date. In the meantime, Vinnie has told me that the mailbox at their apartment building displays both of their names. I guess they want their marriage to be a ceremonial one that's guaranteed to be recognized, instead of a common-law one formed by their cohabitation and 'holding out,' which will be in name only in California.

In a subsequent conversation with Snell he told me that if it wasn't for the fact that I was over the thirty-seven-year limit for incoming FBI Special Agent Recruits, he would have suggested that I consider joining the Bureau. Using my best tactful routine I thanked him for his thought and expressed regret at being 'over the hill.'

If I was a twenty-five-year-old law school graduate I would probably think twice about an offer like that because Special Agents now start in at close to fifty grand a year, and there's no office rent, phone bills, law library or malpractice insurance to buy. But now I'm afraid I could never stand the cut in income. There's more money in being on the defense side, so I guess that Snell and I will have to remain friendly adversaries.

Jack Bibberman has just stepped aboard. He says this visit is to take Suzi and Bernie shopping. As they all leave the boat I ask her if she has enough money in her little purse. Holding up a piece of plastic, she lets me know that everything's okay in the financial department. She points at the dog and gives him a hug.

"We're using his new platinum American Express card." The credit-worthy dog gives a bark in agreement.

About the Author

Gene Grossman worked through high school, college, and law school as a shoe salesman, welder, process server, bail bondsman, tire changer, saloon piano player and 'extra,' appearing in seven motion pictures. He then spent 20 years as a trial lawyer, during which time he served as Dean of a small local law school, where he also taught several classes.

His film & video company produced over fifty special interest DVD titles on everything from boating, to bankruptcy. Now retired from the practice of law, Gene writes aboard his yacht in Marina del Rey, California.

See pictures of Peter Sharp's boats, yellow Hummer, Suzi's e-cart, and Laverne's houseboat at: www.petersharpbooks.com

Editor's Note: If you notice anything you think is a blatant 'typo' or other error, please don't hesitate to contact the author, because he was the last person to sign off on the book: gene_grossman@yahoo.com

The author – always writing. Sometimes in his dinghy, and on often in Avalon, on Catalina Island